# THE NEW WAR WAGON

A Novel by Frank G. Davis

Copyright © 2023
**The New War Wagon**
Book 5 in the War on Crime Series
by Frank G. Davis

## Notice of Copyright

Paperback ISBN: 978-1-954253-59-9

# <u>REVIEWS</u>

I found it to be an intriguing blend of cerebral mind melding, interesting character relationships, time travel and tour-oriented action. Very even pace and flow with an energetic action close. A very imaginative concept to add to your already growing volumes in the Joshua and Caleb, War Wagon series. Looking forward to additional editions and further adventures with the characters. An excellent and engaging read.

Jack Campbell, Clackamas, Oregon

This is the fifth book in the *War On Crime* series and it is by far the most complex. The missions begin with a couple of bad cops in Nogales, Arizona and builds to deal with powerful drug lords in New Orleans. As the criminal characters grow in power, Team Joshua is formed and advanced technology is applied to deal with the increased threats.

Along the way, Caleb, the spirit of Joshua's twin brother, is joined by new spirit characters whose abilities are well beyond Caleb's. Some of them are good, but many are evil.

*The New War Wagon* is an advanced technology demonstrator which is powered by a small, cold fusion reactor. In its most mundane appearance, a large motorhome. However, it can morph into a much more superior combat vehicle. Before it becomes operational, foreign spies attempt to steal the cold fusion technology.

The New War Wagon is manned by an expanded Team Joshua who are tasked with protecting this vehicle and it's designers at all costs.
I found the story intriguing. The technology struck me as being both interesting and plausible in the context of this series. The

descriptions of the numerous combat scenes are well written and exciting to read as well as the degree of detail the author gave to his characters, both humans and spirits.

All in all, I found it to be an entertaining read. The ending of the story gives the impression a sixth book in the series is a possibility.

Gene Carr, Casa Grande, Arizona

The New War Wagon is the latest in the War on Crime series by Frank Davis. Although based on current technology and real life geo-political events, it takes underlying life and alternate reality to new and exciting levels. The book kept me up nights turning pages to the point I read it a second time to completely digest the in-depth workings and associations.

The story line is both colorful and geographically accurate and could easily stand alone as a travel guide, taking the reader from the Pacific Northwest to Alaska, the vast Pacific Ocean, the South China Sea, and Hawaii. The adventure adds new creatures and individuals to the already captivating Team Joshua series. Afterlife questions related to the spirit world are addressed and answered. The reader is left with a comfortable understanding of the development of Joshua, Caleb, and the other characters throughout the series.

The New War Wagon takes the reader in a thrill packed adventure involving every character. The reader can easily identify and bond with the characters to the point that real concerns develop with each of their struggles. Although the book is definitely science fiction, the ties to real world events, technology and potential future conflicts keeps the reader engrossed. The story line leaves the reader both expecting and wanting more. Hopefully, this series will continue.

David S. Davis, Chandler, Arizona (not related to author)

After reading the author's entire Generation series and the War on Crime books, I offered to review and edit the latest book, *The New War Wagon.*

I thoroughly enjoyed the twists and turns of the story line, which frequently took unpredictable turns.

Frequently, I realized I was so anxious to move ahead in the story, I forgot to edit. I had to backtrack and slow down to do the editing.

I admire the author's imagination combined with his technical and geographical knowledge, be it from adventures in outer space to current events right here on Earth, such as illegal smuggling and human trafficking

The common bonus in all the books is that the good guys always win in the end!

Gary Dagan, Renton, Washington

# DEDICATION

This story is dedicated to Gary Dagan, a lifelong friend. We first met as we began pursuing Masters of Science degrees in engineering at Arizona State University. We teamed up as study partners. It turns out we had many common interests. We joined a Shotokan Karate Club at ASU and became sparring partners. We also learned to fly light aircraft together and both got our private pilot licenses.

Gary was responsible for my first job. They were having a job fair at ASU and he sold me on signing up with AiResearch Manufacturing Company of Arizona. We both began our engineering careers designing and developing small turbine engines.

Gary really loved flying and ended up leaving the turbine engine business for the Air Force. He became a flight instructor flying T-38s. I would have liked to join him but it was not to be. I ended up getting my commercial pilot license and was a flight instructor for four years teaching civilians how to fly puddle jumpers.

After Gary left the Air Force he joined up with Bell Aerospace in New Orleans and became a member of an Air Force Reserve unit, the Hurricane Hunters, flying the C-130.

He ended up at Boeing Commercial Division in Seattle initially as a flight training instructor and ultimately as manager of Flight Training for the Boeing 747 introduction, followed by the 777 Aircraft. When I visited him in Seattle he let me fly the 777 simulator. What an incredible rush!!!

When I asked him if he would review this manuscript, he volunteered to edit it. He had previously edited the nonfiction book written by a close friend who was one of the pilots on "The Raid on Entebbe." I was overwhelmed by his offer.

Of course I accepted his offer. He made so many corrections and suggestions on how to make this book better, especially the military aspects of the story. I've loved this man as a brother ever since I met him, but never more than now.

Thank you, Gary. You are one of a kind.

# INTRODUCTION

My name is Joshua Brown. I have a twin brother named Caleb. We have been, and still are inseparable. We were born in the Deep South to my father Moses and my mother Gloria. My dad called our mom Glorious. He claimed she was a blessing from heaven and my brother and I were in complete agreement.

When we were in high school we grew to be big; bigger than our father who was six feet three inches tall. Caleb and I topped out at six feet six inches plus a smidge. When we graduated from high school we weighed almost three hundred pounds and were offered football scholarships to several universities.

Our pops had served in the Vietnam war and suggested we could do a tour or two in the Marines before starting college. We signed up with the U.S. Marine Corps and became part of a recon battalion in Kabul, Afghanistan. A week before the end of our second tour, Caleb stepped on an IED and was killed. Except a part of him lived on. The flesh and blood parts of him were gone, but his spirit survived.

During the next year or so we were able to reunite. Caleb's spirit bonded with me. It wasn't easy and it was very painful for both of us. However, we persevered. In fact, Caleb and I became a dynamic duo. I was approached by a secret government agency as a test case for the War on Crime. They were looking for a well trained killer to take out individuals who considered themselves above the law, like drug cartel leaders, human traffickers and crime bosses. I was assigned to a secret handler. I never knew his name, only his code name: The Apostle.

With the help of Caleb's spirit, I was able to acquire all types of intel on my assigned targets. Over the next few years, the two of us were given ever more challenging tasks. We were able to successfully accomplish all of our missions. Along the way we brought in some additional team members. Each and every one of them was instrumental in contributing to the success of the previous missions. We called ourselves Team Joshua (I voted against that name but was overruled).

Before we start, let me introduce you to our team members. Of course, Caleb and I were the first team. Actually, we weren't even a team for a couple of years. When I was going through special government training, Caleb's spirit was right beside me all the way. None of my trainers had any idea how I advanced so quickly.

When training was over, I was assigned to three successive test missions. It took the better part of a year to complete all three. Caleb's spirit leader did not permit him to accompany me on those missions. That made it a lot tougher than it needed to be, but I survived. When those missions were over, I discovered Caleb had planted a few "suggestions" in my mind which saved my life more than once.

My third mission took place in Portland, Oregon. I added a part-time member to the team. His name is Pham Bin Minh, a former Marine buddy of mine and a damn good attorney. He helped me with the adoption of nearly a hundred young Vietnamese children who had been kidnapped and brought to Portland by human traffickers.

Mark Riley, a second former Marine, was a security guard at Terminal 6, an enormous shipping port on the Columbia River, down river from the city of Portland. He had been a dog handler during the war in Afghanistan. Not only was Mark a highly decorated Marine, so was his attack dog Sarge.

Both these men were combat trained who, at my suggestion, joined Caleb and I in our war on crime. Actually, neither man knew anything about my spirit brother, but Caleb seemed to think the dog had somehow sensed his presence. Both my brother and I thought that was kind of spooky, but if Sarge was okay with it, so were we.

Simone Cantrell was the next to join our group. It turns out she was a DEA agent working undercover at a New Orleans casino assigned to the registration desk. Caleb complained that Simone quickly became a person of interest for me. A romantic person of interest. When I discovered we were both working the same mission, I got to know Simone much better. When our mission was over, she was assigned to our team by The Apostle. She became an important member of Team Joshua. *Stop snickering, Caleb.* I didn't know a spirit could snicker. Of course only I could "hear" it.

The five of us, six if you count Sarge, became the core of Team Joshua. Caleb decided we could be much more efficient if he could communicate telepathically with the entire team. I thought it was a good idea. The remaining team members were in shock when Caleb began to thought/speak to them. However, they adapted fairly quickly.

From time to time we enlisted other resources. Two who come to mind are both Portland cops: Joey Hong and "Buffalo" Bill Cody. Actually, they became special agents for the FBI shortly after we met them. They were part of our team in Oregon when a group attempted to take over the state government. Both men were included when we were informed of a surprise … The Apostle told us Team Joshua was being awarded a three week luxury cruise to Alaska paid for by our government. We were told it was because of the success we had on all our previous missions. However, we all knew it was a cover for another mission, probably more dangerous than the last.

# CHAPTER 1
# GETTING TO KNOW US

### Mark Riley

Joshua asked me to provide him some information regarding the lady who Sarge and I had been spending time with. He thought it would help give the rest of the team some background before we all got together for our first dinner.

I met Maria Gomez and her daughter, Serina, almost six months ago. I hadn't been able to see them once the mission in Antelope, Oregon, began. Once the mission ended and we were released from duty, the dog and I headed over to our old apartment to meet up with them.

I called first and Maria sounded very excited when she heard my voice. When she told Serina we were coming to visit, and that Sarge would be coming too, she went crazy with joy. I guess Maria gave the phone to Serina and the girl asked in almost a whisper, "Mr. Mark, are you really coming to visit us?"

"We sure are, Serina," I answered. "Sarge can't wait to see you again."

I heard a clattering sound as she dropped the phone and squealed with joy. "They're coming Mama. They're really coming! I prayed they would come visit me and my prayers were answered."

"Hello, Mark? Can you hear me?"

I answered yes.

"Serina is running in circles and yelling and screaming. I can hardly hear your voice. Please hurry."

Fifteen minutes later, I was parking the car in the apartment parking lot when I heard the sounds of a little girl yelling and running. She came screeching around the corner of the apartment building and sprinted the last ten yards, leaping into my arms and hugging me tightly.

At first, Sarge wasn't sure if he needed to go into protection mode or join in the fun. I made a brief hand sign just before Serina nearly knocked me down from her jump. Sarge began jumping and yipping with joy as he recognized Serina's scent and joined in the celebration.

I glanced over the girl's shoulder and saw her mother running toward us, a smile on her face and tears in her eyes. She embraced us both and buried her face in my neck as she hugged me even tighter than her daughter. I could feel the wetness of her tears on my face as she looked up at me and whispered into my ear, "I was so afraid you weren't coming back. I… both of us…missed you. And Sarge too."

We walked back into the apartment. I was holding Serina with my right arm, my left arm was around Maria's waist pulling her tightly against my side with Sarge trotting happily behind us. I couldn't remember when I'd last felt such happiness.

Once inside, Serina took Sarge, or as she called him, the doggie, into her room to play a game called dress up. I wasn't sure what the game was about, however I was confident she would be safe with Sarge. Maria and I sat on the couch in the living room. I enjoyed the fact that it was more like a love seat for two.

"You've made us both so happy," she took my hand and smiled. "I was afraid something terrible might have happened to you. I know you can't call when you are on your missions, but I worried anyway." She paused for a moment and her expression turned fearful. She turned her face away from me and asked, "How long can you stay?"

I could sense she was afraid of what I might say. I looked at the side of her face and said, "I'll stay until you kick me out. If I have to leave, I'll take you both with me. I love you so much. All I could think about after I left you was…"

She snapped her head toward me, grabbed my head in both hands and smothered my mouth with kisses before I could finish my sentence. I put my arms around her and pulled her onto my lap.

We hugged and kissed until the door to Serina's bedroom opened up and Sarge walked out wearing a dress, a girl's wig and makeup.

We both burst out laughing hysterically. Serina came out last and looked at her mother sitting on my lap. The little girl smiled and nodded her head in approval. She looked down at Sarge and said to him, "Let's go back to my bedroom and put on other costumes. We need to let the grownups play their own game."

She giggled and ran into her bedroom with Sarge and closed the door behind her. We went back to playing adult games.

I returned to the hotel and picked up all my gear and headed back to the apartment. Once I moved in, it felt like I was back in my own place again. When it was just me and Sarge living there, I have to admit I felt lonely most of the time. I was adjusting to being a civilian and it wasn't easy for me. Just like many of the vets who suffered from various degrees of PTSD, Sarge and I had our own demons to deal with. I was surprised to find out Sarge had combat nightmares just like I did. I even took a night shift job at Terminal 6 trying to avoid the nightmares. It didn't work out so well. No matter when I slept, night or day, the bad dreams returned.

When I moved into the apartment again, I had a ready-made family who loved me. I had a different purpose in life and it was fantastic. For the first few days, Maria and I learned to be comfortable with each other. We examined each other's quirks and mutually figured out a way to live with them.

I felt very fortunate to have so much time together waiting for the next mission to begin. One day I took everybody to the park and had Sarge show off his skills. They never seemed to tire of watching me take the dog through his drills, even the scary ones when I dressed in pads and had Sarge pretend to attack me. We did that three days a week just to keep him tuned up.

When I moved in with Maria, Serina's school was just starting spring break and her mom took two weeks off from work. We used the vacation for what she called "quality time" with Serina and me. When she returned to work, I took Serina to school and picked her up in the afternoon.

It turned out Maria was an instructor at the LA Fitness Spa and she got me a lifetime platinum membership. I would workout at the spa almost every day and hang out with her during her breaks. I knew she was in terrific physical condition, now I knew why.

Once a week we would attend the Team Joshua dinner at one of the great Portland restaurants. She really enjoyed meeting everyone on the team and she became friends with all of them. She even signed up with Simone to begin jujitsu training.

After several months went by, Joshua informed all of the team that we were all invited to go on a two week cruise from Seattle to Anchorage, Alaska. When I told my family the news they went crazy. Maria told me she always wanted to go on a cruise but could never afford it. When I told her we would have a penthouse suite she couldn't believe it.

I had a hard time believing it too. It seemed too good to be true. It also seemed like the beginning of another mission, but I kept that concern to myself.

### <u>Pham Bin Minh</u>

As soon as our mission was completed and we finished our contribution to the After Action Report, Joshua released us to stand down until notified. He added we should plan on getting together at least once a week just to keep in touch.

Simone suggested we could comply with that request and have a nice dinner at the same time. She took it upon herself to be the one to select the restaurants. She picked only the upscale dining establishments so we were to dress nicely and bring a date if we were so inclined. I noticed she stared at me as she said the word date.

I guessed it was to be a combination of work and socializing. I wasn't sure I could find someone who would want to go to dinner with me. I didn't date much when I was going to law school. I decided to visit my old friend and lawyer partner from Vietnam who was recently married. His name was Nguyen Thanh and his wife's name was Cais. I was hoping they might know a woman I could take to dinner.

I called ahead to see if Nguyen and Cais were available. Nguyen said yes and invited me to join them for lunch. Before I hung up, I asked them if they knew anyone who would like to go to a semi-formal dinner with me and the rest of my team. He spoke briefly to his wife then said Cais knew a young lady who might be interested.

An hour later, I met up with Nguyen and his wife at my old law office. Now it was Nguyen's office. When I walked in, I was surprised to see not only my friend and his wife but also another young Vietnamese woman. As was the custom, Nguyen introduced me to the woman. Her name Thong Chau, a very mysterious name which translates into English as Intelligent Pearl.

We bowed to each other and I said in Vietnamese, "It's a pleasure to meet you Ms. Thong."

She replied in English with the faintest of embarrassed smiles, her voice almost a whisper, "Please speak in English, Mr. Pham. I was born in Vietnam, however my family moved to the United States when I was only two years old. I apologize for not being able to converse in Vietnamese. My parents… discouraged me from learning the language. They felt it would be a stigma." With downcast eyes she made another bow, then added, "Both my parents are now deceased and Cais has been assisting me in learning to speak Vietnamese."

Cais added in her broken English, "Smart is she. Hard tries her. Intelligent doctor name her."

I nodded and thought to myself, *Cais' English reminds me of Yoda from Star Wars. Perhaps I should also volunteer to help them both. I've got the time now that the mission is complete.*

We headed out to a nearby restaurant a little after 1300 hours. We all went in Nguyen's car with Pearl and me in the back seat. I had called her Ms. Thong several times before she asked me to refer to her as Pearl. While Nguyen and Cais conversed in Vietnamese, we sat quietly. I spoke first to break the tension, "I think Cais said that you were a doctor. Do you have your own practice, or do you work for a hospital?"

She looked mildly surprised, then smiled. "I'm not a medical doctor, Pham. I have a PhD from Cal Tech."

"Really? What's your specialty?" I asked.

Again in her soft voice she answered, "Nuclear Physics. I'm currently working on a project for a small cold fusion reactor."

I was momentarily stunned. "That's amazing," I finally said. "Is it research, or are you building a power plant?"

"I'm afraid that's classified top secret. I may have said too much already." She reached over and squeezed my hand. "I would be in big trouble if my project became public knowledge. Let's change the conversation. What do you do for a living, Pham? Cais said you're a lawyer."

"She's correct," I replied. "However, I haven't been practicing law for almost a year. I am currently between missions, but I also work for a government agency and my mission activities are classified."

She sat quietly, staring intently at me for an uncomfortable minute, then said, "The attack on the Antelope fortress." She didn't say it as a question, she said it like it was a known fact.

"How could you possibly know that?" I asked, wondering if she was a secret agent for the bad guys.

Her look softened as we pulled into the restaurant parking lot. "I'm not allowed to tell you now, but I'm certain we will be working together in the near future. We'll discuss this more later, if you like. For now let's just have a nice lunch."

Lunch was good, at least I think it was good. Most of my attention was focused on our previous conversation. I was wondering if I should I reveal what she said to Joshua and the rest of the team, or if I should just wait and see how it played out.

I have to admit, this woman really intrigued me. She was obviously more intelligent than I was. She also knew things she shouldn't know. I decided the best approach was to stay close to her and see if I could get more information from her.

At lunch, I made a proposal to tutor both her and Cais. I volunteered to set aside at least an hour every day to help each of them in mastering a new language. Cais would work on her English and Ms. Thong would focus on Vietnamese. Both women were pleasantly surprised by my offer. Even Nguyen agreed it was a good idea.

During the next several weeks I lived up to my commitment and both of the women made great strides in speaking their new languages. It also gave me a sense of accomplishment. Occasionally one of them would have other commitments and I would meet with each of them separately. On those days I met with Pearl, I would stretch the time to chat about nothing in particular.

I noticed when we met one-on-one she seemed to dress differently. I don't know how to describe it, but she seemed more attractive. I also noticed she was beginning to wear a little makeup. Just a little, or maybe it was just my imagination.

She began to open up to me about her personal life. I reciprocated and shared some things about myself. She even laughed out loud about some of my ridiculous misfortunes as a young man.

In addition to the language classes, we began to see each other more frequently. When I invited her to our Team Joshua dinners she was hesitant, but the day of the first dinner she called me and said she would go. She ended up having a great time and so did I and the rest of the team.

After the fifth or sixth of the team dinners, I drove her home as usual and walked her to the door of her apartment. I began to turn away when she called out to me, "Pham, don't go yet. It's still early. Would you like to come in for a drink?"

I turned back and said, "Yes I would. Thank you for the offer."

She was waiting on the top step as I approached and reached out and took her hand. She pulled me in close, put her arms around my waist, hugged me tight and kissed me passionately. I vaguely remember somebody coming up from behind me, but I was so focused on her kiss I barely felt the dart hit me in the neck.

The next thing I remember was waking up on a couch in her apartment with an older man sitting in a chair across from me. Pearl was nowhere to be seen. I struggled to sit up. Once up, I tried to speak, but my mouth and tongue seemed to be out of order, producing a poor imitation of normal speech.

"Don't try to speak, Pham," said the man. "Just listen to me. From now on, you are going to be my confidential informant, CI is the common title. You are going to give me information about the activities of Joshua and his team of misfits. If you don't, I will have you killed and your gook girlfriend along with you. Do you understand me?"

I nodded which turned out to be a bad idea. It gave me a splitting headache. The older man turned to the door of the bedroom and called out, "Carl bring the bitch out now so he can see this isn't some kind of joke." He turned back to look at me as the bedroom door opened. I couldn't see very well, but I was pretty sure it wasn't Carl. My vision was blurry, but I recognized Pearl. She was completely naked with a black eye and a cut on her wrist. She was holding a Beretta with a silencer in her right hand. She held a finger to her lips to keep me quiet as she moved beside the older man. He turned, expecting Carl, and Pearl shot him right between the eyes.

Still holding the gun, she limped to me sitting on the couch. "I'm so sorry, Pham. This wasn't supposed to happen. It's best if you lie down on the couch. The injection from the dart should wear off soon, I hope. We should probably get out of here as soon as possible. Let me know when you are up to walking out of here." She looked back to the bedroom then hurried back inside. I heard the muffled sound of the Beretta again and I managed to stand up and take a few steps when she caught me as I was about to fall.

I must have passed out again. When I came to, we were riding in my rental. She must have carried me down the steps and into the car. *How could she do that?* I was sure I weighed twice as much as her and she was injured besides. She was talking to me a hundred miles an hour. I thought to myself, *Who is this woman? It couldn't possibly be my Pearl. Pearl was a lady, soft spoken and polite. This pretend Pearl was completely different. I didn't know if she was saving me or planning to kill me.* I passed out again.

It was morning when I woke up. The first thing I noticed was we weren't in Pearl's apartment. I thought it might be a motel room; it turned out it was more like a safe house.

The drug had worn off and other than a slight headache, I felt fine. Moving very slowly just in case something was not quite right yet, I turned my head and saw Pearl asleep next to me. She was naked and her body was a mess. Apparently, Carl worked her over pretty badly before she took his gun and killed him. Carl was a huge, strong man. *How could she possibly take his gun away?*

She was facing me and I could see her left eye was swollen shut in a sickening shade of purple and black. It looked like she might have bite marks on her breasts, the rest of her was just as bad or probably worse. I covered her with the sheet and headed for the bathroom.

I relieved myself and washed my face, checking in the mirror to see if I had sustained any injuries when she called out to me, "Pham, can you help me please?" It was the voice of my Pearl. I wondered where the other woman had gone as I hurried to Pearl's side.

She was trying to sit up, but the pain was too intense. Her whole body was spasming. "Just lay back down, Pearl. Do you have any pain meds?"

"Drawer under the sink, right… no, left side."

I ran to the bathroom and found a prescription bottle of oxy and shook out several pills. I held her head up, placed three pills on her tongue and held the glass of water as she drank and swallowed the pills. Five minutes later, she was sound asleep again. I checked her every few minutes to make sure I hadn't overdosed her.

I was wondering what to do next when my iPhone 18 vibrated. It startled me. I would have thought they (whoever they were) would have taken my phone.

It was Simone. She seemed annoyed. "Why aren't you here for the team meeting? We waited for over an hour, then Joshua postponed the meeting and told me to find you. I've been calling you for the last hour and you finally--"

"Simone STOP! Pearl and I were attacked last night, I was drugged and Pearl was beaten, possibly raped. I have no idea where we are. We both need help, Pearl much more than me."

There was a pause then Simone said, "We've got your location from your phone. We're heading out with medical help on the way. ETA to your location is seven minutes. Hold on Pham. We're coming."

I sat on the edge of the bed and checked on Pearl every minute to make sure she was still breathing. Before the seventh minute, there was a rap on the door and I let the team members in along with a medic I had never seen before.

The medic went straight to the bed, placed his med kit on the floor and slid the sheet off of Pearl. Simone had been watching intently as the medic's backup. She gasped in disbelief at the injuries she saw on Pearl's body, then quickly composed herself and followed the medic's instructions. She hooked up an IV drip of saline solution into Pearl's right arm as the medic inspected each of the damaged areas of the woman's body. He said all the bruises would be painful, but there was no permanent tissue damage. She had a mild concussion, but no fractures. The last step was the rape kit. There was evidence of an attempted rape by the bruising of the tissue around her vagina, but he said she had not been raped.

While this examination was going on, Joshua had taken me aside and asked me what had happened. I told him everything I could remember, including Pearl shooting and killing her potential rapist, first name Carl, then shooting Carl's boss between the eyes. I had found the Beretta with the suppressor attached, lying in the bed next to Pearl. I gave it to Joshua.

Caleb briefly interrupted, *Do you know the address of Pearl's apartment?*

I gave him the address. Ten seconds later he transported back and reported to Joshua and the rest of the team: *Two bodies, just like Pham told you. The older victim was seated in a chair across from the couch with a single 9 millimeter wound to the forehead between the eyes. I got his prints and have identified him. I found Carl in the bedroom lying on his back with two gunshot wounds, also from the 9 millimeter. One was in the heart and the other between his eyes. He had a pair of woman's panties stuffed in his mouth as a gag. One novel fact, we found his penis lying next to him on the bed. Upon further examination I found teeth marks on the severed penis. I think she bit it off. There was a substantial amount of blood in the area of his groin but he didn't bleed out. I believe she bit it off, however she shot him in the heart before he bled out. The one in the head was just insurance. My recommendation is to never piss this lady off.*

I was surprised Caleb could get so much information in less than ten seconds. Then I remembered spirits can manipulate time. He could have spent an hour from his perspective during ten seconds of our time.

Joshua went over and spoke to the medic. "Can we safely transport her to a secure facility?"

"That shouldn't be any problem. She's going to need bed rest for at least three days. After that give her 500 mg of Tylenol three times a day until the pain is gone." He packed up his med kit and gave his regards to the team members then left the scene.

"What's next boss? Should we call the police to report the killings?" I asked.

Before Joshua could answer we heard his phone ring. It was The Apostle. Joshua put it on speaker mode so we could all hear. "Do not report the killings to the police. They will eventually find the bodies. In the meantime take care of Pearl. Guard her with your lives. She is one of mine. When she recovers I will have her tell you everything you need to know.

"Joshua, she will become an important part of your team for your next mission. I want you to continue on as if nothing happened. I've already made excuses for her absence from work to her boss and she is on medical leave for as long as she needs it.

"Pham, take care of this woman. She had nothing to do with you being drugged and held captive. Do not withdraw your affection for her. I predict she will be your life-long love.

"Are there any questions? I thought not. Good hunting Team Joshua."

# CHAPTER 2
# CALEB & THE SPIRIT WORLD

### Caleb

Joshua asked me to see what I could find out about the new War Wagon which was supposed to be delivered to us a week ago. Try as hard as I could, I still couldn't find anything about where it was being fabricated or what it looked like. That never happened before. When I asked for help from my spirit guide I got no answer. That had also never happened before. I was stymied.

After I was through butting my imaginary head against an imaginary wall, I received a message from The Apostle. Actually, it wasn't a message, it was more like an ultimatum to cease and desist. He also added a brief explanation, "The delay in delivering the new War Wagon is due to the attack on Dr. Thong Chau. Until she is able to continue her work on the cold fusion reactor, the delivery is on hold. Feel free to share this information with the rest of Team Joshua, but no one else."

I immediately passed on the information to Joshua. He informed me Pearl had been cleared by the doctor for her return to work in a day or two. He communicated to me he had instructed Simone to set up a team dinner for tomorrow evening. Pham would be escorting Pearl to the dinner. He planned to "gently confront" Pearl about her involvement with the new War Wagon.

### Pham

When Pearl was taken to the hospital, I requested Joshua to permit me to stay with her until she was released. I would be her security and I would also attempt to determine why we were attacked. Personally, I needed to know if she had lured me into a trap; if she was somehow connected to Carl and his boss. I didn't want to believe she had been working with them, but I had to be sure. Down deep, what I really wanted to know was if the passionate kiss she gave me on her front steps was part of the setup or if she really wanted to kiss me.

When she woke up in the hospital, she was frightened and confused. She was searching the room to make sure she was safe. Then she saw me and stopped searching. She reached out to me and I took her hand. Her voice was raspy and strained as she said to me, "Oh Pham, I'm so sorry I got you into this. I had no idea they were waiting for me. If I had, I would never have invited you in. I just wanted to kiss you so badly, I didn't think to check the apartment before I invited you in. You must think I'm a terrible person to get you invol—"

I pulled her close and kissed her. It wasn't a passionate kiss. It was a kiss that said I was still her friend and maybe something more. After the kiss, I continued to hold her close. I wanted to hold her to comfort her and to comfort myself. In my heart I felt, no, not felt, I *knew* she wasn't responsible for what happened to me that night. However, a part of me still wanted to know how she'd been involved with people who wanted to hurt us.

"Pham, can you help me up?" she asked. "I really need to use the bathroom. I also want to brush my teeth so I can give you the kiss you deserve."

She wrapped her hospital gown around her as I helped her out of bed and supported/half-carried her to the restroom. She was still in pain, but after a few steps she seemed to get stronger. She closed the bathroom door behind her as a nurse walked in.

The nurse looked around the room, totally ignoring me, headed to the bathroom door and rapped on it with her knuckles, "Ms. Thong, I'm your day nurse, Crystal. Do you need any help?"

"No, I'm fine. Just give me a few minutes to freshen up."

When she came out of the bathroom, she walked slowly to a recliner chair next to the bed and sat down gingerly. The nurse checked her vital signs then asked her to stand up and disrobe so she could check to make sure her injuries were healing. As Pearl struggled to stand up again, the nurse looked at me for the first time and said. "You need to step out until I'm finished, sir."

I shook my head and answered, "Sorry, I'm not leaving."

"Are you her husband?"

I shook my head again, "No. I'm her security and I need to be with her at all times."

Before the nurse could say anything else, Pearl stood, removed her hospital gown and said, "It's okay nurse. He's my boyfriend. He's seen me naked before."

I was stunned and embarrassed by her comments. I could feel my face turning red, but I just nodded my head and stoically watched as the nurse checked her out.

When the nurse was finished, she commented to Pearl, "As far as I can tell, you're healing nicely. You'll still have the bruising for a few more days, but I see no reason for you to remain in the hospital. Of course, the doctor is the one who makes the final decision and he will be making his rounds shortly. I assume your security guard boyfriend will be driving you home?" she asked without looking at me.

Pearl smiled and replied, "Yes, I'm not letting him out of my sight."

The nurse left without another word.

When the door closed, Pearl walked slowly to me and put her arms around my neck and said, "I couldn't wait for her to leave. All I could think about was kissing you again. Did you like looking at my naked body?"

Before I could answer, she covered my mouth with hers and we kissed. Then kissed again and kissed some more. Her knees began to buckle and I wasn't sure if it was from the pain or the passion.

I picked her up in my arms, carried her to the bed and laid her down gently. Being in love was new to me. I wished there was an owner's manual to tell me how to act and to feel. I was so afraid of doing something wrong or saying something that would offend her.

So I left it up to her and she pulled me down next to her on the bed. We hugged gently and we kissed some more. Then the doctor knocked once and walked in.

The doctor didn't seem to mind and waited until I was out of the bed and sitting in the recliner, before he said to Pearl, "Looking at your chart and hearing the nurse's opinion, I think you're ready to go home. If your… security guard doesn't mind, he can take you out in a wheelchair. You both have a good day."

### Simone

Joshua said he wanted me to select a restaurant with a private banquet room large enough to serve eight to ten people. The Ringside Steak House in Northwest Portland was my choice. I let everyone know where the restaurant was located and when to arrive. Special Agent Joey Hong, now with the FBI, and his wife Lili joined us. Mark was with Maria (grandma was taking care of Serina) and Pham was with Pearl. Of course, I was Joshua's date.

Joshua informed me there would be a classified presentation after dinner. My boss said to plan on staying until 10:00 pm. The two women weren't cleared to attend the presentation/discussion portion, however they were cleared to enjoy the Ringside's famous desserts and adult beverages while the meeting was in progress.

Everyone arrived on time and introductions were made during a brief happy hour (more like a happy half-hour). FBI agent Hong had met all of Team Joshua, but Lili hadn't, neither had Maria nor Pearl.

Once the introductions were completed and hors d'oeuvres were washed down with a flute of champagne, we were escorted to the Ringside's private banquet room. The restaurant opened almost eight decades ago and is considered one of the top ten fine dining restaurants in the northwest. It was well known for its steaks, but offered a wide variety of seafood as well as an excellent wine list. It was located within walking distance of Providence Park, initially called Multnomah Stadium when the Ringside opened for business.

Dinner was fantastic. I've eaten in some really upscale restaurants when I was in New Orleans, but the Ringside Steak House had it all. Some of the team had eaten in fine dining establishments, but I think they felt a little out of place until the food was served. Joshua, a big fan of Stake and Shake, commented, "This place is fantastic, why haven't we come here before?"

"Wait until you see the bill," I answered. "I'm glad The Apostle is picking up the tab."

It took us the better part of an hour to finish our dinner. Everyone raved about the food as we ate and chatted with the newcomers. When dinner was over, Maria and Lili excused themselves and left for the lounge area while we set up for the briefing.

### Pearl

Joshua, whom I had just met this evening, introduced me saying, "I'd like to formally introduce you to the newest member of our team. Her Vietnamese name is Thong Chau which translates in English to Intelligent Pearl. To justify that name, she has a PhD form Cal Tech in nuclear physics. She is currently working on a top secret project to develop a small cold fusion reactor. She is going to share with us how this project is an important part of our new War Wagon. Pearl, you have the floor."

I stood and moved to the large screen on the back wall. "Hello again," I said nervously. "I want to thank you all for including me in your team. First, may I ask if anyone has swept the room for surveillance devices?"

Pham spoke up, "Yes, Pearl. While we were setting up I checked for any bugs and the room is clean. I also turned on a jammer that will scramble any transmission from this briefing."

I smiled at Pham. "Very good, Pham. Thank you." I picked up the small controller and pushed the button to show the video. I got the stunned expressions I had been hoping for as the picture of the new War Wagon was displayed on the screen. The image began to rotate slightly as I continued my narration.

"The new War Wagon is about the size of a large motorhome. It is fully armored and carries a large array of both offensive and defensive weapons. Its power source is my cold fusion reactor which provides an unending supply of energy to power all of the vehicle's systems."

I pushed a button and the image began to change. "The new vehicle is a hybrid. It can operate on the ground at speeds up to 200 miles per hour. As you can see, the vehicle can transform into an aircraft using two counter rotating rotors that are collapsed and stored in the roof of the vehicle." They watched as a long narrow door on the roof opened up, and the two counter rotating rotors, each with six rotor blades, rose up and deployed above the roof. At the same time a large propeller with multiple scimitar-shaped blades appeared in the back of the wagon.

"The pusher propeller allows the War Wagon to fly at up to 400 knots. To accomplish this speed, the shape of the vehicle morphs into a more aerodynamic design. The variable pitch blades on the propeller allow the vehicle to fly in reverse or to hover using only the roof mounted rotors."

I pushed another button and the War Wagon transformed into a submarine-looking boat. "Finally, the War Wagon can travel on top of lakes, rivers and oceans, or submerge a hundred feet below the surface. Again, the contours of the vehicle morph to reduce drag, permitting it to travel up to 75 knots on the surface and 50 knots submerged.

"All of this is controlled by a very sophisticated AI system. It permits the operators of the War Wagon to require almost no training to operate this baby."

I paused, then added, "Are there any questions?"

I looked at the audience who seemed to be catatonic. Joshua was the first to speak up, "When will this be ready?"

"Two weeks from now. I have a few bugs to work out in the fusion reactor. I was delayed by the attack of… enemy agents."

Pham commented, "So we're looking at the real thing? I thought it was a computer graphic."

"No Pham," I replied. "What you saw was the real thing."

"How many people can it hold?" asked Mark.

"It depends on how it's configured. It can hold ten to eighteen people."

"When will we get to put hands on?" asked Joshua.

"If you're willing to go to the Seattle area, you and your team can take it out for a trial run in five days."

"Can I go along?" asked Agent Hong.

Joshua answered him. "Absolutely. You're supposed to be on loan to us for the next month."

The questions were endless. There was one question I dreaded to hear and it finally came. "Can you give us any details on who attacked you and Pham?" asked Simone.

Before I could respond, Joshua answered, "At the present time, we're not involved in that investigation. It's just as well. We're going to have our hands full with the War Wagon."


## Caleb

I really enjoyed the dinner party at Ringside. Even though I can't eat, I still get the sensation of eating and drinking. When Joshua ate his fill of delicious filet mignon, I felt full as well. When he gets roaring drunk (a very rare occurrence), I feel only mildly tipsy. I assume spirits aren't allowed to feel drunk… ever.

Once Pearl's presentation was completed, Joshua thought to me, *What did you think of her presentation?*

*Mind boggling,* I thought back. *It kind of reminds me of the armored trucks that transformed into armed APCs during our last mission. Except this is an order of magnitude more advanced.*

*Are you up for some spirit snooping?* he projected.

*Your wish is my command,* I replied. *What do you want me to snoop?*

*Two thing., First, see if you can find out where the new War Wagon is located. Check it out as thoroughly as you can. I want a better sense of when it will really be ready for a test run. Secondly, in spite of what I said at dinner, see if you can get any leads on the two men Pearl shot and killed. I really want to know who they worked for and why they went after Pham as well as Pearl. I'm concerned about sabotage or something worse.*

*What might that something worse be?* I projected.

*The people who ordered Pham and Pearl to be attacked may be interested in stealing the new War Wagon and using it against us,* answered Joshua.

*Roger that.*

My first order of business was to find Pearl. That took about a nanosecond. Sometimes being a spirit has its advantages. She was with Pham in the hotel suite where he was now living. They were talking about her involvement regarding the cold fusion reactor she was working on. It's interesting how when people talk about things they tend to visualize what they are talking about, some more vividly than others. Pearl's visualizations were off the chart. I saw her and her team of scientists, engineers and technicians working on a large variety of things in what looked like a huge building. There were no windows anywhere and the place was as spotless as a clean room.

Behind them was the new War Wagon. I froze the view and zoomed in, only now it looked like a very large motorhome. I saw a different group of techs conducting some tests, so I moved forward in a series of time jumps. Each jump revealed the War Wagon in different configurations, from motorhome to a large armored personnel carrier (APC for short), to an aircraft, ending up with what looked like a very fast boat. What a rush!

I waited patiently to see if Pearl would notice some indication of her location. Five minutes later I saw a sign above her work station. It said:

**Boeing/Everett**
**Advanced Research Laboratory (ARL)**

I quickly transported to Everett in the state of Washington, just north of Seattle. It took me less than a minute of real time to find the building. I could tell it was a secured lab, with two rows of fencing topped by barbed wire and four sets of security guards making circuits around the building every ten minutes. I also noticed armed guards on the roof scanning for any trouble. There was only one entrance. It was located on the west side of the building. People entering had to show their badges and take a retina scan before they were cleared.

I transported inside and noticed it looked exactly like Pearl's vision. And there she was, in all her glory, our new and greatly improved War Wagon. At least a dozen techs were all over the new vehicle running tests and making adjustments. It reminded me of a beehive surrounded by honey bees.

That completed Joshua's first request.

I transported back to see if I could pick Pearl's mind about the attack on her and Pham. What were the bad guys trying to accomplish? I knew they had been torturing her to give them classified information about the cold fusion reactor, but how did Pham fit into it? Was he just in the wrong place at the wrong time, or did they want something from him as well?

I decided to see if I could gently probe Pearl's mind without being detected. Hopefully, she could give us some answers to why she and Pham were attacked. We needed to know who sanctioned this attack. It was worth a try.

I returned to Pham's suite and waited patiently for them to go to bed. Pham waited until Pearl was finished in the bathroom where she had changed into pajama bottoms and a Seattle Seahawk T-shirt.

After Pham had done a quick check of the entire suite, it was his turn for the bathroom. A few minutes later he walked into the bedroom, now also in pajama bottoms, but bare chested. He was carrying his semiautomatic .44 magnum, placed it under his pillow, set the intruder alarm, turned out the lights except for a night-light, and crawled into bed.

Pearl snuggled up next to him. He could tell she was still in pain as she hugged and kissed him goodnight. It was too soon for any romantic action.

I waited until they had both fallen asleep. I continued to wait until Pearl was in REM sleep then gently crept into her mind. I didn't try to probe, only to observe her dreams. Several disjointed dreams sped by, followed by a few romantic episodes with Pham which I ignored until she began dreaming that she was on the top step to her apartment, asking Pham to come join her…

> Pham walks up the steps and she takes his hand, and pulls him close to her, and begins kissing him passionately. Looking through her eyes, she sees Carl fire the dart into Pham's neck. She grabs Pham to keep him from falling and screams at Carl, "What are you doing?!!! she dream/thinks; He's not involved in this. You're not supposed to be here tonight.
>
> Carl drags Pham from her embrace and pushes her hard against the door. It opens and they both fall into the apartment. Pham is unconscious. She staggers to her feet and rushes at Carl screaming, "Did you kill him? You better pray he's not dead or injured or you shall die a thousand deaths by my hand."
>
> Carl backhands her across the face, knocking her back down to the floor at the feet of Carl's boss. As she struggles to stand, she screams at the man in the chair. "Stop this! This is insane, Jefferson. Why are you doing this? I've given you what you want."
>
> Carl picks up Pham and throws him onto the couch. He moans and his eyes flutter open, but stay unfocused.
>
> Jefferson grabs her by the hair and pulls her to her feet. He slaps her hard several times across her face, splitting her lip. He kisses her brutally, biting her lower lip until it bleeds. She tries to knee him in the groin. He hits her again, this time with a closed fist, knocking her to the ground, her cheek cut and her eye swelling.
>
> "You know perfectly well why we are doing this," hisses Jefferson. "What you gave me was crap. My employer knows when he's being lied to. Your cold fusion designs are shit. It took a few days of analyses, but they are worthless. If they followed your instructions they would have been killed by a nuclear explosion. They think you're a double agent. They want you dead. So do I. But Carl wants to spend a little private time with you before you go."

He turns to Carl and says, "She's all yours, Carl. Enjoy, but you've only got fifteen minutes before we have to leave."

"What are we going to do with the gook she was kissing?" Carl asked.

"Kill him of course," answers Jefferson. "I want her to watch when we kill him, then you can kill Pearl any way you want."

Carl smiles, picks up Pearl as if she was a sack of rice, and carries her into the bedroom, closing the door behind him.

The next several minutes was a flurry of incredible pain. He rips her clothes from her body. She fights back, but the blows to her head have given her a concussion and she has little control of her actions. Carl is brutal beyond belief. When he bites down on her breast, the pain is unbearable. She will do anything to make him stop, to make the pain go away, to preserve her womanhood.

Carl looks up as he bites her. He seems to be smiling. When she stabs him in the eye with her pointed fingernail, things suddenly change. He backs away from her breast, but Pearl grabs him with both hands behind his head, pulling him closer, then stabs him in the other eye.

Carl screams in agony as he backs away from her, completely blind. He can't see anything, but he lunges at her and pulls her towards his naked body. His hands grab her around the neck and begins to strangle her, pushing her down his chest to get a better grip on her. Instead of trying to pull away she lets him push her down until she grabs his penis with both of her hands and squeezes as tightly as she can, but Carl's grip on her throat only tightens. She is starting to lose consciousness, she does the only thing she can think of. She bites off his penis and spits it onto the bed behind her as Carl's blood sprays from his wound.

He releases his hands from her neck and falls on his back onto the bed, squeezing what remains of his penis in an attempt to keep from bleeding out. She picks up Carl's gun from the dresser. It has a silencer, and she places it against his chest and shoots him once in the heart. Then she staggers to the bedroom door, opens it, and cautiously walks into the living room holding the pistol and standing behind Jefferson. Pham is sitting on the couch facing her as she puts a finger to her lips to prevent him from speaking. When Jefferson turns his head expecting to see Carl holding Pearl's limp body, she shoots him between the eyes.

She screamed out loud as the nightmare reached its peak, waking Pham. I disengaged as the nightmare ended and Pham began comforting her. He held her in his arm telling her softly it was only a dream, she was safe and he would never let anything like that happen again.

I transported back to Joshua and relayed what I saw. It was one of the worst times in my existence. At first, I was shocked by the brutality of Carl and the indifference of Jefferson. I would have killed them on the spot if they weren't already dead. People like that deserve to die. Their punishment should fit their crime.


## Joshua

When Caleb finished briefing me on the results of his two assignments, I was very pleased at what he had discovered. He had found the location where the new War Wagon was being developed in record time. When he told me the events Pearl and Pham had gone through, I felt his rage and shared his anger.

*Can you use your special spirit powers to identify Carl and Jefferson?* I thought to him.

*Oh my gosh, now why didn't I think about that,* he replied sarcastically. *Of course I identified them both. I had very good pictures from Pearl's dream of Carl and his boss, Jefferson. I also got their fingerprints from the medical examiner's database. I immediately scanned every database in the entire world and got nearly a hundred hits. They all identified both scumbags.*

*Carl was hired muscle with the IQ of a toad. He's been in and out of various jails and prisons. Recently, he was charged with multiple murders, assault and battery, and apparently his favorite, rape. This guy was a real piece of work. He had multiple charges for rape of both women and men. I guess he was an equal-opportunity rapist. However, recently he had gotten off on all the charges filed against him. A team of very expensive lawyers got him acquitted on all charges, mostly because witnesses to his crimes seemed to disappear.*

*Can you find out who paid for his attorneys?* I projected.

*Of course I can and I did. However, I'm waiting for the big reveal after I give you the download on Jefferson,* Caleb thought back to me. He likes being in charge sometimes and since he's my brother, I let him get away with it… occasionally.

*Jefferson is entirely another bag of worms,* he began. *I had to go through some back channels and cutouts to discover anything about him. Here's what I think I know.*

*Jefferson was connected to a deputy director in our state department. However, the deputy director thinks our deceased scumbag was also connected to the Chinese.*

*Now for the big reveal,* he continued. I could sense his excitement in the tone of his thoughts. *The team of lawyers who defended Carl for the last several months also represented Jefferson in some federal charges of espionage.*

*Really?!* I replied with the appropriate amount of awe. *Our own federal government could be responsible for the attempt on Pearl and Pham's life. You need…*

*You don't have to tell me, bro. I'm already working on getting more intel on our state department as well as the Chinese.*

# CHAPTER 3
# TOURING SEATTLE & THE BOEING ARL

### Pham

I wasn't surprised when Joshua approached me and said he wanted the team to visit the Boeing ARL site at Everett, Washington. I was pretty sure Caleb had found the location quickly and Joshua didn't want to wait around to see the new War Wagon prototype.

When I mentioned it to Pearl, she just shrugged her shoulders and said, "I guess it was inevitable he'd want to see it as soon as possible. Just like all little boys, men can't wait to play with their new toys."

She told me, "Make sure Joshua is aware the reactor won't be ready for a day or two after we arrive, however we can demonstrate a lot of the new features using external power.

"I need to be on-site to finish my work on the reactor while they drool over the vehicle. If everything goes okay we can install the cold fusion reactor and take it out for a spin, or a short flight, or maybe search underwater for a pod of whales in Puget Sound."

The next day, we all checked out of our suites in Portland and took a commercial flight from Portland International to SeaTac located about halfway between Seattle and Tacoma. We charted a bus from SeaTac to Everett and checked into a Marriott near the Boeing site around noon.

After we checked into the hotel we were escorted into the secured conference room where Boeing security people read us into the War Wagon project. Of course, Joshua wanted us to go immediately to the ARL facility. I think I detected him pouting when he was told by the head of Boeing's security we wouldn't be allowed to enter the facility until the next morning. They needed the time to prepare the site for our visit.

Pearl was the exception. At her request, the security chief escorted her to meet up with her team and get a head start on finishing the checkout of the reactor. It was suggested we might want to do some sightseeing in Seattle. Maybe check out the Space Needle.

### Simone

Joshua asked me if I could speak to the Marriott concierge to see if we could book a tour of Seattle for this afternoon. She recommended the VIP tour for the four of us plus Sarge. There was an opening for a tour bus in thirty minutes. I signed us up and we all met in the lobby twenty minutes later.

When the bus arrived, the first thing I noticed was it could seat at least twice our number. The second thing was we were the only people on the bus, so everyone took a window seat, including Sarge. The seats were very plush with lots of leg room, which allowed Joshua to stretch out his 6'7" body and ride in comfort. The bus had a transparent roof to allow us to get a great view as we drove the 30 minutes from Everett to Seattle.

Our first stop was the famous Space Needle. We stepped into a spacious elevator car which took us quickly up the 500 feet to the Loupe. The Loupe has a glass floor and high windows which gave us all a terrific view of the city as it made a complete revolution in 45 minutes. As most of us took pictures, the tour guide joined us and pointed out possible stops for our tour.

We decided our next attraction would be Pike Place Market to have a late lunch and watch the employees sling 30 pound salmons across the aisles. The seafood was delicious and freshly caught the same day. After lunch we walked through the rest of the market and bought a few souvenirs. I bought a T-shirt which had printed on the front, *I Survived the 6.8 Earthquake*. Pham opted for a *Go Seahawks* cap. Mark got Sarge toys that looked like small fish and other sea creatures. For the rest of the tour, Sarge walked around with a toy squid hanging out of his mouth, giving a warning growl when Mark attempted to take the squid from him. Joshua decided he needed more seafood and got two orders of king crab to go. Probably for a snack later that night.

When we left the market, the tour guide took us by the dock where two huge cruise ships were tied up. I didn't realize how big they were. Caleb thought to me they were as big as an aircraft carrier and could accommodate over 5,000 passengers and a crew of around 2,000. He quickly checked the ship's manifest and said they were getting ready to cruise to Anchorage, Alaska, making several stops along the way, including the state capitol, Juneau, and the beautiful views at Glacier Bay.

Our last stop was at the underground city. It included the remains of a city under Pioneer Square from a huge fire in 1889. Rather than attempt to rebuild the fire damaged buildings, they raised the streets 22 feet above them and constructed the town on top. I have to admit, it felt kind of spooky.

I was glad when our tour of the underground city was over. It reminded me of my stay in New Orleans, and the deserted homes from hurricanes where ghosts and goblins were reported to reside. It didn't help when Sarge began howling, not barking, howling, his echo reverberating off the overhead ceiling and buildings. It gave me the creeps, especially when Sarge brushed up against my leg in the semi-dark tunnel.

The sun was setting over Puget Sound as our tour guide rounded us up and we got in the bus. By the time we arrived at our hotel in Everett, it was dark with the full moon attempting to shine through the cloud bank which was rolling in over the Sound. Everyone seemed to enjoy the tour, including the spooky part (except for me). Now it was time to think about checking out the War Wagon as Joshua and I shared some king crab.

### Joshua

Simone and I got up early the next morning, had a room service breakfast, and met the rest of the team in the hotel lobby. The Boeing security guard who had read us into the top-secret program the day before handed us badges, emphasizing that they must be visibly displayed while entering the ARL facility and during the stay. He directed us to the large, black SUV parked in the hotel's covered entry area. The four of us, along with Sarge in his therapy vest, climbed into the rear seats and fastened our seat belts.

Our driver and the security guard were dressed like the *Men In Black* agents and were wearing very dark sunglasses to complete the movie image. No one spoke during the short ride from the hotel. We were stopped by a gate as we entered the Boeing property. Our driver rolled down his window and flashed his badge at the guard who turned and signaled to his partner to lift the gate.

We drove about a hundred yards, passing by several multistoried buildings with large code numbers printed on the upper corners. We were stopped again; this time next to a large three story building with no code number. The building was surrounded by two rows of ten foot high fencing with barbed wire on top. I spotted two security guards walking between the fences, each with a large German Shepherd on a leash.

Sarge began to whine and the two security dogs began to bark and pull on their leashes, trying to attack this intruder. The security guard turned to Mark and said in a loud, somewhat agitated voice, "Control your dog!"

Mark gave Sarge a hand sign and Sarge immediately stopped whining as we continued around the side of the fenced building. Caleb thought to me, *Man, that dude is full of himself. As if all this security could keep me out.*

The car had stopped in front of the entry gate and the two armed gate guards came to the present arms position while we got out of the car. Sarge was very docile as our badges were checked and retinal scans were made. We then had to go through a weapons scan before entering the building.

When we reached the entry door after a short walk from the gate, our badges were checked again and Caleb projected, *Do they think we aren't the same people who were checked 10 seconds ago? I believe in being secure, but this is ridiculous.*

Finally, we were inside and Pearl was there to greet us as we entered the lobby. Pham came first with a hug and handshakes for the rest of the humans, and a pat on the head for Sarge.

Each of us had to show our badges again and sign in (not Caleb or Sarge) before we could move through a labyrinth of hallways that led us to another door watched over by a security guard who checked his list of names making sure we were authorized to enter the huge bay. There were several stations that were working on subassemblies, but all eyes were on the War Wagon prototype.

Pearl introduced us to a young man named Jonathan Feelgood. We tried hard not to smile. Jonathan turned out to be very knowledgeable about the prototype. The first thing we did was back off and watched the prototype as it transformed from one type of vehicle to another.

"Please watch closely," he said with a pleasantly deep baritone voice, "as we perform our first transformation from the motorhome configuration to the land version of a hyper combat vehicle."

He turned toward the vehicle and said, "Transform to War Wagon configuration, now!" Without touching any controls, the motorhome began to change. We could hear the whine of actuators as exterior parts of the vehicle began to quickly reconfigure. There was so much movement it was hard to take in the entire process. In less than thirty seconds it had changed from a domestic looking, very large motor home to a very large, bad ass combat vehicle with armor plating, a large variety of visible weapons and six run-flat tires on titanium wheels with independent steering on each wheel.

Jonathan spoke to the vehicle again and said, "Wheel control, all wheels, lateral." At once all six of the wheels rotated sideways until they were facing perpendicular to the vehicle's chassis.

Jonathan said to us, "This improved mobility permits the vehicle to move sideways without turning, allowing it to easily avoid hazardous debris.

"Another feature that improves mobility is the independent control of the front and rear wheels. If you need to make a tight turn just say, 'Tight turn left' and the front wheels turn left, but the rear wheels turn right which reduces the turn radius by sixty percent."

We all watched as the wheels turned just as Jonathan said they would.

Mark raised a question, "Jonathan, Pearl showed us some remarkable videos about how the new War Wagon can also fly, but looking at the War Wagon configuration it looks really heavy with all the armor plating. I don't see how you could get the vehicle off the ground."

Jonathan smiled. "If we used traditional armor you would be right. However, the new armor weighs a fraction of the old ceramic composite material. Everything on the vehicle has a weight restriction and it's been a real challenge to meet the target goal. However, we believe we've actually reduced the weight below our established goals. That translated to the aircraft configuration having faster climb rates and speed than originally predicted."

I felt like I had aged a decade during the briefing. What I considered was the cutting edge of technology was now ancient history. The leaps they made were beyond impressive. No wonder foreign countries were trying to steal the technology breakthroughs.

"Let's look at the aircraft configuration, shall we?" suggested Jonathan.

We all nodded our heads enthusiastically.

Jonathan turned toward the vehicle and ordered, "Transform to aircraft configuration, now!"

Again, we heard the whine of actuators and the War Wagon began changing all over. The six wheels seemed to retract to be replaced by skids, as it became more aerodynamic. We heard the whine of a different actuator on the top of the vehicle as a door opened and a short driveshaft elevated to a vertical position in the middle of the craft. Rotor blades began unfolding from the shaft and two sets of six blades extended to their full length.

"Using counter rotating rotor blades increases lift by fifty percent and eliminates the need for a tail rotor."

As this was going on, we could hear additional actuators at work on the very aft of the aircraft. Another shaft moved horizontally out of the back and eight scimitar shaped propeller blades unfolded. It took a little longer to complete the transformation. None of our team seemed to care. Except for Pham who was frowning.

"What's up, Pham?" I asked.

"It looks more aerodynamic than the APC, but kind of boxy," replied Pham. "I find it hard to believe it can cruise at 400 knots. There's just too much drag on a vehicle with this shape."

Jonathan waited until Pham had finished, then said. "You're absolutely correct. The shape of the aircraft configuration does have a lot of drag." He paused then asked, "Are you familiar with boundary layer control?"

Pham shook his head, "Never heard of it."

"It's a method of dramatically reducing aerodynamic drag. The original technology has been around for decades, but our Boeing engineers have greatly improved the technology. Our analyses and component tests have demonstrated an 80 percent reduction in drag for our aircraft configuration. I'm not qualified to explain how it works, and most of it is classified top secret anyway. With the aerodynamic drag reduced that much we calculate we can reach 400 knots. The planned demo testing will determine just how fast the aircraft mode can really fly. Let me add that we have a completely different type of boundary layer control for our submarine configuration which permits much higher speeds than any known submarines in operation today."

Jonathan looked around at the rest of the team and asked, "Any other questions?"

Mark spoke up, "To the best of my knowledge, none of us know how to fly an airplane, let alone a rotor craft. We will need to add a qualified pilot to the team."

Again, Jonathan shook his head and said, "I have to apologize for not mentioning this up front. You don't fly this aircraft, or operate the War Wagon, or even drive the motorhome." He paused for a moment then added, "I almost forgot, you don't need a captain to operate the vehicle in boat mode either.

"All configurations of the vehicle are controlled by a triple redundant, artificial intelligence computer system. You just tell it the configuration you want, where you want to go, and who you want to destroy and the computer takes over and makes it happen."

He waited a beat, then continued, "All of you will go through a few days of training. That's all it takes."

The rest of our visit seemed as if we had time traveled into the future, way into the future, it felt like Star Trek time.

I had a vague memory about the boat configuration and the propulsors that drive the boat to high speeds and still be able to turn on a dime either on the surface or submerged.

At the end of the day, they opened one of the hatches and all of us climbed aboard. I expected it to look like the bridge of the starship *Enterprise*, complete with all the gizmos and doodads. It was surprisingly sparse with several comfortable chairs facing a wraparound display that I thought at first were windows. Then I remembered I hadn't seen any window on the various configurations. This was going to take a major rethink about how to run the craft. I feared it might be more difficult than it looked.

We rode quietly all the way back to the hotel. My brain was in overload. All I wanted to do was eat the rest of the king crab and have a beer or two and hit the sack. Simone seemed just as stunned as I was.

We were sitting on the couch in the suite's living room when there was a rap on the door. It was Mark.

"Boss, can I invite Maria and her daughter Serina to come stay with me? I really miss them and I'm the only one of the team staying alone. Sarge misses them too, I can tell."

I shook my head. *How could I have been so short sighted?* "Sure, Mark. I should have told you to invite them when we left Portland. My apologies. Fly them up tomorrow."

Mark grinned and said, "They flew in today. Thanks a lot, Boss. I'll make sure they're taken care of when we go back to Boeing tomorrow."

I smiled, closed the door, ate some crab and drank a beer. Simone was already asleep. I turned out the lights, fell into bed and was sound asleep before my head even hit the pillow.

## Caleb

Some of you may be wondering what I was doing while the rest of the team was checking out the prototype for the new and improved War Wagon. On the other hand, you may not really care about my adventures. You just want to find out more about the incredible advances in technologies Pearl and her team have developed. If so, feel free to skip my contribution to the team and go to the part where Pearl is explaining how the War Wagon is powered and all that techie stuff.

Great! I noticed some of you stayed and are curious to find out about who's behind the attack on Pham and Pearl and what their motives were.

So here's what I found out. Jefferson was indeed a double agent. He was acting as a go-between for our state department and the Chinese regarding the joint development of technologies. It seems Jefferson bribed a member of the Boeing Advanced Technology group to supply him with any juicy intel that he could in turn reveal to the Chinese for a substantial fee. Boeing wasn't the only company he approached. I found he had contacts within at least a dozen other corporations who he kept on retainers (aka bribes) to alert him of new technologies.

Our state department became aware Jefferson had been told about the new War Wagon project. They began feeding him bogus information which he promptly sold to the Chinese.

This happened a few months after the assassination of China's president, Xi Jinping. The triad that replaced him made sweeping changes in the leadership of the country. They publicly announced they considered the United States a severe threat to the Chinese economy, and they were planning to sever all contact with the U.S. as soon as possible.

A faction of the new regime took it upon themselves to raid any and all new technologies being developed by the U.S. and their allies. The number one priority on their list was Boeing's development of a small cold fusion reactor. That put Jefferson in the spotlight and made him a very rich man. It also made Pearl, the leader of the cold fusion project, Jefferson's primary target. He offered her a fortune for the reactor design information, which she refused and secretly informed a college friend who worked for the State Department. The friend ran it up the line to a deputy director who suggested that Pearl accept his bribe money and gave her bogus design data to give to Jefferson.

When the Chinese received the bogus design data, they quickly determined it was bogus, actually dangerous. They contacted Jefferson and threatened him with a very painful death if he didn't get them the real data during the next week.

Jefferson then hired Carl as muscle to not only protect himself, but also to torture Pearl to get the real design information. They were planning to kill her as soon as Carl softened her up. Pham was just a loose end who was at the wrong place at the wrong time. They planned to use him as a lever to get her to give them the design information.

What happened at Pearl's apartment is well known and I don't need to repeat it. There is one other thing I would like to share. The medical examiner who conducted the autopsy on Carl gave him a new name: Dickless.

I've just told you what I know. What I don't know is what the Chinese are going to do with Jefferson now out of the picture. The Chinese are well known for playing the long game. When they want something badly enough, they are notorious for waiting for the right time to strike. This isn't over.

## Pham

Pearl called me a little before noon. She sounded very happy. "Pham, can you come over to my lab? I can meet you at the outside gate and get you through all the checkpoints quickly. I want to show you the reactor hardware, explain how it works and tell you how it interfaces with the other subsystems. I hope you can come, I miss you. Now that the reactor is finished and passed all the inspections, I'll have more time to be with you. I can get a Boeing car to the Marriott in 30 minutes. Can you come? Please say you can come."

"I'm out the door now," I replied as I closed the door behind me and headed for the elevator. On the ride to the lobby, I called Joshua and told him what Pearl said, well not everything she said, just the technical stuff.

He answered, "Great, go for it. You can brief the rest of the team so she doesn't have to. Say hello for Simone and me."

The Boeing shuttle was right on time. I was waved on through the first gate and Pearl met me at the gate on the perimeter fence. True to her word, I passed through all the checkpoints with record speed as Pearl held my arm tightly.

We entered a small lab adjacent to the bay where we had been overawed by the new War Wagon. The reactor was a surprisingly small package. At first, I thought it might be a scaled mockup of the reactor, but Pearl assured me it was the real thing.

She didn't bother to give me the technical details of how it worked, it would have been a waste of her time. I am a pretty good lawyer and an even better sniper, but when it comes to nuclear fusion, students in junior high probably know more than I do.

She focused on how the reactor connects to the other subsystems, how the reactor provides the power to drive everything else in the vehicle.

"That must take a lot of power," I exclaimed.

"You're right," she replied. "However the reactor has power to spare. The actual equivalent horsepower is classified higher than top secret, but I can tell you it exceeds 2,000."

"That's a lot of power for such a small reactor. You must have to refuel frequently to put out that much power."

Pearl gave me a gracious smile, then said, "It's estimated it can run at full power for about a century without refueling. Actually, it doesn't refuel like a gasoline or diesel vehicle. It's really too complicated to explain."

I decided to shut up and listen to her explain before I made a complete idiot of myself.

"The power system is the most important module in the vehicle," she said, then paused. "I guess all the other supporting projects feel the same way. Perhaps I should have said it all begins with the power module. In addition to the vehicle structure, there are several subsystem modules," she began, raising her hand and counting off on her fingers.

"The next most important subsystem is propulsion. It consists of three different types of propulsion, let's call them A, B and C. A is the submodule of propulsion used to drive the vehicle on the ground. There are six electric motors, each one driving one of the wheels. B is for aero-propulsion. There are actually two separate electric motors, one to drive the rotors which provides for the vehicle lift, the other to drive the rear propeller which provides the thrust. C is for the naval propulsion subsystem. It is comprised of four high-speed water pumps driven by separate electric motors. They provide not only thrust, but also maneuverability. Each pump is installed in a pod underneath the vehicle. The pods are mounted on each corner when in boat mode. The pods all swivel to provide you exceptional maneuverability.

"The brain of the vehicle is a triple redundant AI computer with a radical new design. It is an order of magnitude faster than any previous AI system. It consists of an all new concept in integrated circuitry. It's voice controlled by the crew and can handle multiple commands at the same time. If the computer senses a threat, it will automatically respond without human orders, however humans can override the automatic responses." Pearl looked at me and smiled. "I think that's enough for now. What are you thinking about?"

I shrugged my shoulders and confessed, "I feel obsolete."


### Mark

I can't believe how excited I was to see Maria and Serina. Sarge was just as excited and danced around the young girl yipping with his tail wagging at supersonic speed. Serina hugged Sarge as he licked her face. Not to be outdone, Maria practically tackled me as I met them at SeaTac. Her hug was so strong, I thought she might have cracked a rib. She kissed my cheek, and her mouth moved up to my ear. Nobody had ever bit my ear before. She said it was a nibble, not a bite. I kind of liked it, whatever it was.

We took a Marriott shuttle back to Everett and took her to my suite. It had only one bedroom, but Serina said she would sleep on the couch as long as Sarge could too.

We decided to have room service dinner, which we all enjoyed. The suite was on the tenth floor and the view from the French doors as we stepped out onto the western facing veranda was outstanding. We could see the boats and ships on Puget Sound as the sun began to set. It was a beautiful ending to the day. Serina ran, got her camera and took a picture of Maria and me with the Sound and the sunset in the background.

Maria took the camera and Serina called for Sarge to join her. We took several pictures which Serina said she would keep forever.

When the sun set, the breeze off the Sound was getting chilly and we decided to go inside. We watched a little TV before going to bed. It didn't take long for Serina to get sleepy. Her first trip in an airplane, the greeting at the airport, and watching the sunset had tired her out. Serina excused herself to go to the bathroom, and came back out dressed in her pajamas.

She looked at her mom, then at me, then climbed up on the couch and whispered something into her ear. Maria smiled, turned to me and said, "Serina says we're sitting on her bed and she and Sarge are very sleepy now."

As soon as we stood up, she crawled onto the couch and pulled one of the cushions to use as a pillow. Sarge needed no invitation. He jumped up on the couch near her feet and stared at the floor lamp then back at me then back to the lamp. "Okay, your majesty, your wish is my command." I turned off the light and headed for the bedroom. Maria had already changed into her nightgown. She smiled at me and said, "I'm not very tired. What should we do now, my love?"

I returned her smile replied, "Me either, why don't we lie down and see what comes up?"

She giggled as I switched off the light, picked her up and carried her to our bed.

The next morning I was up early. Maria was still asleep as I checked on Serina and Sarge. Sarge was wide awake and ready to do his business. I took him down the elevator and out to a small park behind the hotel just for that purpose. It was a little chilly this time of morning, but Sarge was determined. When he had sniffed every inch of the park and did his business he was ready to get back inside. When we were back in our suite, I poured kibble into his bowl and made sure the water bowl was full.

I heard a weak voice coming from the couch, "Daddy Mark, where's Sarge? Where's Mama?"

I picked her up and took her to the bedroom and laid her down next to Maria. She was asleep almost immediately. Sarge joined the party. I kissed Maria on the cheek and told her I was leaving for work. Everyone was snoring as I left the suite.

I met up with the team in the hotel lobby and waited to be picked up by the Boeing shuttle.

# CHAPTER 4
# TESTING THE NEW WAR WAGON

### Caleb

I was really excited about seeing the new War Wagon. I was busy with my own assignments and hadn't had the chance to see it for myself. I'd accessed Joshua's memories of when he was at the Boeing site and I had accompanied the team for their first visit, but somewhere between the first security checkpoint and the last one, he sent me off to another assignment. Joshua's memories of the visit were better than nothing, but I was looking forward to test riding the new War Wagon.

I kind of cheated and skipped over all the security stops and transported to a large bay in time to see Pearl and her team install the cold fusion reactor in the rear of the vehicle. I was surprised to see how small it was, about the size of a large suitcase. I was even more surprised to see there wasn't much radiation shielding. I did a quick scan of Pearl's thoughts and she didn't seem concerned, just very excited about installing the reactor and turning the switch from off to standby.

Actually, there was no switch. I was just thinking metaphorically. Once the reactor was connected, the vehicle's computer switched from external power to running on the juice from the reactor. In the blink of an eye (another metaphor), the computer set the reactor to the standby setting.

Pearl and her team were simultaneously relieved and ecstatic as Pearl announced the reactor's readouts on her wireless monitor (a special, encrypted version of an iPad).

Shortly after that, the members of Team Joshua made it past the last of the security checkpoints. Pearl ran to Pham, making little squealing sounds as she said, "It works, Pham, it really works," or something like that.

The prototype was humming. Seriously, I could hear a humming sound coming from the vehicle. It was a very slight sound, maybe inaudible to the human ear, but I could detect it.

There were the requisite congratulations and a few thankfully short speeches from the Boeing elite followed by several tests of all the subsystems. The vehicle was currently in disguise mode, looking to all the world like a very large motorhome.

Pearl was standing next to the open door near the front of the vehicle and said, "Computer, configuration mode test, now!" Immediately, the motorhome became the War Wagon, and a minute later it transformed into the aircraft mode, the six wheels retracted into the body to be replaced by skids. Once in that configuration, the overhead rotor began to spin and the rear propeller accelerated to what I assumed was the idle setting.

Pearl checked her data pad and nodded her head that everything was operating at optimum. She looked up and raised her voice above the sound of the spinning rotor and propeller, "Computer, boat mode, now!"

I noticed the skids did not retract, however both the rotor and propeller slowed to a stop and were stored away as the shape of the vehicle once again changed. This time, into a more nautical shape that had a gradual taper at the aft end into almost a point. Fins could be seen extending out of the starboard and port side as well as the top deck and keel. As the fins deployed, so did the propulsive pods, one on each corner of the boat.

Again, Pearl checked her data pad and nodded her satisfaction before saying, "Computer, terminate configuration mode test, return to motorhome mode … now!"

Once the vehicle had morphed into motorhome mode, Pearl turned to the people who had been watching and said, "It's time to take the beast out for a pleasure run. The leaders of each subsystem project and the members of Team Joshua, our end user, should board the War Wagon … now!"

I was the first one through the open door. Before anyone else entered, I received a message: *Hello Caleb, I've been waiting to see you. Welcome aboard.*

The message was delivered directly to my mind by telepathy. It was a woman's voice, a deep alto with a sultry touch. If I had knees, they would have buckled. Before I could reply, Joshua thought to me, *I heard her too, bro. Did you recognize the voice?*

I was positive I recognized the voice. It was the Cambodian assassin from our last mission. But how could she communicate to me telepathically? The only human I knew who could do that was my brother!

Before I could answer Joshua, she projected, *Yes, my love, it's who you think it is. Your Cambodian princess. Have to go for now. I'll be back really soon and we can get together again.*

The rest of the team and the project leaders from Boeing climbed aboard behind Joshua. No one gave any indication they had heard the assassin.

The interior of the motorhome looked exactly like you'd expect. There were enough seats to accommodate everyone with a few seats left over. The wraparound faux windows gave everyone a 360 degree view of the inside of the Boeing ARL. Pearl stood and said to everyone, "Please strap in. The vehicle will not move until you are all strapped in." When her data pad indicated everyone was strapped in and secure, she continued, "Computer take us to the test area, now."

The vehicle began to move and the large hangar door on the west wall rolled to the left. The electric motors were so quiet, you could have heard a pin drop as we drove out of the research lab and followed the roads out of the facility. As we approached each checkpoint, the gates automatically rose. Within a few minutes we were on a public road which connected to the northbound I-5. The ride was so quiet, it didn't feel like we were moving at all except for the views of the traffic on the display screens. I thought I could detect the muffled sounds of a large diesel engine, but I was too distracted to be sure.

Actually, it was more than being distracted, more like being really concerned about Chanlina, the assassin. In English her name means Moonlight. I was sure it was her voice I heard in my head. What in the hell was she doing in the War Wagon prototype. Was she working for the Chinese now? Was she going to take control of the new War Wagon and take Pearl and all of her scientists and engineers to China? If that were the case, we really need to stop her … before the test ride is over.

### Joshua

We drove for about thirty minutes then exited onto a surface street. I noticed all the stop lights turned green as we approached them. It made me think our vehicle had some electronic gizmo like the emergency vehicles carry to turn all the stop lights green.

For the next twenty minutes, we continued to drive until we were out of the city and into a forest area with a lot of very large pine trees (or maybe fir or spruce. I'm not a tree person). There was very little traffic as we turned onto a one-lane road that led to an eight-foot-high gated fence with a sign that read in large red letters:

PRIVATE PROPERTY, NO TRESPASSING, VIOLATORS WILL BE
PROSECUTED TO THE FULL EXTENT OF THE LAW!!!

Of course, the gate opened wide and we drove through and stopped. The gate closed behind us. I saw the road had ended. I also noticed the wire fence was electrically charged. Anyone who tried to breach the fence was in for quite a shock (pun intended).

The front monitors displayed a vast open field surrounded by more trees than I had ever seen. Pearl said, "Computer, War Wagon mode, now."

We could barely hear the sound of the actuators as the they transformed from motorhome to War Wagon. When the morphing was complete, Pearl ordered, "Computer, War Wagon demo A, now."

For the next hour the War Wagon put on a show to give us a taste of its capabilities. They were impressive, very impressive. It began by entering the nearby forest and started slalom maneuvers through the trees. At first, we moved at a moderate speed, ducking and dodging trees for a few miles. Then we turned and increased the speed dramatically, without so much as touching a limb or brushing the trunk of at least fifty trees randomly spaced. The vehicle repeated this drill two more times with the final run being made at a little over a hundred miles an hour. Thank heavens we were strapped in tight. I don't know if anyone noticed, but the forest terrain was not smooth. In fact it was very rough, but the suspension system handled the bumps as if the vehicle were gliding on glass.

After that, the War Wagon was put through a number of agility drills, such as left and right pirouette turns where the vehicle pivoted around its center of gravity, moving sideways without turning, ascending and descending 60-degree inclines, raising the vehicle's body six feet to cross a not-so-shallow, fast moving creek, and many other jaw dropping maneuvers.

The last demo in the War Wagon configuration was a drag race— actually, it was not a race. It was a demonstration of the top end speed on a 10,000 foot paved runway. It was just the runway, no airport in sight. I assumed it had been built for these types of tests.

From a dead stop we accelerated to 100 mph in just under three seconds pulling 3 Gs which several of the passengers were not prepared for. The trip continued at a lower G-rate until, based on the speedometer reading on one of the front monitors, we were going faster than 200 mph. During the ride, there had been no sense of motion (other than the initial high G acceleration demo) as we sped down the runway. The only indication of speed was how fast the forest trees on either side were blurred.

We slowly decelerated until we came to a stop at the far end of the runway. A robot carpet cleaner appeared from some unknown storage area and cleaned up the barf from those who weren't prepared for high Gs.

We took a short break, several of the passengers exited the vehicle to stretch their legs and to wait for the smell of the barf to be covered by a mild pine scent mist. Ten minutes later Pearl announced,

"Everyone back in and strap down. We're going flying. We will not be performing any vomit producing maneuvers during our flight for those of you who have delicate stomachs."

She faced the open hatch and said, "Computer, aircraft mode, now." Once inside and strapped down we could hear the finishing sounds of the transformation and I was surprised the interior of the vehicle had not changed, except for the pine tree fragrance.

I guess it really didn't matter. The only noticeable difference was the data display screens located under the window monitors. For the aircraft mode, two additional monitors below the windows were used. One was used to display the normal aircraft instrumentation and the other a moving map showing our aircraft location and the position of all other aircraft within a hundred miles. It was like a combined GPS and transponder.

I was looking at the data display and noticed the rotors were beginning to spool up. If I hadn't been watching the data display, I never would have noticed there was no vibration or the traditional *whop-whop* sound from the rotor blades. A few minutes later, I could tell we were beginning to rise vertically above the ground by looking at the altimeter and watching the ground begin to fall away.

The rotors were not exactly like those on a helicopter which supplies the lift as well as the thrust to propel the aircraft. In our configuration, the rotors were used only to control our altitude. The thrust came from the pusher propeller in the tail of our aircraft. The power that drove both the rotor and the propeller came from electric motors, which in turn received their power from Pearl's cold fusion reactor.

Whatever noise was created by the rotors and the propeller was somehow controlled by advanced stealth technology which also greatly diminished our radar signature. Inside the vehicle we could easily hear Pearl speak to us without using any headsets.

"For this demonstration, our aircraft will climb vertically to an altitude of 20,000 feet. Our environmental control system will keep our cabin pressurized as if we were flying at 5,000 feet, so no one should be bothered by hypoxia. We are currently climbing at a rate of 500 feet per minute to prevent any G-force discomfort, about the speed of a fast elevator. We will reach our desired altitude in 40 minutes. When we reach 10,000 feet we will engage the propeller and begin flying over Puget Sound into restricted military airspace. We are cleared to enter that space for the next 30 minutes. In the meantime feel free to watch the monitors. At 15,000 feet we will begin testing our maneuvering jets located at the tail section of our vehicle. They will be used to rotate the vehicle left and right as we climb."

She paused for a few minutes to speak with Pham, then continued, "Pham asked me a good question regarding contacting the FAA and their military counterparts with respect to following proper radio procedures. In a few minutes, we'll be contacting the military approach control operator to notify them we will be entering their restricted airspace. Our computer's voice feature will be making the call. If there are any issues we need to address, the computer will contact me, and I will contact approach control directly."

She stopped talking and scanned the passengers to see if there were any further questions. There were none, so she took a seat next to Pham and began a private conversation.

I watched the monitor that showed the ground below us. I could tell we were still gaining altitude, but I could also see we were moving westward toward Puget Sound. As I watched, we began to rotate to the left at a very slow rate. I was sure most of the passengers hadn't noticed. We kept rotating until we had turned halfway around and were flying backwards, however I could see we were still flying westward. I wondered how that could happen.

### Caleb

As I was pondering various possibilities, I heard a voice inside my head, *This is your Cambodian Princess again. I can help you with that. The pusher propeller converted into a puller propeller by changing the pitch of the eight scimitar blades. The rate of pitch change is so gradual you couldn't even feel it.*

As she was giving me the technical details, I was watching Joshua. It was obvious this time, I was the only one hearing Chanlina. I could feel she was expecting me to respond to her. I wasn't sure what to say, so I replied with something… neutral. *Hello Chanlina, I thought you and your crew had returned to Cambodia… So, how do you like Seattle?*

I heard what sounded like a telepathic snort followed by, *Really? Is that all you have to say to me? I thought we had something going on… romantically.*

*You're kinda right, excepts it's kinda hard to get romantically involved when I'm a spirit and you're a telepathic human. I just didn't think our relationship would go anywhere, besides, you left me for Cambodia. Long distance relationships seldom work out.*

*Things have changed, lover boy. I'm no longer human. I was killed by Fat Man. That son-of-a-bitch cut off my head with his machete just because I was sleeping around. So I'm a spirit now. We're free to be lovers.*

I really needed to change the subject. *How did you end up in the new War Wagon?*

*Couldn't you figure it out? I'm the ghost in the machine.*

My mind was really overloaded, more accurately it was my consciousness that was overwhelmed. I thought she had more to say, so I waited for her to continue. Then she thought to me, *Sorry, I have to go for a while. I have work to do. See you later, lover boy.*


### Joshua

I attempted to contact Caleb. He wasn't responding. He almost always responds to a hail from me. When he doesn't respond, his consciousness is usually busy on some important task or he has accelerated his time reference (for those of you who haven't been paying attention, that means he has slowed down time for us, maybe nearly stopping time while he examines something in great detail. Any attempt at trying to communicate with him during those events is impossible). I wasn't too concerned that I couldn't reach him, he'd get back to me when he could.

I began to focus on what was happening with our aircraft. We entered the restrictive airspace at 20,000 feet altitude doing 400 knots. Just a friendly reminder, when we are driving the motorhome or the War Wagon, speed is measured in statute miles per hour. When flying an aircraft or sailing a boat, speed is measured in knots. A knot is based on a unit of distance known as a nautical mile equivalent to 1.15 statute miles. If you ask me why they do it that way, I have no reasonable answer. Perhaps tradition is the best explanation.

Once inside restricted airspace, Pearl gave us a running description of which maneuvers we were going to be undertaking just before we undertook them. It was good to know in advance what was going to happen. It was also good to know we would be treated like commercial airline passengers, not like a fighter pilot in the middle of a dogfight. Maybe that would come later during other test flights.

Pearl gave the order for the flight test, "Computer, commence flight test demo 1A…now."

For the first time, the computer responded, "Roger that, Captain. Commencing flight test demo 1A…now."

It was the same woman's voice I'd heard in my mind when we climbed aboard. I felt a cold chill run down my spine. Chanlina was dangerous. Had she taken control of Caleb? Maybe that was why I couldn't contact him.

The computer's voice brought a chuckle to many of the passengers. True to Pearl's promise, the demo flight tests mirrored what an airliner would go through. We went through a series of maneuvers that simulated a transport aircraft landing at a commercial airport, only it began at 20,000 feet and ended with a simulated touchdown at 18,000 feet. The landing approach was repeated, this time simulating the landing of a large helicopter.

At 18,000 feet our aircraft approached a spot in the sky descending to 17,000 feet as it reduced speed and came to a hover at the desired location. Then it descended vertically another 500 feet to simulate touchdown. The process was then reversed to simulate a helicopter takeoff.

Our aircraft successfully demoed five flight scenarios with a few minutes to spare before having to leave the restricted airspace.

Instead of flying out of the restricted area, our aircraft descended vertically at a relatively slow rate until we were hovering over the surface of Puget Sound. Pearl stood up from her seat and faced the passengers, "This concludes the aircraft configuration demos. We will transition to boat mode for our last set of demonstrations."

She turned toward the port side wall and said, "Computer, boat mode, now."

The computer responded in the same female voice, "Aye aye, Captain. Transforming to boat mode, now."

There were more giggles from the passengers this time. However, I noticed Pearl wasn't one of them, instead she looked concerned.

As the aircraft continued to hover just above the surface of the water, we could all hear the aircraft begin to transform into a boat, actually more like an amphibian. In boat mode it could operate on the surface as well and underwater as a mini-submarine.

As the aircraft configuration continued to change, the rear propeller system folded up and withdrew into the aft of the vehicle. A pressure tight door closed over the opening as the boat propulsion pods descended on each corner of the boat, followed by the retraction of the aircraft skids.

The rotors slowed and the boat lightly touched down on the surface of the water. As the boat floated on the surface, the rotors stopped, the blades retracted and the rotor assembly folded away into the top of the cabin.

Pearl stood and said, "Computer, all ahead full, execute demo packages 2A through 2G."

The voice of the computer responded, "Aye Captain, all ahead full, executing demo packages 2A through 2G as ordered."

As the boat smoothly accelerated for the first demo, Pearl added, "We are now in restricted naval waters. We are limited to 60 minutes of demonstrations to prove the sea worthiness of the boat configuration. We have three boat configurations to evaluate. We will spend up to 20 minutes for each configuration. The first two demonstrations will be for the standard flat bottom configuration, the second for the hydrofoil configuration…"

I raised my hand and waited for Pearl to notice, when she did she asked, "Yes Joshua, you have a question?"

"Sorry to interrupt, some of us may not be familiar with the hydrofoil. Could you briefly describe what it is?"

She nodded as she said, "Certainly, Joshua. The hydrofoil configuration uses foils to lift the hull of the boat out of the water like water skies. The foils are shaped like a section of an airplane wing. For an aircraft, the wing provides lift to get the plane into the air. For our boat, the four hydrofoils lift the boat out of the water to greatly reduce water contact reducing the drag which substantially increases the speed of the boat. The Boeing Marine Systems group out of Renton, Washington, designed the hydrofoil for boat mode. Projected estimates for increased speed indicates a 50% increase in speed from the flat bottom design. One of our demonstrations will determine exactly how much speed improvement we will achieve. Does that answer your question?"

"Yes," I replied. "Thank you."

"During the last demo, we will submerge the vehicle and become a mini-submarine. Before we do, we will pressure check the boat to ensure hull integrity."

One of the passengers asked another question, "What does 'ensure hull integrity' mean?"

Pearl smiled a small smile, then said, "It means we want to make sure the ship doesn't leak and send us to the bottom of the Sound."

There was some nervous laughter, some expressions of concern. as the boat continued to accelerate westward.

The boat performed flawlessly as expected. Even when the water got choppy, the ride was pretty smooth. I was later told the flat bottom hull speed exceeded 75 knots on the last high speed run. I was also told the actual hydrofoil speed was classified, but it was well over a hundred knots. Part of that speed increase was due to the pusher propeller from the aircraft mode that was employed to assist during the hydrofoil configuration.

I'm happy to report no leaks were detected when we submerged the boat. In fact our ride was quite comfortable. This configuration was considered way above top secret so I can't really share much. However, I'm allowed to share some data from the demo.

We dove to the bottom of the Sound and rested there for five minutes. The average depth of the Sound is 270 feet. During one of the submerged speed runs, the boat exceeded 50 knots. The latest American nuclear submarine is rumored to have a maximum submerged speed of 35 knots.

Lastly, during our last submerged demo we came across a pod of killer whales. They seemed curious about us and several of the large ones approached us singing one of their songs. We managed to capture the whole song using our advanced underwater camera systems with audio pickup. It was breathtaking to see these mammoth animals so near to our boat. Unfortunately, for security reasons the pictures cannot be shown to the public.

When the submarine's demos were completed, Pearl ordered, "Computer, return to home, now."

The computer did not respond this time. The boat began to surface. Once on the surface, the vehicle transformed into the aircraft configuration. We rose from the surface of the Sound and flew back to the test grounds. We landed on the road in front of the gate and transformed into the motorhome configuration. From there, it was a relatively easy drive back to the Boeing ARL.

It had been an eventful day. I felt like I had been in a science fiction movie and my brain was considerably overloaded with all the advanced technology. I really missed my old War Wagon. Even with all the updates to the original War Wagon, I always felt like our team was in charge, the wagon was just an extension of our weapons. We were in control.

When we were in the new War Wagon, I felt like we were just passengers with little or no control of the vehicle or its weapons. It made me feel uncomfortable.

A short debriefing was held once we were back at the ARL, then we were driven back to our hotel in Everett. Pearl would be joining us later after she wrapped up her summary report of the demonstrations. On the ride back, I posed the question, "So what did y'all think of the War Wagon demo?"

Mark was the first to answer. "I kinda felt obsolete, boss. Like, what do they need us for when they've got this incredible machine to do it for us?"

Simone nodded and added, "I'd like to find out how we're expected to integrate the new War Wagon into our next mission, or any of the next missions. Are they going to give us some type of training on how to deal with the AI computer interface?"

Pham didn't add to the other concerns. He just sat there quietly as we rode in the shuttle, however I thought I noticed a look of concern on his face.

As we rode in silence, Caleb finally contacted me, *Is this a good time for me to communicate with you? I don't want the others to know.*

*Now's fine. I was worried about not hearing from you. Are you okay?* I projected.

*Not sure yet,* he answered, *I think Chanlina has control of the computer system which means she has complete control of the War Wagon prototype. That was her voice repeating Pearl's commands during today's demonstrations. I really don't know how's she connected to the AI. I can't figure out how she can communicate with me. I thought you and I were the only ones to have human/spirit contact. All I know for sure is she wants to be my girlfriend!*

# CHAPTER 5
# TRAINING BEGINS

### Pham

For the next three weeks, Team Joshua learned how to operate the greatly advanced War Wagon. As complicated as the multitude of systems for the various configurations were, from a user standpoint they were fairly straight forward. Mostly, it involved becoming familiar with the verbal commands.

The first week of training was programming the AI computers to recognize our voices. All commands were voice activated and each member of Team Joshua was authorized to instruct the computer system. Each of the three AIs that made up the computer system had to learn to recognize each of our voices.

Caleb was a special case. He was a spirit and had no voice, however he did have the ability to contact the computer system and instruct the AI. Don't ask me how he accomplished that. I have no idea how the spirit/AI interface works. Joshua was also a special case. The AI would accept both voice and thought commands from him. Again, I had no idea how that could happen. I quizzed Pearl to see if she could explain it to me, but she just smiled and shrugged her shoulders and said, "I haven't a clue how it works. I'm not a computer person, my specialty is limited to cold fusion reactors."

Pearl was the leader of the overall project and was tasked with training Team Joshua. The first day of training for the team was very interesting. When the team climbed aboard we were greeted by the AI. It had the same voice we had heard during the demos. "Welcome aboard, Team Joshua," it said. "I can't wait to get started with your training. Listen carefully to what Dr. Pearl has to say to you. If you have any questions, please ask her. She's an incredibly intelligent woman and can answer all your questions."

Once I'd finished downloading all my voice commands to the three AI computers, I took Pearl aside for a private conversation. I tried to ease my way into expressing my concerns. "Pearl, I couldn't help notice the same voice was used for all three AIs. I thought each computer would have their own voice."

She shrugged, but I noticed a look of concern on her face. "I would have thought so too. I asked the project leader on the AI system about it. I wasn't aware the computer would be replying to our orders. It caught me off guard when she began speaking during the demos."

"What did he say?" I asked curiously.

"I was shocked by his answer. He said he had no idea the computer systems would speak to us at all. He knew they would respond to our voice commands, but there were no speech subroutines downloaded into any of the three computers. He thought maybe the computers were smart enough to decide it would be best if they could talk to us, like it was another crew member. He said, 'We created the computer to have the ability to grow in intelligence, to generate software that would optimize performance.'"

Pearl stopped talking and I just stared at her for a moment while I gathered my thoughts. Pearl waited patiently for me to respond. After a pregnant pause, I asked, "Do you remember an old science fiction movie called *2001: A Space Odyssey?*"

"I'm a scientist, my focus is on science, not science fiction. When was it released?"

"I'll take that as a no then. The movie was released in the late 1960s. It was about two astronauts on a mission to Jupiter. The flight of the space vehicle was controlled by an AI computer called HAL, a play on words for IBM, the world's largest manufacturer of computers at that time. The two crewmen spoke to HAL like he was a human being."

"How did the movie end?" Pearl asked, in spite of her professed disinterest in science fiction.

"HAL killed one of the astronauts and tried to kill the other one. The surviving crewman had to remove all of HAL's memories, both RAM and ROM. Essentially, he had to kill HAL in self-defense."

Pearl looked surprised, she composed herself and replied, "That was fiction. Not reality. I have every confidence our computers will perform flawlessly."

"I hope so," I said and paused, not sure if I should mention my real concern or wait until I had more information.

"What's going on, Pham? Why do you seem so negative all of a sudden?"

I had been staring at the deck of the War Wagon while considering my options. I looked up and scanned the walls of the vehicle looking for some sign, but of course I saw nothing. The three AIs' circuitries were imbedded in the walls. I looked over at Pearl and said, "Can we step outside for a moment?"

She nodded and we left through one of the forward hatches and moved across the wide hangar floor away from any prying eyes or ears. I turned my back to the War Wagon and confessed quickly and quietly, "I know the voice of the computer. It's the voice of a Cambodian assassin from our last mission."

Pearl's eyes opened wide as did her mouth, finally she asked, "Are you sure? How could that be? We have the tightest secur—"

"I know, but I'm 90% sure I'm right. I'm going to talk to Joshua to confirm."


### Joshua

Pham requested a private meeting with me. I was pretty sure I knew what he was going to ask me. I still wanted him to speak first. "What's up, Pham?"

"I'm not sure, boss. I think we may have a problem and I'm hoping you can confirm or deny what I'm about to ask you."

"Okay, what's your concern?"

"At the risk of sounding ridiculous, I suspect the AI voice is Chanlina's, the Cambodian assassin."

I said nothing and waited for him to say more. After a moment, he continued. "If it's her voice and somehow she gets control of the War Wagon's computer system she would have access to all of the secret technology, especially the small cold fusion reactor."

"I share your concern, Pham," I replied. "I want Caleb to tell you what he found out about the voice."

*Hi Pham,* projected Caleb. *You have a right to be concerned. Just between the three of us, I'll tell you what I know. I don't want this information to go any further than us. Do you understand?*

"It may be too late for that. I told Pearl about my suspicions. I don't think she's shared our conversation with anyone else."

"Get her in here right now," I ordered.

As he left to find Pearl, I thought to Caleb, *We may have to introduce you to Pearl.*

*I was thinking the same thing, Josh.*

*Before we take that step, I want to see how she reacts,* I replied.

A few minutes later, Pham and Pearl joined us. I told her not to share her fears with anyone else. At the present time we needed to restrict the information until we determined what was really happening. She wasn't too happy, but agreed.

I was glad we didn't need to introduce her to Caleb or the fact the members of Team Joshua can communicate with him. Now wasn't the right time.

## <u>Caleb</u>

I was in the middle of a conversation with Joshua when all of a sudden, I was back in Wonderland. The setting was still the same. It was a lovely spring day with puffy white clouds in a bright azure sky. There were massive trees interspersed with an abundance of flowering plants. The flowers were of every color imaginable and their scent filled the air with a sweet aroma. A large variety of birds were there, and their songs gave the final touch to a paradise no eye had seen before.

The best thing about being in Wonderland was feeling like I was in my old body again. I knew it was only temporary, but I really enjoyed it, especially being able to see and interact with the temporary bodies of other spirits. This time, I was all alone. Captain Collins, my Marine company commander, was nowhere to be seen. He had been my spirit guide every time I visited Wonderland, but apparently not today.

I sat down on a blanket of rich green grass and waited. A few minutes passed before I noticed someone in the distance walking toward me. I thought it might be a woman, but I couldn't be certain. I was so focused on trying to determine if the approaching person was a man or woman, I was startled by a voice behind me. "What an attractive woman. A real beauty."

I jumped up, turned around and assumed a defensive posture, only to discover The Apostle standing close to me. I had suspicions he was similar to Joshua and could communicate with spirits as well as humans, but I thought only spirits could enter Wonderland. Could he have died? I had no idea. Maybe it wasn't him. Maybe this was another spirit who chose to look like him. I needed to make sure it was really him.

I always thought The Apostle was a good looking man who always dressed professionally. This spirit's avatar looked exactly like him. He wore a perfectly fitted gray suit with a white shirt and starched collar. He had a dark red tie with a double Windsor knot that matched his pocket square. He was clean shaven with the slight aroma of Giorgio Armani cologne and his haircut looked like he had just stepped out of a barber's chair. Everything about him made me think it was really The Apostle.

Unfortunately, I just looked like Caleb Brown. No big deal as I was dressed in business casual. Actually more casual than business. However, I thought they got my avatar right. I looked and felt really muscular just like I looked when Joshua and I signed up for the Marines, quite literally a lifetime ago.

I spent too much time checking out The Apostle. When I turned back to look at the woman, I wasn't sure who she was. The Apostle was right, she was a real beauty with just a touch of makeup and a form-fitting, blue, sequined dress that accented her feminine figure. She looked familiar, but I couldn't quite place her. She smiled at me and said, "Well hello lover boy! Aren't you the stud?"

Holy crapola!!! It was Chanlina, the Cambodian assassin, however she looked nothing like the Chanlina I knew. That woman was skinny as a rail and covered with welts and bruises. On her best day, I would not have thought her attractive. It was her, I was certain of it, her voice was unmistakable. I wondered if she looked this hot when she was younger.

Before I could return the greeting, The Apostle said, "It's time to get down to business. We've got a lot to cover and very little time to accomplish our goals."

"Wait!!!" I interrupted. "I need some background on how Chanlina became a spirit and why you trust her to become the overlord of the new War Wagon's computer system."

The Apostle slowly turned his head and stared at me. I didn't like his look. It made me feel… uneasy. "Caleb," his voice was low and menacing, "don't ever interrupt me again. If you do you will find it… uncomfortable for you."

I was surprised when Chanlina stepped between us and said, "Apostle, I think it would benefit Caleb if you granted him his request. I know he can be a bit brash, but we are dumping some heavy shit on him. Would you consider letting me give him a brief overview about what happened to me since he and I last met?"

The Apostle gave me a withering stare, then turned and gave her the briefest of nods and added, "I'll leave you to it then. I will return when you have completed bringing Caleb up to speed," and he vanished.

Chanlina smiled and said to me, "Let's sit down and I'll tell you what I know. When I finish, you can ask me all the questions you want."

I was about to say there wasn't any place to sit when I noticed a picnic table and two chairs materialized at the wave of her hand. I thought to myself, *This spirit woman is well beyond me with her abilities.*

We sat down at the table across from each other as she waved hand again. Two ornate glasses filled with crystal clear ice appeared, along with a pitcher of a dark reddish liquid with sliced lemons and oranges floating on the surface.

"It's an old Cambodian drink," she said as she filled our glasses. "In ancient days the blood of our enemies was a major part of the drink along with some blends of local wines and stronger native drinks."

She raised her glass and I joined her with mine. "A toast to a long and happy life… oh wait. That's not correct. To a long and happy existence and good times in these avatars."

I took a sip and it was delicious, before I could comment, she said, "I know you must have many questions for me. Let me guess what the first two are. First, is there any blood in the drink? The answer is no, of course not. None of this is real. Wonderland is a construct where spirits can play at being human again and pass on information and receive awards.

"Second, you would like to know if this body I'm wearing is what I really looked like when I was much younger before I became an assassin. The answer is yes. I was the belle of the ball when I was in my twenties. When the wars and revolutions began, I… changed."

She paused to take another drink and I joined her. The wine was excellent, I was wondering if there would be something to munch on while she began her story. Immediately, large silver trays materialized on the table full of snacks and little sandwiches. I looked at her and she smiled back at me. "Yes, I was reading your mind and your desire for food, I hope you enjoy the food. Eat while I begin my tale."

She selected one of the small sandwiches and ate it in one bite, took another sip of the drink and started, "I was born in the late 1800s."

I was so shocked by her comment, I gagged on my snack and began coughing. I was bent over and she slapped me on the back and added, "Perhaps I shouldn't have been quite so abrupt. Let me start over."

"In the early 1600s, there was a community in the middle part of what is now Cambodia. The residents who lived there were well known for their long lives. The vast majority of the community lived to be a hundred. A portion of the centenarians were found to be great thinkers and a sub group of the great thinkers came up with a plan on how to extend their lives as well as their knowledge.

"They studied the animals and discovered when they bred the pairs of the oldest, smartest animals, their offspring usually lived longer and learned faster. They thought they should try this approach with humans.

"They paired up the smartest, longest living humans and found it worked for human beings, too.

"Of course, their breeding methods were a carefully guarded secret. By the time I was born, several of us had life expectancies of over two hundred years. That's when the wars began. When we were invaded by warring tribes from Laos and Vietnam, they discovered our secrets. They wanted to double or triple their lifespans and they wanted it now. They believed we must have had an elixir that would give them this long life instantly. When we tried to explain the process, they thought we were lying and many of us were slaughtered. I was part of a handful who managed to survive the wars.

"We migrated to various Asian countries and tried to start over, but we needed a critical mass for the breeding process to work. Unfortunately we never were able to build a critical mass again. When I first met you there were less than ten of us over the age of two hundred years.

"Just before that I was approached by a man who called himself The Apostle. He knew all about me and my Cambodian soldiers and wanted to train me for a mission. He was willing to pay us more money than we ever thought possible. He told me about Joshua and you, Caleb, and how your spirit was bonded to your brother.

"Almost all of Southeast Asia believed in spirit worship, but no one had ever believed humans could communicate with the spirits of their dead relatives. I was an exception. I believe The Apostle discovered a small group of our ancestor spirits who routinely communicated with their living descendants. I frequently asked my parents and grandparents for advice. Their assistance kept me alive during the worst of times.

"The Apostle told me there would be times I would have to begin communicating with you. In spite of all the nasty things I said to you, I never intended to harm you. My original mission was to assist you and the rest of Team Joshua to accomplish a specific mission. We were to take out two key figures, a Pol Pot wannabe and a specific individual in the Army National Guard. We had to determine who that would be. We successfully accomplished our mission, were paid an embarrassing amount of money and returned to Cambodia. That about sums it up. Do you have any questions?"

"Yes," I replied. "Did Fat Man really behead you?"

"Yes, but not for sleeping around. My body was dying. Bit by bit my body parts were ceasing to function. My mind was as alert as ever, but I couldn't continue. I reached the point when I couldn't mask the pain any longer."

I noticed the tears forming on her avatar's eyes and running down her cheeks. I reached out and took her hand in mine. She gripped my hand tightly as she continued, "Fat Man is one of my children. He was the only one I trusted to make a clean cut. At first, he refused, but eventually he agreed. My death was painless and completed in an instant.

"The Apostle was there and quickly captured my spirit. I have no idea how he did that. However, he combined my spirit to this avatar you see before you today. Any more questions?"

"None than I can think of," I said.

"Great, Caleb," she said as she jumped up, moved around the table and sat in my lap. "I've been waiting for so long to kiss you."

She grabbed my avatar head and laid one on me. I had almost forgotten what it felt like to kiss a pretty girl again, even if we were only avatars. It felt real, very real, as she continued to kiss me passionately, pressing her delicious body against mine. She had just thrust her hand down between my legs when I heard someone behind us say, "Play time's over, boys and girls. It's time to get down to business."

As usual, The Apostle was all business. He went through in great detail why Chanlina was involved with the new War Wagon's computer system. The Boeing computer design group was having problems integrating the three AI computers even though they were supposed to be identical. He mentioned he remembered how I was able to access some of the most sophisticated computers in existence and tied them together in nanoseconds to produce a cohesive set of data.

While what I'd done with the computers was very impressive (his words not mine, but I love it when someone says nice things about me) the merging of three identical AI computers was subtly different. I had other responsibilities and The Apostle decided to offer Chanlina's spirit the opportunity to come up with a solution to the integration problem. She wasn't a computer expert, but she may have been one of the smartest people/spirits on the planet. She had a knack for thinking outside the box. She solved the problem in less than a day. She discovered each AI computer solved the operational problems in slightly different ways and each one calculated the answers to every problem to six decimal place accuracy. The solutions always agreed within three decimal place accuracy, but since the last three decimal places always differed, the solutions were considered inaccurate.

Chanlina's avatar asked a question of the computer experts: Was it necessary to have six decimal place agreement between the three AI computers in order to predict accurate solutions to all possible situations for the new War Wagon?

Their answer was, the NASA Space Shuttle required at least two of the three onboard computers six decimal agreement to perform all operational procedures. They assumed it was the same for the new War Wagon.

Chanlina's avatar suggested the requirements of the War Wagon traveling at a maximum of 400 knots might not be as stringent as a Space Shuttle traveling at 17,000 mph to acquire orbital speed.

The computer experts grudgingly acquiesced and reran all the War Wagon's operational requirements using solutions with three decimal place agreement between all three of the AI computers. As the Marine private, Gomer Pyle, once said, "Surprise, surprise, surprise!"

There was complete agreement between all three AIs for all vehicle configurations operational requirements. In fact, they had rerun the analyses with four decimal point accuracy and two of the three AIs agreed 95% of the time.

It took the better part of two days to make the necessary adjustments to the computer system, just in time for the initial demo runs. The Apostle was so impressed with Chanlina's performance, he offered her spirit to be the onboard computer coordinator for all of the new War Wagon missions.

"That's all I have to say," said The Apostle abruptly. "I have other projects and programs to take care of. One more thing before I go. I feel Chanlina should be considered part of Team Joshua. Caleb, that's on you to make the suggestion, understand?"

I nodded my head and replied, "Yes sir, I will get right on that when we finish here."

There was a slight smile on The Apostle's face as he closed with, "I'm looking forward to observing your missions. I must be leaving now, but Wonderland will be open for you both for at least two hours subjective time. Enjoy each other before you return to reality."

He abruptly disappeared, to the squealing delight of Chanlina who jumped into my lap. It was the most wonderful two hours of my spirit life. It was the greatest substitute existence I had ever experienced and I hoped Chanlina and I could return to Wonderland sometime soon.

### Joshua

The members of Team Joshua sat in stunned silence inside the War Wagon as Caleb debriefed us on his meeting with The Apostle and Chanlina. Pearl was not present since she had not yet been informed of Caleb's spirit abilities. When he was finished, Chanlina added her own comments, mainly reinforcing everything Caleb had already revealed. I suspected there was something going on between the two of them which they decided not to share with the team and I didn't press them for any personal information.

When the briefing concluded, we spent the better part of two weeks running various scenarios in each of the vehicle configurations. We were also introduced to the weapons available in each configuration and we took turns tracking and destroying target drones on the ground, in and under the sea, and in the air.

Pearl had joined us for the training and gave special attention to our actions in aircraft mode. "When the War Wagon is in aircraft mode, think of her as a bomber, not an attack fighter. The vehicle is not equipped to handle high G forces common to fighters. We have two fighter drones available to defend us from enemy aircraft or ground anti-aircraft weapons. Both Mark and Pham will undergo special training to control the drones. The drones are designed to withstand 15 Gs, well in excess of what the human body can take."

Pham and Mark were in hog heaven playing video games to help them hone their computer game skills. By the end of the week they were comfortable with the drones' limitations as well as some of the newer tricks the drones could utilize.

### Caleb

When our final training was complete, The Apostle made a surprise appearance to Chanlina and me in Wonderland. We had spent the better part of our first day of what was supposed to be a week's vacation together. We were getting better acquainted, it felt like we were Adam and Eve in the Garden of Eden. Then from out of nowhere, the serpent also known as the tempter, the accuser, or perhaps even The Apostle, suddenly appeared. "Oh my goodness!" he cried out loud. "Is that all you two can think about? Put on some clothes, for heaven's sake."

Instantly we were clothed in loose fitting robes. "That's better, much better. I will keep you only a moment from your frivolities. Now that your training is over, you will all be rewarded by a three week vacation to Alaska. You will be cruising from Seattle to Anchorage on the inside passage, taking the War Wagon to Fairbanks in motorhome mode, returning to Anchorage, then taking another cruise back to Seattle on the outside passage. A list of invitees will be sent to Joshua. All of the invitees will have the most luxurious penthouse suites each with spacious verandas. Your country wants to reward you for your efforts in this very important program. I'm leaving now. Please continue your vacation without further interruption."

He vanished and so did our robes. A week later we all boarded the *Wonder of the Seas.*

# CHAPTER 6
# GETTING READY FOR A CRUISE

### Joshua

The invitation list included some unexpected guests. The government paid for five large top deck penthouse suites with all the trimmings which also included land excursions at every port-of-call on our way to Alaska. We were taking the inside passage, which meant we would be cruising between the mainland on the starboard side of the ship and a series of small islands on the port side that acted as water brakes, resulting in very calm seas. The return trip on the outside passage could get a little rougher. However, our ship was the largest cruise liner afloat traveling to Alaska. It was so big it would be smooth cruising even in rough seas.

We were sailing on the Royal Caribbean's *Wonder of the Seas*. This would be the ship's first cruise from Seattle to Anchorage. Extensive upgrades had been made to the various ports of call in the Pacific Northwest, now accommodating this massive ship at most of the larger ports.

I did some research on just how big *Wonder of the Seas* really is. When it became operational in 2022, it was the largest cruise ship in the world. For comparative purposes, the USS Gerald R. Ford aircraft carrier is 1,106 feet long. *Wonder of the Seas* is longer at 1,188 feet. It can accommodate up to nearly 7,000 passengers plus a crew of 2,300. We were all booked in a series of the best accommodations called The Royal Luxury Suites, the largest of which was a two-story apartment that could sleep up to six people.

To the best of my knowledge, none of the invitees had ever been on a cruise before. I know for sure neither Caleb nor I ever even thought about going on a cruise. Us poor black folk from the South wouldn't even know cruise ships existed.

A travel agent contacted by The Apostle made arrangements to educate us on what to expect on our cruise. The Apostle gave me a list of the names of the adults who were invited plus potentially others to be named later.

We met in the banquet room at a posh Seattle restaurant. Of course, the dinner was wonderful and I felt guilty Caleb couldn't enjoy the feast. I hadn't heard from him in several days and I noticed a change in his behavior. He seemed to be gone frequently, but he was entitled to break away and be on his own for a while now that the Oregon mission was over.

The invitation to the agent's cruise preview included the following whom I expected: Simone and me, Pham and Pearl, Mark and Maria, Maria's daughter, Serina, and Sarge. The unexpected guests were those who were involved with the Oregon mission. Detective Jerry Hong and his wife Lili, and Detective Bill "Buffalo" Cody and his girlfriend were all on the list. The unidentified guests failed to show up. Or so we thought.

The travel agent took a few minutes to introduce himself to us as his assistant set up his presentation material. When everything was ready, the house lights were dimmed and the presentation began. It was a stunning thirty-minute video presentation showing us things we could never imagine. The opulence was incredible and gasps of surprise were routinely heard. I was so engrossed in watching the presentation, I vaguely remember Simone slowly standing up and moving behind me, followed by a few murmured comments before she returned to her seat.

When the presentation was over, the agent followed up by handing out our boarding passes along with newly minted passports and what looked like a credit card to each of us. He emphasized not to lose the card. It was the key to each suite, as well as the means of paying for any and all expenses that might not be included in the price of our tickets.

I snuck a look at the boarding pass receipt because I was curious. The contents shocked me. All fees were to be charged to a special government account and we all had unlimited credit. That was my idea of a fantastic surprise.

The agent ended up with a handout giving suggestions on how to dress, what to take as well as what to avoid. We also were told we wouldn't have to go through the tedious registration process. All we had to do was show them our cards and be escorted to our suites.

The agent took me aside just before he left. "Mr. Brown, would you do me a favor?"

"Certainly," I replied, "whatever you want."

He smiled, but looked somewhat uncomfortable as he handed me two extra packets and said, "Simone asked that you personally deliver the packets to the two individuals who showed up after dinner. If you'd be so kind, I'd really appreciate it."

"Of course, I'll take care of it right away. Thanks again for that wonderful presentation. I can hardly wait for the cruise."

The banquet room remained mostly dark after the presentation ended and Simone guided me to where the two unannounced guests were standing alone in the shadows with their backs toward us.

As the two turned to face us, Simone said, "Joshua, let me introduce you to Caleb and Chanlina."

### Chanlina

The look on Joshua's face was priceless! Caleb was all smiles when he slapped his brother on the shoulder and asked, "I'd bet good money you never thought you'd see me again, did you? Well, you can thank Chanlina for making this happen."

He grabbed his brother in a bear hug and squeezed him until Joshua said, "Easy bro, you're breaking my ribs."

"Oh! Sorry, I didn't realize I had that much strength. Actually, it's not my strength, it's the avatar's," Caleb apologized timidly. "There's so much I… we, not just I, Chanlina and I need to tell you."

"Don't you realize everyone is watching us. I don't think now is—" Joshua whispered as he quickly looked over his shoulder to see who might have been looking toward our small group.

It was time for me to break in. "Don't worry, Joshua, we're in the fringes of a Wonderland bubble. No one can see us in here unless we want them to," I interrupted. "Look around, the rest of the party are starting to leave. They'll assume you had to leave for some important reason and you'll catch up with them tomorrow."

Joshua's expression turned doubtful. "Why would they assume that?"

"Because Simone is going to step outside the bubble fringe and tell them you had to leave. Go on Simone, step out."

She nodded, turned, and made her excuses to the rest of the party. Joshua was still concerned. "Aren't they going to see Simone suddenly appear out of nowhere?"

"Nope," I replied. "Leaving and entering a Wonderland bubble looks like someone gradually fading into or out of a dark shadowy place."

Simone rejoined our small group. "That went well," she said in a whispering voice.

I couldn't help but giggle a bit about Simone's concern. "Simone, honey, you don't have to worry about being heard. Once you enter the bubble's fringe, it's soundproof. No one on the outside can see *or* hear what's going on inside the bubble. I suggest we enter the main bubble and remain inside for a while so Caleb and I can try to explain what you can and cannot do once inside."

"Don't you have to move the bubble out of the banquet room?" asked Simone. "If we stay inside for too long, someone is bound to discover us."

Caleb just shook his head and said, "No, Simone. We don't have to move the bubble, because the bubble isn't inside the banquet room. The bubble exists in spirit-space, outside of real physical space. It's complicated, but you entered and left spirit space. We never existed in the banquet room. Bear with us and we'll explain how it works and most importantly, how the avatars in the Wonderland bubble have physical bodies."

It was time for me to take charge. Caleb was so pumped being in contact with his twin, I knew he wouldn't be able to stay focused on the information the humans would need to know about Wonderland. Besides, I'd been in and out of Wonderland (Caleb's name for the spirit bubble, not mine) as both a human and spirit for over a hundred years.

"Joshua, Simone, close your eyes. When humans move from the fringe to the inside of the bubble the shift can be disorienting."

BAM!!! When they opened their eyes they were in the standard Wonderland bubble where everything was beautiful.

"You can open your eyes now," I said in as soft a voice as I could manage.

Joshua was looking straight down at his feet as he slowly, very slowly opened his eyes. He continued to stare down at his shoes, the same shoes he had worn to the banquet. After a few seconds he looked over at Simone's shoes. They were also the same high heel shoes she'd worn.

"Why are you staring at my feet?" Simone asked. "Do you think they look different?"

Caleb interrupted, "Oh for heaven's sake, Joshua. Get your head up and look around. Nothing about you or Simone has changed. The only difference we wanted to avoid was the quick transition from the banquet to the Wonderland bubble."

"Oh my God!!!" squealed Simone. "This is fantastic, Joshua. Just look at this place, It's perfect, absolutely perfect."

"I'm not a big fan of the supernatural," he said in a very low whisper. "It brings back memories, more like feelings, of what I went through when I found out Caleb was dead and his spirit was trying to take over my body."

"I understand exactly what you're going through," I responded. "It's been almost two-hundred years, but I still remember how unsure I felt when I was human and forced to visit the spirit world. It took me many visits before I felt comfortable. Eventually, it became second nature to move back and forth between reality and the spirit world."

I paused to check Simone. She seemed to embrace Wonderland without the reservations Joshua was going through. That was a plus. I focused on Joshua. "Let's all take a seat at the picnic table," I suggested. "Caleb, maybe you can add comments about your time in Wonderland?"

The picnic table magically appeared with all types of snacks and drinks and Simone helped Joshua sit down then sat beside him. I took Caleb's hand and sat down next to him as he began to speak to his brother.

"Joshua, please open your eyes and look around you. What do you see?"

His head came up slowly and he began to scan the entire area from horizon to horizon. He reminded me of our time as Marines on a recon mission in Afghanistan, taking in the entire terrain, looking for possible enemy locations.

When he'd completed his surveillance, he looked at me and said, "It looks like a perfect place… for an ambush."

"Give me some detail," I said softly. "What do you feel about this place?"

Without hesitation, he began debriefing me on what he saw. "The burned out remains of a small village. I can hear the sound of a tank moving into the battle zone, probably one of the Russian tanks stolen by the Taliban. Any minute they will be on us. We need to retreat or we'll be killed."

"Freeze that picture in your mind," Caleb ordered and waited a beat before continuing. "Josh, what you are seeing is exactly the same thing I saw the first time I visited Wonderland. Our old commander, Captain Collins, was trying to tell me something, but all I could see was the war. I had to die again and it was even more horrific than the first time. Eventually, as I made additional trips, I was able to see Wonderland as a safe place, an idyllic escape to withdraw from the pitfalls of reality. I hope you let Chanlina tell you how to make that transition."

"Thank you, Caleb," I said as I squeezed his hand. "That helps a lot. Joshua, please look at me. I need your full attention. This is the time to listen, focus on my voice and the words I use to describe Wonderland. Do you agree to this?"

He began to look at Simone, but she turned away. He turned back to me and nodded. "You have my complete attention," he said in a strong, commanding voice.

"Wonderland isn't real," I began. "It's a construct, however everything is a construct. Humans live in one set of constructs while spirits, at least some spirits, exist in an entirely different, mutually exclusive construct. Wonderland is a conduit between human reality and the spirit world.

"There are rules that govern how things will be in each construct. Some of the rules are cast in stone, others are more flexible. Wonderland permits both life forms to coexist.

"Every human born comes with a spirit attached. The spirit in the human helps to form the personality of that human, but it operates on a subconscious level until the human dies. Here's where it gets complicated. When the human dies, there seem to be a couple of spirit options. Options may be too strong a word. As far as we know, spirits have no say in their path of existence. The majority of spirits are separated from their humans never to reconnect again. There is little known regarding the duration of their existence. It could be only a brief moment or it could be millenniums.

"The other option is what happened to Caleb, Simone, myself and probably hundreds of thousands more. These spirits continue to have some contact with their close human counterparts. A substantial portion of these continue to exist even after the humans have passed away. Some call these spirits ghosts. For others, they must be bonded to a human to continue their existence. I will be focusing on this type of spirit and their interactions with humans.

"A few decades ago, there was a very old spirit who bonded with his great grandson. The great grandson had made a name for himself in various government agencies. He became disenchanted with the greed and corruption that ran rampant within our federal government. He gathered together like-minded high-level members of government, business and military, a few of whom also had spirit bonds. They began a search for a champion who would lead the war on crime. They felt the optimum team would consist of a human and bonded spirit to maximize the potential in making substantial inroads in the battle against crime.

"Three years later, the great grandson and his spirit found a possible candidate. Of course, as you know, you and Caleb were the team that began the war on crime. I'm also sure you know the great grandson was the man called The Apostle. What you don't know is the old spirit was my father."

"What?!!! Wait a minute. Was your father Ang Tong?" asked Caleb.

"Don't interrupt me, lover boy. We'll discuss that later. Let me finish." I looked at Joshua and Simone and they were even more stunned than Caleb. "Sorry for the outburst. Let me wrap this up by explaining Wonderland. As I mentioned before, Wonderland is a relatively new construct. It was created by some of the most ancient spirits and their bonded humans. It allows for humans and spirits to co-exist in a safe environment. The default appearance is the one we are in now. However, it can take on any desired appearance based on the will power of humans and spirits involved.

"Caleb has visited Wonderland several times. He would meet with spirit guides to get questions answered, received awards for improved performance and other things like that. When he was in Wonderland he was represented by an avatar which had a physical body that duplicated a fully functional Caleb Brown before his untimely passing. I chose to pick my avatar as what I looked like in my mid-twenties. Call it vanity, but I always thought of myself as being something of a hottie.

"When humans step into the Wonderland bubble they retain their current appearance. They can interact with the avatars as if they were human. That's why Joshua felt Caleb's rib-cracking hug.

"You may decide that all of your main team members need access to Wonderland. That will be your choice, however be sure to prepare them first and get them to swear to secrecy.

"One last thing, time doesn't exist in Wonderland. You could spend a thousand years in Wonderland and not one second would go by in reality. It's the ultimate getaway place. Once the bubble is locked, no human or spirit can touch you."

### Joshua

The Wonderland bubble meeting with Caleb and Chanlina took me back to the time my brother bonded with me. It was exceptionally difficult for me to accept. Our papa taught us that when you die, your spirit goes to heaven or to hell. He never mentioned anything about the possibility that the spirit of a dead man could join up with a human, no matter how closely related they were.

It took me a long time, almost two years, to accept Caleb was truly the spirit of my dead brother and we were somehow connected. To tell you the truth, I gave up trying to understand what happened to us and just went with it. After a while, I just accepted this was the way things were going to go for us, I would be able to telepathically communicate with Celeb. He became invaluable to me regarding our missions and it was a blessing to feel he was with me between them, but I never expected to see him again or to have him hug me until it felt like he cracked a couple of my ribs.

In some ways it was like starting our human/spirit interface all over again. I wasn't sure I'd ever get over seeing him in a physical body again. His avatar looked exactly like the real body of my brother. In fact, everything about him matched with the Caleb I knew. Except I knew it wasn't really him. I decided to look at the positive aspects of what was going on between us. For most of the time, we would interact like we had been doing ever since we bonded. I would only have to accept the avatar Caleb when we were together in the Wonderland bubble. Maybe I would gradually adjust to seeing him that way. I hoped so. In so many ways I've missed seeing him.

### Pearl

A few days after our banquet and the presentation on our upcoming cruise, we all met in the lobby of our hotel to await our shuttle to Emerald City Seaport. We arrived at noon and I had my first real look at our cruise ship. I knew all the dimensions of the *Wonder of the Seas*, but when I saw it in person for the first time, it was truly a shock. To say it was a large ship was a gross understatement. It was longer than several city blocks and taller than an eighteen story building.

The shuttle dropped us off at the aft end of the ship and after a very short wait, we were ushered into what was called a transport pod. The pod was about the size of a large apartment providing ample room for everyone, including the dog and all our luggage for our three week vacation. The pod reminded me of an elevator, a very large elevator, with lots of windows so we could watch as we were whisked upward to the very top floor (I was told I should call it a deck, not a floor). It gave us a breathtaking view of the city, the seaport and the ships in Puget Sound.

When we reached the top deck, we were escorted by several teams of stewards to our individual luxury suites. They ensured all our luggage made it to the correct suites. In addition, they gave us a detailed explanation of all the accommodations included in our suites. They were exceptionally well versed in answering any and all of our questions not only about our quarters, but also about the ship in general.

As our travel agent briefed us, we were given the SVIP treatment (that's my acronym for Super Very Important Persons). We didn't have to go through the registration process and have our passports verified. Nor did we need to wait in the hours-long line to finally get aboard and hunt for our rooms.

All the suites had spacious verandas which gave us incredible views of Seattle. Once Pham and I were settled in, we decided to enjoy the view. The stewards had provided some refreshments before they left, and Pham and I sat together in the cushy love seat and sipped fruity cocktails laced with several types of rum. They were delicious as were the snacks of various cheeses, assorted sausage slices and a variety of salted nuts.

"I could get used to this," Pham said as I snuggled close to him.

I took a sip and replied, "Me too. How long before we get underway?"

He checked his watch. "If they're on schedule, about three hours from now. After we finish our drinks, how about we stroll around and look at all the onboard activities before the peasant passengers come aboard?"

I giggled and elbowed him in the ribs. "Since when did you turn into one of the rich and famous?"

He took another sip, turned to me, and answered, "Since I met you."

We finished our cocktails and headed out. We decided to limit ourselves to the top deck for our excursion and where we were not too surprised to run into Joshua and Simone. It took us almost an hour to walk from the aft end of the ship to the bow, then back again. It gave us perspective of just how big our ship was. And we only covered one deck. There were more than a dozen more to explore, but not today.

When we arrived back to the lobby area for all our suites, Mark stepped out of his door and waved to us and said, "I'm so glad to see you guys. I want to show you our suite. You won't believe this place!" he said enthusiastically.

We entered the foyer of the two story luxury family suite. The back wall was made of floor-to-ceiling (deck to overhead) windows with verandas on each floor. There was a stairway from the living room to the upper level where Serina and Sarge would sleep. The second floor was a spacious loft which extended about two-thirds of the way to the glass windows, leaving the living room open to the ceiling of the loft. Mark and Maria's master bedroom had an adjoining master bath on the first floor. Serina had her own bathroom on the second floor with a good sized potty area for Sarge.

From the landing at the top of the stairs was a large multicolored tube about three feet in diameter and twenty feet long, curving to the first floor in back of the living room. When we entered the suite, Maria, Serina and Sarge were all waiting impatiently to greet us.

Mark was grinning from ear to ear as he said, "Serina, why don't you and Sarge show us your little game?"

The young girl let out a piercing squeal and headed for the stairs followed closely by Sarge. They ran up the stairs and dove into the tube which activated loud music and colorful flashing lights as they slid down and out onto the carpeted first floor. As soon as they were out of the tube, the lights and the music stopped. Serina was sprawled on the floor laughing uproariously as Sarge came bursting out of the tube and headed for the stairs again.

Sarge was fast as he streaked up the stairs, diving into the tube again.

We all began laughing at their antics, and after they completed three more circuits, Sarge slid to a stop next to Serina with his tongue hanging out the side of his mouth.

As we headed back to our own suite, I asked Pham jokingly, "Are you sorry we don't have a tube slide in our suite?"

He answered, "Not really. Maybe it would be okay without the loud music and flashing lights. I'm satisfied with our own suite. It's more… I guess refined would be the best description."


### Joshua

After our hour-long stroll around the top deck, I felt like I'd worked up an appetite. I asked Simone, "Are you hungry?"

"I'm not starving, but I could eat. How about you?"

"I'd like to get everybody together for lunch. How many restaurants does the ship have?"

She picked up a fact sheet, scanned for restaurants, and smiled. "What a shame," she said in snooty voice. "They have only twenty restaurants, how *bourgeoisie* of them. How can we possibly enjoy our vacation with only twenty restaurants? Even worse, most of them don't open until we sail. For now, your choices are hot dogs, tacos or the buffet. I'd prefer the buffet, it has extensive choices."

"How far from our suite is the buffet?" I asked.

She turned to the smart screen on the wall and asked, "How long a walk from our suite to the buffet?"

A pleasant sounding female voice answered, "You are among the first passengers to board so traffic will not be heavy. I estimate you could walk there in less than twenty minutes. I've sent a map to your smart phone so you don't get lost. Would you like to know more details about our ship's entertainment features?"

I answered as Simone began contacting the rest of the extended team regarding lunch. "Yes," I said to the smart screen. "How many swimming pools onboard?"

"We have nineteen swimming pools and a wide variety of other water park features including hot tubs, slip and slide pipelines and a place to try your hand at surfing called Surf's Up. In addition to the water attractions, we have several spa areas for weight training and aerobic equipment, massages and hair salons. We also have a huge casino if you like to gamble and a replica of Central Park on the main deck. Would you like to hear more?"

I saw Simone looking at her smart watch and gesturing towards the door. "Not now. We're leaving for lunch," I answered.

"Enjoy your meal with the rest of your team, Joshua."

As we joined the team and headed to the buffet, I thought to myself, *The smart screen is really cool, a little creepy, but definitely cool.*

### Simone

There were only a few, small additional groups of passengers scattered throughout the buffet restaurant, but far enough apart not to overhear any conversations.

I was overwhelmed by the varieties of food offered. I was sure they could supply dishes to satisfy every palate. I noticed Pham and Pearl took small servings of a variety of tastes including seafood dishes from Southeast Asia. They topped it all off with slices of pepperoni pizza. I knew better than to question their choices even though they looked surprised to see the variety of Mexican foods on my plate. What can I say? I have a passion for red chili burritos, enchilada style, with a side of both beef and chicken tacos with frijoles smothered in cheese.

As we ate, we carried on conversations regarding our suites and how overwhelmingly posh they were. Maria's daughter was having the time of her life eating deep fried chicken fingers and French fries that she shared with Sarge. I was very surprised at how delicately he took the food from her hand.

As time went by, more and more groups of people began drifting into the buffet. When we finished up and were ready to leave, it still looked like less than a hundred passengers getting their food.

With our belly's comfortably full, we headed back to our suites while Pham and Pearl went to oversee the loading of the War Wagon into the ship's cargo hold.


### Pham

Pearl and I took one of the many freight elevators down into the crew's quarters and followed directions to the aft cargo holds. Some holds were designated for storing baggage, others for food, or in our case, storing our multi-billion-dollar motorhome.

We walked down the cargo ramp to the dock and unlocked the War Wagon storage container. Once the motorhome was clear of the container, we climbed onboard and Pearl gave voice commands to the AI system. It drove us up the ramp and into the designated location in the hold. Once it was parked, Pearl ordered, "Maintain all systems at standby. All security systems to full alert."

After a short pause, Chanlina's voice responded. "Confirming. All security systems activated. *Bon Voyage.*"

# CHAPTER 7
# BEGINNING THE CRUISE

### Special Agent Joey Hong, FBI

The sun was on its way to the western horizon and had ducked behind a cloud bank moving in across the Sound. Bill and his current girlfriend, Naomi, joined Lili and me waiting for the ship to begin its voyage. We were standing at the rail looking down at the last-minute passengers scrambling to get aboard.

It was an unusually balmy afternoon for Seattle. I was looking around the crowd gathering on the upper deck where tradition dictated passengers were to throw tons of confetti and streamers over the side as the ship began to move away from the dock. Even noise makers were encouraged.

I noticed Mark, his fiancé Maria, and her daughter were moving through the crowd so I waved them over. They were accompanied by Sarge who was wearing his therapy vest and providing Serina with a security detail.

"Is this your first cruise?" I asked Mark as we leaned against the rail.

"Not really, I was on a Navy ship moving through various locations in the Middle East during my tours in Afghanistan. I don't think that counts as a *pleasure* cruise. How about you?"

"Not hardly," I replied. "I took a ferry boat across the Sound to Bremerton once to question a witness in a robbery case. This trip is so far above our pay grades, I can't believe this is happening."

"How about you?" Mark asked Bill.

"Same for me," answered Bill. "When we walked into our suite, my first thought was that we were in the wrong room. Then I decided I was having a beautiful dream. It had to be a dream because there was a box of two dozen donuts on the kitchen counter."

"I think that was a surprise from Joshua. I got two dozen donuts too."

We felt a slight shudder go through the ship. I looked over the side and saw jets of foamy water shooting out from the stern at midship and at the bow. "What's going on? Is this normal?"

Mark spoke up as the roar of the jets increased. "These big ships use propulsor pods instead of propellers and rudders, just like the new War Wagon, only much larger. The big cargo ships that docked at Terminal 6 in Portland all had pods. It allows the ships to avoid using tug boats to assist in docking and moving the ships."

There was a thunderous roar from the ship's horn as the ship began to move sideways away from the dock. I noticed all the huge rope lines were being cast off from the ship and the passengers on the upper deck began yelling and screaming, blowing on party horns and tossing confetti over the side to the dock below.

"How many of these pods does this ship have?" I shouted to Mark above the noise of the crowd.

"At least six major pods," Mark yelled back. "Each pod would be rated around eight thousand horsepower. They probably have additional smaller pods to assist with maneuvering."

Once we were safely away from the dock, the pods swiveled and we began to slowly move forward. It took us several hours to navigate through the numerous islands in Puget Sound and across the border into Canadian waters before transitioning into the inside passage of Alaska. Sometime during the night we reached our cruising speed of 20 knots (23 mph).

Early the next morning, we were awakened by a very loud alarm. All four of us had been up late. Did I mention Buffalo Bill and Naomi were sharing a suite with us? It was a mutually acceptable arrangement. Both Bill and I were pleased everyone got along so well. Naomi was a friendly, outgoing, charming woman and of course she was stunningly beautiful, not at all like the dogs Bill normally dated.

Bill came bolting out of their bedroom in his underwear with his gun held at the ready. He stopped short and had this dazed look as he scanned for perps.

I lowered my own gun as Lili came up behind me. "What's happening?" she asked. "Are we sinking?"

The alarm ended abruptly as Naomi came up behind Bill and placed her hand gently on his shoulder. "Put your gun down, baby. It's only a drill."

The announcement for the lifeboat drill followed quickly after the alarm ended and we retreated to our respective bedrooms and threw on some decent clothes. As we headed out to the express elevators, Bill grumbled as the elevator doors closed, "We're in the luxury suites. We should be exempt from the damned lifeboat drill." We left our weapons in the lockboxes next to our beds.

Once on the main deck, it took the better part of an hour getting everyone into the right locations. Apparently, we weren't the only ones to sleep in. A substantial part of the passengers were still in their pajamas and nightgowns. A very few were in their underwear with blankets wrapped around them.

Once the head count was confirmed and everyone was in the right place, a quick recorded message apologized for the inconvenience. They stressed after numerous voyages they have never had to deploy the lifeboats. However, the federal government required the drill.

All of Joshua's extended team were grouped together and after the drill was completed he suggested we meet in the buffet for breakfast and a short meeting. He arranged for a private room off the main buffet.

### After-Breakfast Meeting—Joshua

After the servers had cleared our breakfast plates and placed water pitchers on the table, I stood at the end of the table and began what I thought was going to be a brief meeting. "I want to welcome you all to this fantastic cruise ship. With the exception of the life boat drill, are you enjoying your first day at sea?"

There were a few chuckles but mostly smiles and nods of agreement.

"For the next three weeks you are going to be treated to an incredible vacation. We will spend the first week cruising from Seattle to the port of Whittier, Alaska, the port city located about sixty miles from the city of Anchorage. During the first leg of the trip we will make stops at Ketchikan, the Alaskan capitol city of Juneau, and Skagway, a town with Russian heritage. We will also spend time in Glacier Bay. There will be shore excursions at each port of call and the opportunity to visit the top of a glacier by helicopter for those interested. Once we dock, we will spend another week traveling from Anchorage to Fairbanks with a layover at Denali National Park. In Fairbanks you will get to pan for real gold and you get to keep all the gold you find."

That raised a few eyebrows around the room.

"At the end of that week we will head back for a return trip on *Wonder of the Seas* and—"

I had to pause, Caleb interrupted me. *Josh, it looks like we have visitors at the War Wagon. How do you want to handle this?*

*I'll meet you at the cargo bay in ten minutes. I'll bring friends.*

I refocused and said, "We have a security issue to deal with. As soon as I can, I'll continue this meeting. I need a few of you to assist. Mark and Sarge, Pham, Pearl and Simone please join me."

"Wait!" said both Hong and Cody at the same time.

"We'd like to go with you," added Hong.

I nodded in agreement. "Welcome aboard."

One of the ship's security people met us outside the banquet room and escorted us to the cargo bay. As soon as we entered, a message sounded: "Warning! Warning! Warning! Step away from the vehicle. Attempting to enter the vehicle will result in a powerful electric shock which could potentially lead to death." The message repeated in several different languages, interspersed with the sound of a siren and flashing lights.

A very large, muscular man closed in on me. He was big. Not as big as me, but I didn't want to deal with him just yet. He wasn't smiling and yelled, "Turn your damned alarm off or I'll dump your death trap into the ocean."

Pearl touched a key on her encrypted smart phone and the warning message stopped abruptly.

We saw three people lying on the ground next to the motorhome. All three were being treated by the ship's equivalent of EMTs. I could see flash burns on the hands and face of one of the men. The other two had similar damage. Without looking at the obnoxious large man, I walked passed him and continued toward the motorhome.

"Hey, buddy, you've got some questions to answer."

I continued to ignore him so the man reached out and grabbed my arm. Big mistake. Simone quickly grabbed the man's wrist, ripped his hand from my arm, twisted her body as she swept his legs out from under him and dumped him onto the deck with a resounding crash. She stood over him with a small knife pressed against his neck.

She leaned down and in a very soft voice said, "Be very careful. Your next move could end your life."

The man froze as I continued on to look at the injured bodies next to the motorhome.

"What happened?" I asked the nearest EMT.

"Apparently, these three men ignored your warning and attempted to enter your motorhome. One of them had a crowbar and it looked like he was about to pry a door open when he was hit with an electrical charge that blew him about twenty feet from the vehicle."

"What about the other two?" I asked.

"Not sure. You need to see the CCTV footage. I think at least one of them tried to place an explosive charge under the motorhome and got the same treatment.

"Can you ID the three men?"

"Security is working on it. You need to talk to the big guy on the floor. He's the head of this cargo bay's security team."

I glanced over at the man on the floor with Simone standing over him, her knife lightly touching the man's throat. "What's your prognosis for these three?" I asked as I turned back to the EMT.

He shrugged. "I don't think any of them will die, but they may have had their brains scrambled for a while. We're going to take them to the infirmary in a few minutes."

"Can you put them in restraints? I would consider all three of them as flight risks."

"Sure we can restrain them, but hey, we're on a ship, where are they going to go?"

I shrugged. "Contact me as soon as they regain consciousness. These men are to be treated as armed and dangerous."

The EMT looked at me and said, "I'm sorry mister, but I have to ask, do you have the authority to arrest these people?"

I pulled out my cred back and said as he looked at my creds, "My name is Joshua Brown, I'm from Homeland Security, Special Agent in Charge. I consider these three men as extremely dangerous. Is that sufficient for you?"

"Absolutely, you're the boss."

I left the EMT and walked back to Simone and her captive. "Let him up, Simone. Thanks for having my back."

Simone stepped back and let the man struggle to his feet. She continued to stay within striking distance.

I turned back to the chief of security for cargo bay three and said, "Let's go to your office. We need to talk."

Without saying a word, he led Simone and I to his office. Special Agent Hong joined us while the rest of the team entered the motorhome to check for any damage. Cody, Mark and Sarge followed the EMTs and their prisoners to the infirmary.

### Inside the Motorhome—Chanlina

Caleb and I transported inside the motorhome as soon as the alarm sounded. Our spirits had been at the banquet meeting with Joshua and the extended team, listening to the travel plans.

Once inside, our first order of business was to determine if the attackers had somehow breached our security system. Our outside cameras tracked the three individuals from the moment they were within fifty feet of our motorhome. We could see they weren't wearing any masks and Caleb identified them as Asian. We could hear their conversations through the external audio pickups. We agreed they were speaking Chinese, Mandarin Chinese to be exact.

One of the invaders pointed something that resembled a Taser at the side of our motorhome near the front hatch and pulled the trigger. Two projectiles from the weapon stuck to the skin of the motorhome. The projectiles trailed thin wires back to the weapon. The shooter pushed another button on the side of the weapon and our security system shut down, including the alarm.

The other two men approached the motorhome and attempted to open the hatch. I manually activated the security system while Caleb manually turned the alarm back on. When the two men touched the door, I fired a 250,000 volt charge through the outside skin. The two men exploded away from the door with the sound of a thunder clap and landed in a smoking pile twenty feet from the motor home.

Their bodies were twitching violently as the man with the weapon ran toward the door and attempted to attach what looked like an explosive device. We assumed he was going to blow the door and gain access to the interior. I gave him a double tap of the 250,000 volt charge. There was a double thunder clap as the man was hurled backwards near the other two attackers. Like his friends, he was smoking and twitching.

The alarm continued to scream out its warning and we observed several of the ship's security people running toward the alarm. A very large man led the security team. We noticed Joshua and the team running into the cargo bay. The large man attempted to grab Joshua, but Simone gave him a very quick and effective lesson in jujitsu.

We waited patiently for Pham and Pearl to enter to determine what damage might have occurred to our subsystems. Joshua, Simone and Special Agent Hong followed the ship's cargo bay security chief back to his office while Special Agent Cody, Mark and Sarge followed the EMTs as they pushed the attackers' gurneys to the ship's infirmary.

### Who Were the Attackers?—Joshua

As the three of us followed the cargo bay security chief back to his office, Caleb and Chanlina gave me a quick briefing on their side of the story. The office was small, however large enough to seat the chief behind his desk and the three of us in folding metal chairs on the other side. I noticed a name plaque on his desk identifying the chief as Björn Larsson.

"Chief Larsson, let me introduce ourselves and show you our creds," I began. "My name is Joshua Brown, I'm from Homeland Security and the Special Agent in Charge of this operation." As I spoke I laid my cred pack on his desk to verify my title.

"With me is Simone Cantrell, Special Agent with DEA whom you met earlier." As she presented her cred pack, Chief Larsson touched his injured right arm. "Also joining us is Special Agent Joey Hong with the FBI."

The chief briefly looked at Hong's credentials as I began. "What can you tell me about the three men who attacked our vehicle?"

He shrugged his shoulders and looked mildly embarrassed. "I'm sorry to say I know nothing about the attackers. I had never seen them before," he replied with a heavy Swedish accent. "When your alarm went off, I left my office to see what was the problem. When I first saw them, all three were lying on the bay deck smoking and shaking."

"So you didn't see their attack?" asked Hong.

"No sir, I did not," he answered emphatically.

"Do you have CCTV cameras in your bay?" asked Simone.

"Of course. This bay has four cameras which scan continuously. Unfortunately, I have not yet seen the footage."

"Would you have some way of identifying the three attackers?" I asked as I gathered our creds and handed them back.

"Yes, of course. Everyone who boards the ship has to have a passport. However, we occasionally have stowaways who manage to sneak on board. I believe our medical people found none of the men had any identification on them."

Hong turned to me and said, "Joshua, I brought a fingerprint scanner with me. I could take their prints and see if they're in any of the data bases I have access to."

Simone smiled at Hong and said, "Really? You brought a fingerprint scanner on your vacation?"

He shrugged his shoulders and answered, "Once a cop, always a cop. I believe in being prepared, even on vacation."

"It may be our only lead to finding out the identity of these people. Do it while these clowns are still unconscious," I interjected, then turned back to Chief Larsson. "Do you have a brig aboard for when they regain consciousness?"

"Yes," replied the chief. "However, only the captain or first officer are authorized to imprison anyone in the brig."

"I'll take care of that. Thank you for your time, chief," I said as we stood up to leave. "Sorry about the misunderstanding. Take care of your arm."

As I walked to the door, I paused, turned back to the chief and added, "Would you please keep an eye on the motorhome, just in case there are more stowaways? It's a very special vehicle, the only one of its kind."

### Who Are You? I Really Want to Know—Joey Hong

I hurried back to our suite to pick up my portable fingerprint scanner. It's about the size of a smart phone and has a direct line to the bureau's data bases. I also picked up the special camera I use for facial recognition scans. I decided to take our guns out of their lockboxes. I knew Bill would appreciate having his weapon with him while guarding the three men when they woke up.

Lili stopped me before I could leave our suite. "Where are you going, Joey? What happened in the cargo bay that's so important?"

Before I could answer, Naomi added, "I'd like to know too. Where is Bill and when will he come back?"

I was anxious to get the fingerprints and pictures of the three attackers; however, I really needed to give the two ladies an explanation. They were both made uneasy by not knowing.

"We have a very special vehicle stored in one of the ship's cargo bays and some men attempted to break into it. They were taken to holding cells and we are attempting to identify them. I think they could be Chinese spies. I'm going to take their fingerprints and pictures to assist with identification. Bill is currently guarding them. We should both be back in less than an hour."

From the look on both women's faces, I thought I may have given them too much information. Lili looked at me for a long minute then said, "Thank you Joey, please take care of yourself and Bill too. We'll stay in the suite until you return. Be careful Love, hurry back."

I closed the door behind me and headed to the infirmary, all the time thinking what a smart woman my wife was. She understood that being a cop could be dangerous work sometimes. I essentially told her not to worry, at least not yet. I hoped Naomi would agree.

The three men were still unconscious when I arrived. I gave Bill his Glock and shoulder holster. I'd already put mine on in the elevator while I was still alone.

Bill helped me get the prints, holding the perps' hands with fingers extended. It took only a few minutes to take the prints and send them back to the bureau for analyses. It took a little longer to get the pictures for the facial recognition scans.

There are a number of data bases used to identify a variety of people. It used to be each of the security agencies had their own separate data bases, however, with the formation of Homeland Security, all the data bases were combined into one extremely large database. They also had shared access with European agencies.

It took only fifteen minutes to get confirmation of the three men's identities. They were agents of the Chinese Ministry of State Security. MSS is similar to our CIA and FBI rolled into one. MSS was well known for cyber-crimes as well as attempting to acquire (more like stealing) secret technology. The known leader of MSS is Chen Yixin.

By the time we had identified each of the three attackers, they were beginning to wake up. They were very disoriented and experiencing considerable pain. The doctors in the infirmary wanted to give them some pain pills, however we suggested they hold off on the meds until we had a chance to question them.

Each man was restrained in a separate gurney. Bill and I moved them far enough apart that they couldn't communicate with each other. Bill watched as I began questioning the first perp in Mandarin. I addressed him by name. *"Good afternoon Wo Fat Ling. It is so good to meet you. Your boss, Chen Yixin sends his greetings. He also asked me to inform you your failure in your mission is unfortunate, therefore he has no further use for you in the Ministry of State Security."*

I went on to the last two men and gave them the same message, being sure to address them and the minister by name. There was a look of fear on the faces of each man as they were transferred to individual cells in the ship's brig. The ship's captain approved the move to the brig with the understanding that the three prisoners would be turned over to the FBI at the first port-of-call.

We rejoined the women in less than an hour and shared with them what heroes we were. They made us promise we wouldn't be bothered with more attacks for at least a few days, hopefully a week. Bill and I promised. We may have had our fingers crossed.

After we enjoyed a couple of donuts we headed out to enjoy as many entertainment venues as we could until dinner time.

### How Did They Knockout Our Security System?—Pham

The first thing I did once I arrived at the motorhome was confiscate the Taser-like device that quickly short circuited our alarm system. With the help of Caleb and Chanlina, we were able to figure out how it worked and what mods we needed to make sure a similar attack would not be successful. I was able to reverse engineer the device and make some adjustments to the security circuits, then tested the system several times before I was satisfied that form of attack would never work again.

While I was working on the security system, Pearl, Caleb and Chanlina did a thorough diagnostic exam of all the subsystems. Pearl paid special attention to the cold fusion reactor and was relieved to determine it had not been affected by the security breach. Chanlina gave an all-clear to the computer system. Caleb was concerned that the morphing configurations might have been affected, but we decided we'd have to wait until prying eyes were no longer an issue.

# CHAPTER 8
# NORTH TO ALASKA

### Ketchikan, First Port of Call—Lili

After Joey and Bill returned from the cargo bay, we spent the rest of the day and most of the evening enjoying all the wonderful things our ship had to offer. It was warm enough to try many of the outside water attractions, from one of the numerous swimming pools, some with swim up bars, to hot tubs, and slip & slide tubes where I almost lost part of my swimsuit. That would have been very embarrassing.

Speaking of embarrassing, Bill decided to try out Surf's Up. Joey told me Bill had never surfed in his life, but when he saw the little kid from Hawaii doing it, he figured how hard could it be? It turned out, it was much harder than it looked.

He started out okay, until another surfer bumped into him and sent him into the fast-moving water. He went one way and his suit another. Naomi had to throw him a towel to cover his body as he climbed out of the water. I just wish I could unsee what I saw. Joey teased him about it for a while until Bill threatened to hide the rest of his donuts.

We went back to our suite, changed into our casual evening clothes, and went to a fine dining restaurant for dinner. The food was terrific, I especially liked the tiramisu dessert. Between courses we were entertained by singing servers who sang everything from romantic ballads to rock and roll. I was pleasantly surprised when two Chinese waiters came to our table and sang a very famous song from a Chinese opera. Both Joey and I were very impressed.

To end the evening, we attended a Broadway-like show in the ship's magnificent theater. The performers were very talented, and we all loved the music from *The Phantom of the Opera*. I think Naomi and I had a little too much champagne during the intermission because we giggled all the way back to our suite. Joey had to carry me into our bedroom. Sometimes my husband can be very romantic.

I awoke the next morning to the sound of Joey shouting, "Where are my donuts, Bill? This isn't funny, give me back my damned donuts!"

I was still in my nightgown as I walked out onto our private veranda and noticed we had already docked at Ketchikan. Time to enjoy another beautiful day in the Pacific Northwest.

I was still full from last night's dinner, however I nevertheless wanted to eat a little something before we went ashore. Joey contacted room service for coffee, tea and a fruit plate. When they arrived, Bill brought out the hidden donut box. Both of our men had coffee and donuts, while we ladies enjoyed the fruit and a hot cup of delicious green tea.

We took the VIP elevator directly to the main deck and walked through the security checkpoint. I was informed that they would check us out as well as check us back in. This was a safety requirement to make sure everyone who went ashore was back on board before our ship sailed to our next port.

I should mention, both Joey and Bill had taken their weapons with them, which resulted in them having to go through a separate screening. They were permitted to disembark, provided they showed their credentials as federal agents.

Once we were ashore, we looked at the various excursions available to us. We decided to just browse the numerous shops along the shore. Our ship wouldn't sail until late evening so we had plenty of time to explore.

The second shop we visited was called the Outlet Store. I was looking at the T-shirts with pictures of Alaska on the front when Joey said to me, "Lili, come look at this. You won't believe it."

I walked around the corner and came to a dead stop. Bill and Naomi were staring at an enormous stuffed polar bear on a raised platform covered in simulated snow. Joey said to me, "I had no idea they got that huge."

"Was this a real bear?" I asked.

Bill was reading a plaque underneath the bear. "It says it was shot by a hunter who said the bear attacked him. He claims to have shot the bear in self-defense. It's a little under thirteen feet tall when standing up and weighs close to a thousand pounds. What a monster!" We bought several postcards with a picture of the bear and Bill bought T-shirts for Naomi and himself.

We strolled along the shops picking up little mementos that caught our eye. I noticed the two men had dropped a little behind us and were scanning the crowd. Joey raised his smart phone and began snapping pictures of what I thought were random individuals as they walked by.

A couple of hours passed and I was getting tired of walking. "Is anyone ready for lunch?" I asked, as we neared an open-air restaurant that claimed to have the freshest salmon in all the world.

Naomi agreed saying, "I could eat. How about you, honey?"

Bill turned from Joey. "I'm sorry, were you speaking to me, babe?"

"Do you want to have a fresh salmon lunch here?" she asked again.

"Sure," he smiled. "I need to sit down a spell anyway. My hip is a little tender after my fall at Surf's Up yesterday."

We sat at a table next to the crowded walkway and waited for our salmon salads. Bill and Joey were usually very talkative when we were all together, but not today. They were both checking their phones and occasionally snapping pictures of people passing by. When a young man delivered our salads, Naomi asked, "Why are you two taking so many pictures?" She sounded perturbed.

Before Bill could answer, Joshua and Mark came out of the crowd.

"Hello, may we join you? Salmon salad sounds good," said Joshua, as the two of them sat down beside us.

Without thinking, I asked him, "Are you searching for more possible spies too?"

"Is that what they're doing? I was wondering why they're acting so weird," fumed Naomi. "I'm going back to the ship. Let me know if you catch anybody." She stood up abruptly and started to walk back to the ship.

I yelled back to her, "Wait up, I'll join you." I scooped up our salads and ran after her.

### All Hands on Deck—Joshua

I called a meeting of everyone from the extended team, with the exception of Serina and Sarge, who would act as her bodyguard while I explained to the adults what was going on.

We met in Mark and Maria's family suite. Before anyone arrived, Mark scanned the room for bugs before declaring the suite safe.

"Thank you all for coming. This shouldn't take too long. First, I want to assure you all we are on a legitimate vacation. As most of you know, we have also brought onboard a very special vehicle with the intent of doing some field testing once we leave the ship at Wittier, Alaska. That will be five days from now. That vehicle is currently in a restricted cargo bay of our ship. Unfortunately, three foreign agents attempted to break into the vehicle yesterday.

"Those three men were restrained, arrested and turned over to the FBI immediately after we docked at Ketchikan this morning. They will no longer be a concern for us; however, just to be sure there aren't any similar break-in attempts, this morning our two FBI agents took it upon themselves to identify any additional foreign agents that might be masquerading as passengers on our ship.

"With the help of our ship's security people, special agents Hong and Cody have checked every passenger and crew member aboard. They used facial recognition software to scan the passports of every person on board and I'm happy to report no foreign agents were detected.

"Based on that information, I don't anticipate any further interruptions."

Naomi raised her hand. "I have a question, am I allowed to speak at this meeting?"

"Of course, Naomi. What's your question?"

"Is there any chance we could be attacked once we are off the ship and heading toward Fairbanks?"

Without hesitation, I answered her. "Yes there is."

My reply raised a few eyebrows around the room. "However, I consider it highly unlikely. If any of you feel we have put you in possible danger and want to return to Seattle, that is your prerogative. We will be able to fly you back from our next port-of-call. That would be Juneau. We're due to dock there tomorrow morning."

Naomi nodded and said to the group, "I have no intention of leaving the ship and I look forward to the entire vacation with all of you. I just wanted to be sure I had some options if things started going sideways. Thank you, Joshua, for taking the time to explain the situation to me and anyone else who might have concerns."

The meeting was adjourned. I hoped and prayed I hadn't misled anyone.

Later that night we set sail for Alaska's capital city. We arrived in Juneau early the next morning.


## Capital City, the Port of Juneau—Pearl

I woke up early the next morning. I wanted to watch how they docked this huge ship into the relatively small docking area. This far north, the sun rose early and set late during the summer. It was a little past 4 a.m. when I stepped out onto the veranda holding a cup of coffee in one hand and grasping a blanket around me to keep me warm in the cool of the morning.

I sat down in one of the cushioned chairs and placed my coffee cup on the nearby table and stared out at Taku Inlet, one of the many rivers and creeks that are near Juneau.

Taku is the Tlingit name for Fierce Winds. As I sipped my coffee, I accessed Wikipedia on my iPad to find out just how fierce the winds really were. There was a video showing Taku Inlet in the winter when all of the rivers in the Juneau area are frozen solid. The text indicated the wind speed could reach 220 mph blowing down the frozen river.

I was amazed! No wonder the natives had named it Fierce Winds. Fortunately, during the summer months when the rivers were flowing, the wind was very subdued.

The Taku Inlet flowed into Gastineau Channel with the city of Juneau on the east bank of the channel. It was also where the cruise ships docked during the summer months. The Juneau Cruise Ship Port can handle up to five cruise ships at the same time, however one of the ships has to anchor away from the dock and use small boats, called tenders, to taxi the passengers to the dock area. Because *Wonder of the Seas* is so large, it takes up space for two smaller ships. During its maiden voyage to Alaska it was given privileged docking rights. That meant two ships had to anchor and tender in their passengers ashore in the small motorized launches.

*Wonder of the Seas* had been slowing down from its cruise speed of 20 knots to barely moving over several hours. The ship used its thruster pods to bring the ship to a full stop and then move it sideways toward the docking area. It took a little more than an hour to bleed off the ship's momentum and come to a dead stop. The thruster pods were shut down and many large ropes where thrown down by the ship's deck crew to the shore crew waiting on the dock below, who secured the ship to the large metal bollards.

"You're up early," said Pham as he joined me on the veranda. He had on a heavy bathrobe with warm looking slippers. He brought out a pot of steaming coffee and filled my cup before filling his own. "What do you feel like doing today?" he asked.

"We're going to be in Juneau for a day and a half," I replied. "I've been looking at all the shore excursions, and there are several I'd like to try."

"Which ones?" Pham asked as he sipped his coffee and took a croissant out of the pocket of his robe.

Before I answered, I put out my hand and waited. He put down his coffee cup and reached into his other pocket, pulled out another croissant and handed it to me.

"I'd really like to take the helicopter ride to the Mendenhall Glacier and then go for a ride in a dog sled."

He looked surprised. "Really? I didn't think you were that adventurous." He paused, then added, "I'd like to take the cable car to the top of the mountain and then zipline down."

"What about whale watching?" I asked, getting excited about the excursions. "How many things can we do while we're here. Maybe we need to speak to an excursion agent. We should see what the rest of the team wants to do. It would be fun to go as a group. First, we should get dressed."

Pham started laughing. "Whoa, slow down, Pearl. It's not even 0600 hours yet. They won't be letting us off the ship for a couple of hours."

"You're right," I said with a pout. "We've got plenty of time," I added as I got up from my chair and slowly walked over and sat in his lap. I put my arms around his neck and kissed him on the cheek.

"That's it? Just a cheek kiss? I was hoping for something more," he said playfully.

"Oh, you'll get more. Lots more. But first I need to brush my teeth," I replied in as sultry a voice as I could manage at six in the morning and headed inside to the bathroom.


### Excursions in Juneau—Simone

Joshua asked me to organize our excursions in Juneau. I found out our VIP status allowed for us to have one of the ship's excursion agents to help us plan our activities for the day and a half we were in Juneau. All of us met in a VIP conference room at 0800 hours and by 0830 we were done with the planning. By 0900 hours we were on our way.

As you can imagine, there were a few things we all wanted to see. A one hour city tour was one of them, as was whale watching and a visit to the Mendenhall Glacier. While at the glacier, some of us opted to take a helicopter ride to the top of the glacier and ride in a dog sled. Others were interested in the history of Juneau and wanted to visit museums, and still others decided to take a zipline trip through a forest on Douglas Island, west of the Gastineau Channel across from Juneau by bridge.

We were told by the agent to dress warmly. In the summer months the temperature seldom got above 60° F, on top of the glacier it would be a lot colder.

Every one of us climbed aboard the open-air tour bus for our trip around the city. Our guide informed us of some interesting information regarding the ride. For example most of us didn't know the only way to visit Juneau was by boat or aircraft. There are no roads in or out of the city. All cars and trucks are usually brought in by cargo ships. Juneau is one of the largest cities in Alaska with a population of just over 32,000 residents. Fairbanks is slightly larger. There are five different types of salmon in the world and Juneau has all five. Bald eagles love to eat salmon, as do grizzly bears and other wild animals. Speaking of bald eagles, there are more of that breed of eagle in Juneau than anywhere else in the world. We stopped to look at a huge tree near the river. There had to be hundreds, maybe a thousand of the white-headed bald eagles roosting in the branches.

Most of us must had taken hundreds of pictures of the city during our tour. We tipped the driver and the guide as we got off the bus and headed for our other excursions. Whale watching was next for me and several others of our group.

We boarded a large powerboat and headed out to open water to look for whales. We were told this was the time of year when whales migrated to Alaska to breed. Ten minutes later, we ran into a pod of five whales who came up out of the water about ten feet from the side of the boat. Serina squealed with delight at the sight of the enormous mammals until one shot upward out of the sea and came crashing down very close to us, spraying salt water over all of the passengers who chose to stand on the open deck to get a better view. We were drenched with ice cold water, but fortunately we were given hooded rain gear to wear when we came aboard, along with life jackets.

The last thing I will cover is our trip to Mendenhall Glacier. It was only a 12-mile drive from downtown Juneau. Our bus rounded a curve in the forest and suddenly it was there. The glacier was composed of the prettiest shade of blue ice. As we got off the bus, a large piece of ice came loose from the glacier and crashed into the large lake at the end of the ice flow. I was later told that was called calving and it resulted in a towering spray of water which shot up into the sky and then thundered down into the lake. It was a very exciting beginning to our excursion.

There was a relatively large log building that housed a combination store and museum with a fifteen-minute film being shown, continuously presenting the interesting history of the glacier.

The store had a small cafeteria and we all bought sandwiches, chips and drinks and we took them outside and sat at picnic tables to watch for more calving. When we were done with lunch, we hiked a trail that took us almost to the face of the glacier, and ended at the perfect spot for a photo op.

About half of us decided to head back to the city to visit other excursions. Joshua and I, Pham and Pearl, plus Mark and his crew, including Sarge, decided to take the helicopter ride to the top of the glacier. We decided our last excursion in Juneau would be the dogsled ride.

We climbed aboard a refurbished, bright red Huey helicopter, which had ample room for all of us. The doors had been removed and replaced with a web netting to give us a better view as we flew up to a relatively flat spot on the top of the glacier. The pilot set us down without so much as a bump. We waited for the rotor to wind down before he let us climb down to the rock hard, bluish ice.

It was cold, very cold, as the wind blew down the valley created by the slow movement of the ice flow. The surface was flat and rough, but hard as rock as we made our way to three waiting dogsled teams. Sarge was uncertain how to deal with the sled dogs, however Mark got permission from one of the drivers to introduce his dog to the dog team. There was a lot of sniffing, but the sled dogs were used to strangers, both two legged and four.

The drivers all wore heavily insulated parkas and thick gloves. I wished I had added another layer to my clothes. As I stood shivering, the lead driver spoke to Joshua, "Do you want to drive or ride?"

The question seemed to surprise Joshua for a moment before he responded. "I'd like to drive. What do I need to know to not to kill my passenger or the dogs?"

The driver smiled and said, "Hold on to the handles at all times. When you go up hills, run between the runners. When you go down hills you can step on the runners and ride. Never let go of the handles. If you have to make a panic stop, dump the sled on its side."

Joshua looked at me, then back at the driver. "What happens to the passenger if I dump the sled?"

"Hard to say. First priority is the dogs," he answered. He looked at me and said, "Climb in the sled, miss. Cover up with the bear skin. It'll keep you warm. Time to go. Don't worry, the dogs know where to go and when to stop. Don't try to steer them. They'll see any ravines before you can. I'll be waiting for you here. One of my dog handlers will go with you just in case something goes wrong."

He gave a shout and the dogs all stood up. He shouted again and the dogs took off with Joshua, as he held onto the handles, running full speed between the runners. I looked to the left and saw Pham driving Pearl as the runners of their sled kicked up snow. On the right Mark was driving with Maria sitting in the sled, holding tight to Serina both covered in bear skin. Sarge ran beside the sled dogs on the right side, barking along with the sled dogs as they ran. They were having a blast.

I tilted my head back to look at Joshua. His face was almost covered in snow, but I could see his smile. He looked down at me with a silly grin on his face, then looked up at the dogs and yelled at the top of this lungs, "Mush! Come on you huskies, mush!"

They were running up a slight grade for almost fifteen minutes. I was very impressed, all three of the men ran the entire way until the grade got steeper and the dogs began to slow, and finally stopped near an outcropping of rocky terrain. Sarge joined them as they laid down to rest.

I climbed out of the sled, keeping the bear skin rug wrapped around me as I looked at Joshua. He was bent over, hands on his knees, trying to catch his breath. I asked him, "So, Nanook of the North, how are you feeling now?"

He straightened up, using his gloved hand to wipe the snow off his face, and gasped, "You get to drive back."

"No way, José! That looks like too much work."

"It's all downhill on the way back. You won't have to run at all. Just put your feet on the runners and glide back."

"Let me see what Maria and Pearl think," I said, as I trudged over to speak with the two women. I turned at the familiar sound of a helicopter and noticed it wasn't red. It was black, and by the looks of it, a newer model.

The helicopter came to a hover close to the two drivers and the side door slid open. I stopped and watched as a man stood in the open doorway and fired two shots with what I thought could be an assault rifle. Both men dropped to the ice, not moving.

Joshua was also watching and yelled to Pham and Mark, "Dump your sleds and take cover behind the rocks. Leave the dogs. They're not the target."

The black helicopter was about a mile away and it began to close the distance between us. We had spread out amongst the huge boulders and Joshua asked, "Is everyone armed?"

Both Pham and Mark had pistols, so did I, and, of course, Joshua had his two Desert Eagle .50 AE Magnum Research pistols with several magazines of ammo. He yelled at Mark, "As soon as the helicopter is on the ground send out Sarge. I'm going to try to flank them and take out their turbines. On my order, everyone commence firing at the chopper's pilot."

The black chopper continued up the glacier with both side doors opened with armed men scanning for targets. About half way up, the remaining sled dog driver came out from behind one of the large granite boulders that lined the sides of the glacier. He held both hands high above his head, as he walked slowly toward the black copter, which had stopped moving and now rotated toward the man.

I couldn't believe he would expose himself like that, but it did dawn on me that perhaps he was acting as a distraction, giving us the time to get into position to counter any attack they might attempt.

Whatever the man's motives were, it gave Joshua the time he needed to move behind the rocks and get into position to open fire.

Josh popped up and had a clear shot at the side of the chopper. He wasted no time and fired 14 rounds of .50 AE bullets into the engine compartment. He reloaded with new magazines as the engine compartment burst into flames. The pilot attempted to put the gyrating chopper on the ground as the remaining sled dog driver dropped to his knees, rolled to his back and pulled out two .44 caliber Auto Mags. He began firing into the open side door of the 'copter.

While Joshua began firing at the pilot side, Mark, Pham and I saturated the front windows of the bird with everything we had.

Sarge streaked by me, jumped into the open side door, and went to work on whoever remained inside. We could hear screaming just before the chopper crashed into the glacier, scattering rotor blades in various directions. Just before it exploded, the screaming stopped and Sarge bolted out of the destroyed helicopter and ran to Mark with blood dripping from his mouth.

It became very quiet as we cautiously made sure no one could hurt us. Another chopper arrived about 15 minutes later with local police on board and a couple of EMTs. It was followed by another helicopter with three crime scene investigators. They pulled out five bodies from the attacking chopper, three of them burned beyond recognition. Only one man survived the crash, but he passed away before the EMTs arrived.

A total of seven people lost their lives that day, including the two sled dog drivers. It turns out the surviving sled dog driver was ex-FBI.

If it hadn't been for his distraction, things might have turned out very differently.

A rescue chopper picked us up on the glacier and flew us directly to a landing pad on our ship. None of us felt like going on any other excursions that evening. We stayed in our respective suites and ordered room service.

# CHAPTER 9
# WHO IS OUR ENEMY

### After Action Report—Caleb

Chanlina and I created a report for the police based on reading memories of everyone involved in the incident on Mendenhall Glacier. We also included the autopsy reports performed on the five men who were killed inside the black helicopter and the two dogsled drivers who were murdered.

The autopsies were performed by FBI medical examiners who were flown into the Juneau airport from the Seattle office two hours after the attack. There was a sense of urgency to identify the men from the helicopter.

The cause of death of the two dogsled drivers were gunshot wounds from a military grade assault rifle. Each driver was shot through the heart with a single bullet. Ballistics confirmed the assault rifle found in the remains of the helicopter as the murder weapon.

The pilot and copilot of the helicopter were identified as suspected mercenaries. Both were American citizens currently living in Canada. Both men were suspected of taking part in kidnappings and murders-for-hire in the Pacific Northwest. Cause of death of the two men was multiple gunshot wounds to the head and body from a variety of weapons.

The remaining three men were identified as Chinese nationals, suspected of ties to the MSS. Their names will not be released to the public, however they were well known spies operating throughout the Americas.

Cause of death of one of the men was multiple gunshot wounds fired from a .44 Auto Mags owned by the chief dogsled driver. Witnesses confirmed the former FBI agent fired in self-defense.

The second Chinese man was killed by an attack dog. The dog, a former decorated Marine, attacked to prevent the shooting induced death of Joshua Brown. Cause of death was the removal of the man's throat by the dog and the subsequent loss of blood.

The third Chinese man was killed by the explosion of the helicopter's gas turbine engine. Flying debris from the explosion resulted in the decapitation of the victim.

It is believed the motive for the attack was to kidnap Ms. Thong Chau.

Details of the reason for Ms. Thong Chau's attempted kidnapping are considered Top Secret and will not be presented in this report.

<u>**The Following Report is Classified Top Secret**</u>
<u>**Distribution is Limited**</u>
<u>**Code Name: The Apostle**</u>

With the successful development of a small cold fusion reactor by Dr. Thong Chau and her team of scientists and engineers, I believe she has become a target for kidnapping by the Chinese Ministry of State Security. MSS is well known for illegally acquiring advanced technology from supposedly friendly countries, as well as for attempting to steal information related to artificial intelligence. This includes both hardware and software.

The Top Secret research vehicle known as the War Wagon, and the scientists and engineers who created it, have been attacked with increasingly violent methods. I believe this will continue as the recent attacks show. I strongly recommend that 24-hour armed surveillance be employed for the War Wagon. That also includes the protection of all members of Team Joshua, as well as the scientists, engineers and technicians at Boeing's Advance Research Facility located in Everett, Washington.

I further recommend all non-essential members of the expanded Team Joshua currently on board the *Wonder of the Seas* cruise ship be removed from the ship and sent home at their earliest convenience.

A member of the Chinese tribunal speaking in closed session before MSS leaders has been quoted as saying they desperately need this new technology: "It is a critical part of our plan to make us the strongest nation in the world, both technically and militarily. We must not fail if we are to meet our goals of world domination."

## Who Wants to Go Home?—Caleb

Joshua asked Chanlina and me to do a subtle probe of each of the minds of the extended team to see who should go home and who should stay.

Joshua and Simone were at the top of the stay list, as were Pham and Pearl. Mark, Joey and Bill wanted to stay, but they wanted their loved ones out of harm's way. Maria didn't want to go home but she wanted Serina to stay with her grandmother. Lili was very adamant she was going to stay with her husband and, surprisingly, Naomi wanted to stay with Bill. Reading her thoughts, seeing Bill in action really impressed her. However, at the request of Mark, Joey and Bill, and with Joshua's consent, the women were to be sent home. It was just too dangerous to have untrained non-combatants in potential combat situations.

The non-combatant women would remain on the ship until we docked at Whittier.

## Visiting the Chinese MSS—Chanlina

At the request of The Apostle, I transported to Beijing to have a secret visit with the Ministry of State Security. By secret, I mean they didn't know I was coming and they never knew I was there, probing their collective minds regarding their feeble attempts to steal our advanced technology.

I'd been to Beijing several times, both as a human and a spirit. I really liked the general population, but their government, not so much. My appraisal of their government was it was just a little less oppressive than North Korea.

The MSS is housed in a large building located in Xiyuan, next to the Summer Palace near the Beijing Zoo. It's a massive structure harder to get into than a maximum-security prison is to escape from. Fortunately, they have not developed the technology to scan for spirits so I had the run of the place.

Unfortunately, anything of any importance to us was compartmentalized. Only a very few of the top echelon had access to the big picture. The top echelon is divided into two groups: the Tigers and the Dragons. Based on the hierarchy of the lunar calendar, the Tigers are the lower level of the elite bosses, while the Dragons are the *crème de la crème*. The Dragons further breakdown their power structure by color. The Minister of the MSS, Chen Yixin, is code named Red Dragon.

Trying to locate Red Dragon was like trying to find a needle in a hay stack. When I finally found him, I discovered he had delegated the information I was looking for. I had to settle for White Dragon. He alone was responsible for the attempts to acquire all the new technology packed into the new War Wagon.

The White Dragon didn't look all that powerful. He was a short, plump middle-aged man with thick glasses and little hair on his head. He also had a ridiculous mustache. As it turned out, he had the power of life and death, and he wasn't afraid to use it. That was bad news, but even worse than that was he had a very old, very wise spirit guiding his every move. The spirit traced his ancestry back to a very nasty distant emperor, not a very nice fellow at all. He ranked right up there with Pol Pot.

I had to be very careful how I handled myself. My goal was to find out as much as I could without letting either White Dragon or his spirit guide find out I had gone traipsing through his memories. I decided the best time would be when he was sleeping and his spirit guide was otherwise occupied.

I waited until he'd fallen asleep. Fortunately, he slept alone and took a strong sedative before retiring. I took my time as he fell into a light sleep, followed by REM sleep with a few very disgusting dreams. Finally, he transitioned into a deep, restful sleep, and I began a very delicate probe.

There was nothing there. Absolutely nothing. He had no memories. *How can this be?*

A voice began to resonate into my essence. It was in an ancient Chinese dialect, but of course I understood it perfectly. *Who dares to probe the mind of my servant? It is a waste of your time, infidel. He has no memories, I am the keeper of memories. Think of me as my servant's cloud.*

I tried to back out of White Dragon's mind, but I was trapped. The spirit was too strong for me. There was a deafening roar and suddenly I was back on the cruise ship, totally alone and struggling to recover.

*Caleb? Are you there? Can anyone hear me?*

I strained to hear, to sense any spirit. After what seemed like an eternity, I could sense a voice, a distant, barely audible voice. It was The Apostle. *Don't ever go there again. Never again!*

### *Speak Softly and Carry a Big Stick; You Will Go Far*—Joshua

On September 2, 1901, this famous quote of Vice President Theodore Roosevelt's was said just two weeks before his inauguration. It outlined his ideal foreign policy. Team Joshua embraced it as our own.

Since the attack at Mendenhall Glacier, the team was always alert, always carried weapons, and always made sure Pearl was protected. She never left the ship until it docked at Whittier. Wherever she went while onboard, she was always escorted by at least two armed team members. Outside of her suite, she always wore body armor under her clothes. If she needed to use one of the ship's public restrooms, Simone would clear it before Pearl entered and remained with her until she was ready to leave. As for the new War Wagon, we didn't leave it unprotected. Two of the team, most often Caleb or Chanlina, took turns inside the vehicle. The vehicle's security system was upgraded to lethal voltage and barriers were used to prevent access by anyone not a part of Team Joshua.

### On The Road Again, In Our Billion Dollar Ride—Jacob

We were told we were going to have a three-week vacation. Originally, all of us were going to take the train from Anchorage to Fairbanks with an overnight stop at Denali National Park. After a two-day stay in Fairbanks, we would take a nonstop train back to Whittier and sail the outside passage on board the *Oasis of the Seas* back to Seattle, making a few stops along the way. The last stop before Seattle would be at Victoria, British Columbia.

Because of the attacks during our cruise on *Wonder of the Seas,* that plan was no longer tenable. Our non-combatant women had grudgingly accepted the inevitable and would remain on the ship until it docked at Whittier, two days from now.

We left Juneau on schedule and there were no announcements within the ship regarding the shootout on Mendenhall Glacier, however most of the extended team was traumatized by the shootout and loss of life.

We had two more days before we were scheduled to dock at Whittier. The ship made two stops along the way. The first was at Sitka, a small town that predated becoming American property; its Russian heritage still remained intact. None of the team went ashore. The last stop was not at a city nor a town. It was at Glacier Bay.

When we arrived at the bay, there were two other cruise ships already in place. The view was breathtaking. Glacier Bay is made up of over a hundred separate glaciers. The John Hopkins Glacier ends with a towering wall of ice, 250 to 300 feet high and a mile long. We spent several hours about a mile from the wall, slowly rotating the ship so all sides got a spectacular view, especially when an iceberg-sized chunk of ice would calve and come crashing into the bay.

After about six hours of picture taking, we headed out of the bay following a pod of whales and continued to Whittier. Once we arrived, the entire team escorted the four non-combatant women to the airport. The remainder of our group got special permission to walk their loved ones onto the airplane. It was a sad time with many tear-stained faces. Eventually, it was time to depart with promises we would stay in contact everyday by vid phone. It was the best we could do under the circumstances, but it still hurt.

## On The Road With The New War Wagon —Mark

The seven of us plus Sarge took the VIP elevator to the crew area and entered the cargo bay. We checked in with Chief Björn Larsson and let him know we would be leaving the ship as soon as we completed the inspection of our motorhome. The spirits of Caleb and Chanlina were already aboard. They shut down the security system and began bringing all the subsystems from inactive to standby.

Pham assisted Pearl in the walk-around inspection. She checked the vehicle's external arrays and Pham swept the vehicle from front to back and top to bottom to make sure there were no bugs or locator transmitters attached.

Chanlina had reconfigured the interior of the vehicle with seven captain's chairs in the front half of the motorhome and sleeping quarters in the rear. Pham, Pearl, Simone and Joshua had the front four seats and Joey, Bill and I had seats spaced behind and between the four front seats. Sarge claimed the space next to me, close to the front hatch on the port side of the vehicle.

There were simulated windows completely encircling the motorhome's front compartment, giving everyone a 360-degree view of what was going on outside. Below the sim-windows were displays which let us all see the vehicle's performance data.

Chanlina's voice announced, "Everyone please strap in. I'm bringing the motorhome online, switching from standby to active. If you are interested, feel free to monitor the displays. As soon as we have all green lights we are ready to move." In less than a minute, all the situation lights changed from yellow to green. Chanlina announced, "Chief Larsson has cleared us to disembark from the ship and suggested we might want to follow the cruise line buses that run between the docks at Whittier and Anchorage. It's a sixty mile ride and should be very scenic."

## A Relaxing Ride—Joshua

We moved toward the cargo bay hatch, onto the ramp that ran from the bay to the dock, and then joined a convoy of buses heading to Anchorage. Even though I'd been in the new War Wagon before, I was still amazed at how smooth the ride was. It was almost too quiet, kind of spooky, really.

Caleb must have been reading my thoughts. *You want to hear something really weird?*

*If it has something to do with what you and Chanlina do in the Wonderland bubble, I don't want to hear about it,* I answered.

*No man, nothing like that. Did you notice how quiet our ride is? Listen to the outside audio pick up where the engine would be if we had an engine.*

I pushed the button on the rear exterior audio system and it sounded like a big diesel engine. *What the hell is that? Why do I hear engine noise?*

*It's a recording so that we sound just like a real motorhome. The Boeing people thought if we were too quiet people might get suspicious.*

*Damn, doesn't that sound a little paranoid to you?*

*Not really. I just think it's funny.*

All of a sudden, it got noticeably darker. Before I could ask what was happening, Chanlina announced, "We just entered the Anton Anderson Memorial Tunnel. It's two-and-a-half miles long and goes through the Chugach Mountains and exits into the Potage Valley where the scenic vista begins. Sit back and enjoy the ride."

When we came out of the tunnel, the view was truly stunning. It reminded me of Wonderland without the bubble. It was early afternoon; the sun was behind us, illuminating everything in vivid detail. The sky was a pristine blue laced with puffy white clouds. It reminded me of when I was a kid. Caleb and I would look up at the sky and see all sorts of images in the clouds. We'd watch the cloud images morph into all sorts of things, from fish to airplanes to a dog and his bone.

Mark drew our attention when he asked, "Are those moose? Over to your left, close to the water. Do you see them?"

"I had no idea they were that big" Simone exclaimed in awe.

With Chanlina and the AI driving, all of us were free to be observers. It brought back memories of a trip Caleb and I took the summer before our senior year. One of our alumni supporters paid for all of the team to spend a weekend at Disney World. We went from one amazing ride to another. Except that was all fake. It was still very entertaining, but seeing the moose, then a few minutes later, seeing a bunch of bald eagles diving into the river and catching large salmon to feed on was something else entirely. It was spectacular. A little further down the road Simone spotted a herd of wild sheep running on narrow paths up and down the mountain on the other side of the river.

To top it off, we were only a few miles from Anchorage when we saw a pod of Beluga whales swimming in the widest part of the river. They were playing. I swear they were playing, coming out of the water and crashing back down, blowing jet streams of water from their spouts high into the air and slapping their broad tails to make wave after wave.

Once we entered Anchorage, we left the bus caravan and turned onto the George Parks Highway also known as Interstate 3. It would take us at least four hours to get to the entrance of Denali National Park. We had a light dinner on board and watched the sunset around 10:00 p.m. before we went to bed, fully confident Chanlina and the vehicle's computer system would drive us safely to the park.

### Denali National Park, Getting Ready for Action—Simone

I awoke to the aroma of coffee brewing. Joshua was still sleeping as I got up and used the bathroom, brushed my teeth and slipped on a long warm robe, then headed for the small kitchen area.

"Good morning, Simone," Pearl greeted me with a smile as she spread jelly on a piece of toast. "There's coffee brewing and orange juice in the fridge. What would you like to eat?"

"Just a cup of coffee for now," I answered and looked at the window screen. "Where are we?" I asked.

"We're parked in the lot adjacent to the park's visitor center. Pham needed to speak to the people who set up the park tours. He should be back soon." She gestured at one of the sim-window screens. "Take a look to your left and you can see Mount Denali. It's the largest mountain in America. Most of it's covered in snow, even in the summer."

The rest of the team began emerging from their respective bedrooms, still dressed in pajamas. Both Joey and Bill were wearing sweatshirts with FBI written in large letters across the front. Mark was dressed in shorts and a T-shirt and Sarge had on his therapy vest. Joshua was the last to show up. He was wearing a heavy robe with a hood pulled up over his head. He looked at Joey and asked, "Where are the donuts?"

"No idea, Joshua. Bill's supposed to bring the box."

"That's not true," Bill protested. "You were supposed to get the donut box refilled before we left. Did you screw up again?"

"What do you mean? I didn't screw up. I never screw up. I filled up your box with two dozen donuts from room service and left it on the kitchen counter in our suite for you to pick up."

"You didn't tell me the donuts were on the counter," Bill shouted at him. "I didn't see the box on the counter."

Before Joey could rebut Bill again, Joshua intervened. "Gentlemen, please. You don't need to argue about a box of donuts. We can have something else for breakfast."

Pearl laughed as she opened the door to the small pantry and pulled out the donut box. "I did a quick check of all the suites before we left and picked up the box. I forgot to mention it while we were getting ready to leave.

While the three men finished their donuts and coffee, Pham returned. "I found out all the tours have been canceled for the next few days. I tried to get an explanation from the director of tours, but he wouldn't discuss it until I pulled out my creds and identified myself. Even then he was reluctant to say much until his boss showed up. He looked at my creds and told me why the park was temporarily closed.

"Apparently there were two different groups in the last tour, and they began arguing. One group got violent and attacked the other. The driver stopped the bus and told everyone the tour was canceled. The violent group, about twenty Asian men, went crazy and kicked the other group off the bus, beat up the tour guide and driver, and kicked them off too. Then they stole the bus and drove off into the park. They had taken all the phones and the bus radio was destroyed so no one could call for help. They weren't expected back for several hours. They had to walk back to the center and didn't arrive until late last night. The tour guide was pretty badly beaten. They called the forest rangers and the state police this morning. The director said they should be arriving soon.

"I told the director to cancel the rangers and the police. We would handle this."


### It's Time To Dance—Joshua

I contacted The Apostle and briefed him on what had happened in the park. His response was surprising. "You realize this is a setup, don't you? They want you to chase them into the park, but those twenty men are just the tip of the iceberg. We've got some sketchy intel that says a substantial number of troops are heading your way. Unfortunately, we don't know how many or how soon they will show up."

He paused for a minute then added, "This will be a good opportunity to find out just how powerful the new War Wagon can be in real combat. On the other hand, you cannot let it fall into enemy hands. If you are outgunned you need to bug out. Is that understood?"

"Yes sir," I answered. "We won't let you down."

We drove past a line of empty buses and onto the road into the park. We drove until we were out of sight from civilization before we stopped and transformed into the War Wagon. We launched a number of small drones to search for the stolen tour bus. We also launched a larger drone with very sophisticated search capabilities that could identify potential enemy aircraft over 500 miles away. Mark and Pham launched the two attack drones and had them orbit at 5,000 feet. I felt pretty confident no one was going to sneak up on us.

We moved the War Wagon off the tour bus road to avoid any potential land mines. Our opponents might have buried IEDs in the dirt road. We continued to move west toward Mount Denali at 60 mph.

We drove for an hour and found nothing but fantastic scenery, several herds of moose, six grizzly bears, not counting three bear cubs, and many other wild animals.

*Maybe we should morph into aircraft mode,* Caleb suggested. *We can cover more land at 400 knots then…*

Mark interrupted, "Tally ho. Target bus at four klicks on heading 073 degrees relative. Attack drone 1 making ID run."

One of our sim-windows changed to show the view from drone 1 as it descended toward the tour bus. At the bottom of the display, the readouts indicated the jet powered drone was moving at 450 knots and descending at 1000 feet per minute. The drone leveled off at 50 feet above the rolling terrain and slowed to 100 knots to give a better view.

Mark narrated as the drone descended and approached the bus on the driver's side. "This could be a set up. There was no attempt to hide the bus, it's sitting in the open and I'm not seeing anyone around it. It looks deserted."

Even though Mark was sitting next to me, he was wearing VR goggles, and to him it appeared he was a pilot inside the drone. Pham was wearing similar goggles and had stayed at 5,000 feet providing close air support if needed.

"Don't get too close," I ordered. "It might be booby trapped and I don't want to lose the drone."

"Roger that," said Mark as he did a pitch-out maneuver to distant the drone from the bus. Two seconds later, the bus exploded.

"Scratch one bus," reported Mark. "No human casualties that I can see."

Chanlina announced, "We've got visitors. They just showed up coming around Mount Denali. They're flying low and slow. I count ten bogies, ETA thirty minutes."

Special Agent Hong asked, "How did they know we'd be at this place, at this time?"

His partner answered, "It seems to me somebody must be tailing us and passing on our location. Somehow, they knew we were going to be at Denali National Park today. Who knew our itinerary?"

Pham replied, "I swept the motorhome before we left the cruise ship in Whittier. I'm sure there weren't any locator bugs on us and we never stopped driving until we parked last night in the visitor center parking lot."

I turned to Simone and said, "We need to check for locator bugs on our War Wagon."

Caleb spoke up. *No need. I just finished and found three locator bugs. They must have been put on last night.*

I projected to Caleb, *I thought you'd be watching our six.*

*I was,* he replied defensively, *except for about an hour when I was... off duty.*

*Why didn't Chanlina cover for you?* I asked.

*She was busy too. Let's move on. I'll remove the bugs from the War Wagon and trash them.*

"No. Don't destroy them," I said aloud so everyone would hear. "Take the bugs and attach them to three small drones. Have them fly nap of the earth in a tight formation to simulate the Wagon. Find a place at least ten miles from the road the tour buses use. I want our enemy to think they know where we are. We can set up an ambush and take them out when they arrive. We've got twenty minutes. Let's get ready to surprise them."

# CHAPTER 10
# LET'S GET READY TO RUMBLE!

### Senior Colonel Fang, Peoples Liberation Army

"Are you positive we have not been detected yet?" asked Li-Jun, a high ranking pain in my butt from MSS.

"You've asked that question several times and I have replied with the same answer. Do you not remember?"

He stiffened at my insult. "Of course I remember, and you will not address me in that tone. I'm your superior for this mission, do *you* not remember, Senior Colonel Fang?"

I ignored his counter insult and said, "We are five minutes from our target and we still have not been detected based on our most superior surveillance equipment. Let me recite my orders from the general of the PLA land forces just so you know I haven't forgotten what we are to accomplish on this mission. Number 1, we will capture Thong Chau and return with her to Beijing. Number 2, capture the vehicle known as the War Wagon and return it to the PLA facilities at Xiamen for evaluation. Number 3, kill all of the American agents known as Team Joshua with the exception of Joshua Brown. He will be returned to MSS for interrogation. And before you ask me again, all twenty of the elite PLA troops have been recovered and will gladly forfeit their lives if this mission is not carried out as ordered."

Before Li-Jun could reply, one of my subordinate officers approached and waited for me to acknowledge her. I turned toward her and asked in a polite voice, "Yes, Lieutenant Li?"

"We have visual contact of our target, Senior Colonel. We believe it is the target, but it no longer looks like a motorhome, more like a heavily armed armored personnel carrier. We have not detected any enemy drones, and to the best of our knowledge they have not detected us. They are located in a small valley surrounded on three sides by low mountains."

"Thank you, Lieutenant Li," I said and turned to my second in command, "Order battle stations."

### Surprise, Surprise, Surprise—Caleb

In describing the new War Wagon's capabilities we focused on its offensive weapons. I completely forgot to brief the team on its defensive capabilities. I guess I was too distracted by Chanlina. In setting up our attack plan, I briefed the team on the very advanced defensive features. *How many of you remember the Star Trek TV series?* I asked.

Joshua shook his head. "Not now. We don't have time for—"

I interrupted, *We have a cloaking device. Just like the Klingons, only better. The enemy could be standing right next to us and never see us. We've been cloaked ever since our long range surveillance drones detected the Chinese helicopters.*

I let that percolate for a moment then continued with, *The second item is the SIP, that's the nickname for the Simulated Image Projector. We can project the image of the War Wagon anywhere we want and you'd swear it was the real thing until you tried to touch it.*

Once I made them aware of the two defensive features, Joshua and the team quickly put together the battle plan. All of us remained in the War Wagon as we transformed into aircraft mode. The fake noisemaker was deactivated. We needed complete silence if this was going to work. Chanlina made sure all of our drones, including the two attack drones, were cloaked as was our aircraft. Before the Chinese arrived, we projected the image of the War Wagon into the middle of the valley surrounded on three sides by low mountains.

The enemy had to approach us through the opening in the mountain range. We hovered at a hundred yards from the opening and 2,000 feet above the ground. Pham had one of the drones just above the mountains on the left and Mark had one on the right. Then we waited.

## The Attack—Senior Colonel Fang

We split our group into three parts. Our eight attack helicopters will divide and go left and right around the mountains and then enter through the opening, curving back near the mountain side forming a near-circle of attackers. Each of the attack 'copters will carry two land soldiers who will storm the War Wagon and make entry. My helicopter will pull up over the mountain and hover directly over the War Wagon at 5,000 feet to become a command center for the mission.

Once we have control of the vehicle, the heavy lift helicopter will fly in at a low altitude through the opening in the mountains and use slings to lift and carry the War Wagon 150 miles to a waiting cargo ship of ours just off the coast in international waters.

Something didn't feel right about our attack. It all looked too easy. Truly, the three trackers our man at the visitor center had planted on the motorhome led us to this place. Why would they have this vehicle, this War Wagon, just sitting out in the open? Granted, it was shielded on three sides by the mountains, but why didn't this supposedly very advanced war machine not detect us as we flew around Mount Denali? Once around the mountain it was a thirty-minute flight. It was hard for me to believe we weren't detected. Even if they didn't see us, they would be able to hear the noise of our ten helicopters when they began their approach. If I were in their place, I would make some attempt to escape or at least fight back.

I turned to Li-Jun and said, "I think we should abort the attack, it's a trap."

"Ridiculous," he cried. "You must continue the attack. This is no time to get cold feet, Senior Colonel. I forbid you to cancel the attack."

"We will have another opportunity, but this is a trap. I'm sure of it."

"You are a coward!" he yelled at me. "I relieve you of your command. First Officer, you are now leading this attack."

### <u>Come On In, Said The Spider To The Fly—Joshua</u>

The eight attack helicopters were first in. Four went to the left and the other four to the right as a larger helicopter, probably a command center, came up over the mountain ridge and climbed to 5,000 feet before hovering directly over the image of the War Wagon. Once the command center chopper was in position, the eight attack 'copters opened fire.

"Return fire," I ordered, and Pham and Mark opened fire with a combination of mini-machine guns and rockets. They took out the two choppers closest to the opening, then moved on to the next ones until all eight were smoking piles of rubble. The last two tried to shoot down the drones, but it's hard to shoot what you can't see. In a desperate attempt to escape over the low mountains, one of the attacking craft was inadvertently shot down by the other attack helicopter on the other side of the fake War Wagon.

Mark sang out, "Like shooting fish in a barrel. All the bogies are down and out."

Several of the land force soldiers managed to get out of the attack helicopters before they were destroyed and began an assault on the image. They raked the side of the image with assault rifles and a couple of heavy duty .50 caliber machine guns. They ended up killing each other as the bullets passed through the image and took out their own troops on the other side. What a pity.

That left the command center above us and their heavy lift 'copter well below. I knew what I should do, but I hesitated. Chanlina projected to me, *Let me do it, Joshua. After all, I've been an assassin for longer than you've been alive. These men were going to kill all of us, besides we can't let any of them get back and tell the MSS what we are capable of.*

She was right. *Do it and destroy any evidence this ever happened. Let MSS wonder what happened to their people.*

The command center above us had started to bug out. We turned off our cloaking device and demolished them with our onboard weapons. When we were done, there was nothing left.

The heavy lift helicopter was another story. It was huge. We forced it to land and Chanlina made sure the entire crew on board was eliminated. With the help of Caleb, they programmed the autopilot to send the heavy lifter on a course out to sea. Checking the history of their flights, we were able to determine all of the helicopters had been launched from a Chinese cargo ship. We loaded all the bodies onto the giant heavy lifter and locked them into a storage area. When they sent it out to sea, they made sure it would be far from the cargo ship when it ran out of fuel and crashed into the sea.

It was the best we could do. There was substantial debris, but at least it was off the road and hiking trails. We hoped it wouldn't be found. I contacted The Apostle and gave him a verbal after-action report. He said not to worry about the debris. A team of cleaners would sanitize the site.

When I was finished he said to us all, "Congratulations on successfully protecting Dr. Pearl and keeping the Chinese from getting access to this new breakthrough in technology. Unfortunately, these Chinese are very persistent. There may be more attacks, so stay frosty."

### Calling Home, Then Off to Fairbanks—Mark

We drove the ten miles from the battle site across rough terrain to the dirt road that led back to the highway. On the way back, several of us called home to let everyone know we were all right. Of course, we didn't go into great detail about the attack and our counterattack, but Joshua gave us his approval to tell them in a general way about what went on. He wanted us to emphasize that none of us got hurt, not even a scratch.

It would take us a couple of hours to reach Fairbanks. Joshua decided to take a break from traveling and we stopped at a roadside diner. It was evening, however the sun wouldn't set until around 11:00 p.m. in this part of Alaska.

The diner had a large parking lot and picnic tables were plentiful along the north side of the diner extending into a forested area with numerous huge pine trees. Sarge took one look and bolted into his version of Wonderland. He quickly disappeared into the forest, only to show up for brief periods when he would stop to mark his new territory.

I let him run for about 15 minutes while the rest of us took seats at one of the picnic tables where we could keep an eye on our motorhome while we scanned the menu. Most of us decided on broiled salmon, guaranteed to be freshly caught the same day.

A waitress came out to our picnic table to take our orders. I looked over at our motorhome and did a double take. Our motorhome was gone! Then I realized it *was* our motorhome with a brand-new paint job. Well not exactly paint, Pearl explained to us, the designers of the exterior used some type of nanotechnology to coat the exterior surface when our vehicle was in the motorhome configuration. She said the AI computers could select from six different color schemes to reduce the possibility of being identified. Ah! The wonders of science!

When the server brought out our dinners, Sarge magically appeared from the forest. He sat very close to me and kept scooting nearer until his muzzle rested on my knee. He gave me a pleading look. As usual when we eat at a restaurant, I had ordered two helpings of salmon. The rest of the team watched in amusement as I took turns feeding Sarge, one bite for him then one bite for me, until it was all gone.

When we finished our meals and Sarge made one more pass through the trees, we climbed back aboard the now three-tone blue motorhome and continued on our way to Fairbanks.

As I climbed aboard, I heard the sound of a large turbodiesel engine coming to life at the rear of our ride. It sounded so real!


### In The Heartland Of Alaska—Caleb

The first thing I noticed as we entered Fairbanks was a large cemetery. There was one feature that I found a little confusing. I had no idea why there was a ten-story structure on the edge of the cemetery property. Having access to every database in the world, I quickly accessed the answer to my question. Apparently, it was common knowledge to the people of Fairbanks. In the winter months, the ground freezes solid and grave sites can't be dug. The caskets are stored above ground in large storage units until the ground thaws and they can give the dearly departed a proper burial. A couple of other anomalies came to my attention. The first was a large pipeline that runs right through the center of the city. Another search identified it as the Alyeska Pipeline. It runs from Prudhoe Bay in the North to Port Valdez in the south.

I also noted many of the cars had what looked like extension cords peeking out from under their hoods. At first, I thought they were for charging electric vehicles, but then I noticed those cars had exhaust pipes. I searched again and found out the cord was for a device called a block heater. When a driver leaves their vehicle out in the winter cold for any length of time, the lubricating oil freezes solid, and the engine doesn't work. When the driver plugs in the block heater cord to an electric outlet, a bolt in the car's engine block heats up and keeps the oil liquid so the engine can run.

Joshua and I were born and grew up in the deep south. We stayed there when we were training with the Marines, and when we went into battle in Afghanistan, it was blisteringly hot with very high humidity. Once we began our missions, they were all in the southern states: Arizona, Mississippi and Louisiana. Portland was the farthest north of any state we'd been in, and they have mild winters for the most part. How was I to know about block heaters?

I found all this information to be very interesting, however when I shared it with the rest of the team they didn't seem as enthused as I was. I decided there was no point in educating them any further. Chanlina told me to quit pouting as we pulled into a military armory to replenish our supply of ammunition. We'd used almost all of it during our skirmish at Denali, but I considered it was ammo well spent.

Once we were rearmed, we were ordered by The Apostle to park the War Wagon in a highly classified and well protected facility for an extensive inspection of all the systems. A shuttle took us to a nearby hotel where reservations had been made in advance. It would take at least two days for the techs to finish their inspection and upgrades and we were told to stand down for R & R.

Chanlina and I transported to Wonderland immediately.

### Taking a Tour of the City—Agent Bill Cody

Joey, Mark and I decided to take a bus tour of the city. Joshua and Pham both had their women with them. With ours at home, we became part-time bachelors. Sarge joined us wearing his therapy vest. Each of us carried at least one gun. I think Mark had a knife and a baton as well. We made sure none of the weapons were visible.

Our tour bus was two levels, with the second deck being an open-air configuration. The three of us climbed the stairs and took seats in the middle of the bus. We all brought heavy coats with us since early on we discovered summer in Alaska was cooler than Portland or Seattle, a lot cooler.

As the bus began our tour, we all slipped on gloves and wool knit hats pulled down over our ears. At 30 mph it was down-right freezing. Even Sarge curled up close to Mark to share body heat. Our tour guide came up the stairs to greet all the passengers wearing a short-sleeved polo shirt and no hat or gloves. He wasn't even shivering. What a show off.

We started down the street and the first place we stopped was at the Alyeska Pipeline. Then he did a ten minute presentation on block heaters. We drove a few blocks away to a cemetery and the guide talked another fifteen minutes on how coffins had to be stored in the winter because the ground froze.

We couldn't believe it. An hour ago, Caleb gave us the same briefing. We could have saved a few bucks if we just listened to him.

The next stop was a tourist trap, but it did have some novel gifts that you couldn't find anywhere else in the world. For example, how about moose turd jewelry. "Hey guys, come here. You have to see this to believe it," I yelled to Joey and Mark who were browsing the other side of the store.

"Watcha got, partner?" asked Joey as they came over to see what I was so excited about.

I held up the necklace to show my friends. "It's moose turd jewelry," I answered.

"No way!" Mark exclaimed. "That's got to be a joke. Real turds would be a health issue, all kinds of bacteria."

"No problem at all gentlemen," said a salesmen as he walked up to us. He was big and portly, dressed in bib overalls with a black and red checkered wool shirt underneath. He had a long black beard and mustache, but his head was bald as a melon.

"Boys, I guess you haven't heard about our annual Moose Dropping Festival held nearly every July in a little town called Talkeetna. It's close to Mount Denali."

"No sir. We just left the Denali park a day ago, but we didn't hear anything about a moose festival," replied Joey.

"You don't have to call me sir, Bart's good enough. The festival is usually in July, you might be a bit early," Bart replied.

"They don't really drop moose, do they?" teased Mark, with Sarge sitting beside him seemingly listening in on Bart's every word.

Bart scratched his beard and answered, "Not anymore. Them fellers from the ASPCA have no sense of humor. Now they make a game of dropping moose turds on a huge target. Mostly it's an excuse to consume as many adult beverages as you can during the festival week.

"About ten years ago, an enterprising individual, a ranger at the Denali Park if I remember it right, came up with an idea to sell shit to our summer tourists. He coated the turds with clear plastic, added a few fools-gold fittings, a synthetic diamond here and there, and turned them into bracelets and necklaces. Our store has some smoking deals on some of our best pieces."

We walked out of the store, each with a bag of goodies. "Can you imagine their faces? How our women will react when we give them jewelry made of actual shit?" laughed Joey. I laughed along with him.

Mark just shook his head. "I would never even consider buying real turd jewelry for my wife. The postcard pictures are bad enough. Maria will think buying that stuff was a waste of money."

"You're right," I replied as we climbed aboard the tour bus. "However it's not a waste of *our* money, Uncle Sam is covering all our expenses on this trip and the necklace I got cost only twenty-five dollars."

The next stop was a gold mine. Not a real one, but they guaranteed we'd get at least *some* of our money back. First there was a short video showing how to use a pan to find the gold. You pour dirt into a pan that might have gold in it, then you pour in a little water and swirl it around sloshing out the wet mud and tiny rocks. Gold is a lot heavier than dirt or rocks, so, if you're clever about the way you swirl the water, tiny pieces of gold sink to the bottom and remain in the pan.

Each one of us had a couple of practice swirls then went out and got a bucket of dirt. We walked over to a nearby trough of running water and proceeded to swirl. It took us about fifteen minutes before we ran out of dirt and each of us came away with $20 to $25 dollars of gold. They placed our tiny pieces of gold into a tiny glass tube filled with clean water and capped it off so we could display our treasure when we got back to Portland.

Panning for gold was the last stop on our tour and we headed back to the hotel to show the rest of the team what we had acquired. They laughed at the moose turd jewelry and checked out our tubes of real gold. Everyone wanted to go back to the gold mine the next day. Joshua said, "Who knows, maybe we'll strike it rich."

Then Caleb burst our bubble. *The panning for gold place you went to is a scam. Every bucket of dirt is filtered. Any gold they might find is collected. Then they salt the filtered dirt with a few flakes of gold worth no more than $25.*

There was total silence for a moment until Simone said in a disappointed voice, "Well shit! Isn't that illegal or something?"

Caleb replied, *It's not illegal but it's a rigged game... How would you all like to win a small fortune tomorrow, just before we leave town?*

## A Fortune in Gold—Joshua

We checked out of our hotel rooms and picked up the motorhome at noon the next morning. Before we boarded, one of the technicians demonstrated three new color configurations for the external non-paint paint job. They cycled through all nine of the potential color combinations. It happened so fast it didn't seem real, more like special effects in a movie or TV show. It gave me a few moments of vertigo.

Chanlina was in control of the three AI computers and took charge of driving the motorhome to a large parking lot where we could familiarize ourselves with the upgrades. We had a leisurely lunch aboard and waited for Caleb to show up. It was almost 1500 hours when he contacted us. *Are you all ready to make some real money?*

Everyone agreed they'd like to have a little more spending money.

*So this is the plan,* Caleb began. *We drive to Panning for Gold, but spread out, get some tourists in between you. They might recognize the three bachelors so don't go in as a group. All seven of you go through the whole intro and practice. When they give you your bucket of dirt, make sure you aren't standing next to a team member at the water trough. Stagger the time when you start panning. Make it look random. Have fun!*

I had been the first one of the team to pick up a bucket of dirt. As I carried it to the trough it seemed to get heavier. I scooped out a handful of dirt and put in the pan, added water and began cautiously swirling the dirt away. There was no gold in the first handful of dirt and I was already reaching for the next one when I heard a woman screaming. I recognized her voice, it was Pearl, and she was jumping up and down holding a golf-ball sized nugget of gold.

There must have been twenty people panning with us. Several of them also found gold nuggets in their dirt. I was the first one to find multiple nuggets. The rest of the team was just as lucky. I suppose luck had nothing to do with it. *Somehow had Caleb discovered a real mother load somewhere and transported the nuggets into the dirt buckets for us?*

Most of the people in our group were lined up to swap their nuggets for cash, some decided to keep the gold. Before any of our group of thirty could leave and get paid, a man in a business suit stood up holding a microphone. "Ladies and gentleman, may I have your attention please. I'm so sorry to have to tell you the nuggets you have found today are not gold. It's fools-gold; its mineral name is iron pyrite. It's not worth anything."

The room suddenly became silent and remained that way until someone spoke up in an angry voice, "The hell you say? My name is Cary Clarke, Professor Cary Clark. I'm the director of the College of Geology at North Dakota State University." He held up his hand holding a nugget the size of a tennis ball. "This is not iron pyrite, it's gold, real gold. Are you trying to cheat us?"

The room exploded and the man in the suit with the microphone shouted, "Hold on… Hold on please. I have a government assayer on his way to determine if this is real gold or iron pyrite."

The professor shouted back. "He better bring his credentials. I want to verify he's really certified."

The man with the microphone shouted back in return, "Where are your credentials, sir? How do I know you are who you say you are?'

The professor reached into his coat pocket and raised his cred pack high. "Here are my credentials. Examine them as closely as you like, call my office, and the office of the president of the university. I am exactly who I say I am."

I could understand why the man in the suit was trying to get away with trying to convince us it wasn't really gold. He was going to make a substantial profit. He was either that greedy, or perhaps he just didn't have the cash to pay everyone.

Panning for Gold closed their operation early that afternoon. The assayer showed up and verified each nugget was really gold. A banker came in and issued bank vouchers for those who turned over their gold to the store. I have no idea how much was found, but the certified bank vouchers for all seven of us totaled a little over $100,000. That came to just under $15,000 per person. It wasn't exactly a huge fortune, but it sure beat a poke in the eye with a sharp stick.

Once we were safely back aboard the motorhome and headed out of town, I asked Caleb. *Where did you find all that gold?*

*It wasn't just me, Chanlina was a big help too.*

*Yes, but how did the two of you find more than half a million dollars in gold in one night?*

*You're forgetting time distortion,* he replied. *It took us the better part of a month to locate the gold. By the way, it was closer to three-quarters of a million. Chanlina is an older spirit with a lot more skills. We worked as a team. She would find a rich vein of gold and I would extract it. We stored it in our Wonderland bubble until we thought we had enough.*

*When people began picking up their buckets of dirt, both Chanlina and I began slowing down time and transported the gold nuggets into various levels of dirt in every bucket. It took us almost three days of our time to get every bucket fixed.*

*What about the professor of geology from NDS? It seems highly unlikely he would show up just in time to keep us from being cheated.*

I could sense his smile. *No coincidence, bro. Chanlina did a quick search to find a geologist who also was a certified assayer. Once she found him, she made sure he really wanted to go Alaska and pan for gold, sort of a whirlwind vacation.*

*So she reprogrammed his mind to cover our tracks?*

*Yup. Something like that. He was well paid for his troubles. His nugget was worth about $20,000.*

*That's an amazing story, Caleb, tell Chanlina we really…*

*Chanlina's right here,* she thought to me. *I've been here the whole time listening to how my man told the story. Oh, by the way, if you thought this was a private conversation between you and Caleb, think again. The entire team listened in, even Sarge. Did you know he can read your thoughts too? That is one smart dog.*

Mark interrupted, "Are you messing with me? I haven't heard any of his thoughts."

*I said he could read your thoughts, not that you could read his. We're working on getting you up to speed. Give it a month.*

# CHAPTER 11
# PIRATES? REALLY, PIRATES?

### Beginning the Trip Home, Sort Of—Pham

It was evening, and after a quick dinner we headed back toward Denali National Park. We were going to do some more testing of the various War Wagon configurations before resuming our trip back to Anchorage. We planned to use some of the remote portions of the park for ground testing, then head out to sea to conduct more rigorous testing of the three boat configurations.

It finally got dark around midnight. Since it never got really dark this time of year, it felt more like twilight. Traffic was light with only a few cars passing by. One of our sim-windows was focused on the sky above us and I thought I caught a glimpse of the aurora borealis. It was hypnotic as it flashed slowly across the sky in a kaleidoscope of colors.

Pearl had gone to sleep an hour ago. Most of the crew were also asleep. Only agent Hong and I were still awake but even I was beginning to fade.

I assumed Caleb and Chanlina were still fully alert since they don't have to sleep. It occurred to me, perhaps they had transported to Wonderland for some additional R & R. However, I wasn't worried. With their time dilation abilities they could spend a day or two in less than a minute in our time.

Just before I was completely asleep, I noticed a softly flashing red light on one the monitors. I vaguely remembered it was a signal for an emergency alert. Then I heard Caleb's voice in my head, *I got this, you and Joey go back to sleep.*

I seemed to remember a vague image of Caleb with Wonderland in the background. He was totally naked, as was the image of Chanlina who was standing behind him. Both were smiling. I must have slipped into a dream.

### Up, Up And Away!—Chanlina

The alert notice was from The Apostle. We transported out of Wonderland to the motorhome configuration before responding. Caleb didn't want The Apostle to see us naked … again. Sometimes men are such prudes.

The alert was to update us on some potentially dangerous activity. It had to do with a relatively new ship called the Zumwalt-class destroyer. It's a very stealthy, guided missile ship with more fire power than a World War II battleship. It appeared someone may have stolen one of them.

The Apostle asked, *Are you familiar with the Zumwalt-class destroyer?*

*Not me,* I replied. *How about you, Caleb?*

*Never heard of it.*

*Not a problem,* The Apostle telepathically assured us. *I'm sending you some pictures of the ship. It doesn't look anything like a conventional warship. The reason being, it was designed to be nearly invisible to any and all forms of surveillance techniques currently in service. That includes all types of radar, infrared, and sonar.*

*How do they get around sonar?* Caleb asked.

*They use integrated electric propulsion, usually referred to as IEP. That's all I can tell you. They must have gotten rid of the propellers somehow. However, I was never read into the details.*

*Is their stealth as good as our cloaking device?* I asked.

*We don't think so. Unfortunately, we don't know for sure. There have been a lot of changes from the original design. It's called a destroyer, but its larger than any current cruiser in the Navy's fleet.*

*The ship's original mission was for land attack, however, the program for the development of the Advance Gun Systems was canceled due to escalating costs caused by technical difficulties. In 2023, the AGS was abandoned and replaced with hypersonic missiles.*

*Isn't hypersonic supposed to be Mach 5?* Caleb asked.

*Not really. Hypersonic is anything above Mach 5. They could be a lot faster.*

*The original order was for 32 ships. Due to cost overruns, that number was reduced to 24, then to 7 and then finally to 3. This significantly raised the cost per ship to $4.24 billion. That's more than twice the cost of our largest nuclear-powered submarines. The two major contractors were not happy. Each of them had invested heavily for the research and development phases of the program. One of them was facing bankruptcy.*

*A few years ago, a rumor was making the rounds in our various government agencies that a foreign power wanted to buy four newly built Zumwalt-class destroyers. They were willing to pay $5 billion per ship, provided they were built in their country. There was a significant bonus if the ships could be built in a year. There were further rumors that the foreign power would place an order for another four ships if the first four met the performance requirement.*

*Our State Department and the Department of Defense went ballistic when they heard about the rumor. The admirals protested most of the technology developed for the Zumwalt was classified top secret and could not be made available to any foreign powers... ever!!*

*It was obvious which country had made the offer. Since the decline of Russia, the only country who could afford to make such an investment in military equipment was China. The other shoe fell a few months later; North Korea would foot the bill for one of the four destroyers.*

*The President secretly ordered the CIA to send spies into China and North Korea to determine if either country had the necessary shipyard facilities to handle the construction. The spies who went to China discovered there was considerable expansion of the military shipyard in Xiamen, China. Xiamen sits directly across a relatively narrow ocean strait from Taiwan.*

*The spies who were sent into North Korea were never heard from again.*

*The Department of Justice issued a warning. Anyone who accepts the offer of a foreign government for any information about the Zumwalt will be charged with first degree treason. If convicted, the penalty is death. The Justice Department ordered the FBI to immediately seize all contractor documents pertaining to the design, development and fabrication of the Zumwalt-class destroyers. That step seemed to put the kibosh on the rumors and it was noted the expansion of the shipyard in Xiamen ceased.*

*For the next two years nothing happened … until last week. While on a routine transfer mission from San Diego to Pearl Harbor, the ship disappeared. The normal crew requirement was 175, but for transfer missions only a skeleton crew of 50 was on board.*

*There was a brief moment of contact with what could have been the Zumwalt, but it seemed unlikely. A fishing trawler off the coast of Alaska reported they saw "a weird looking ship that seemed to disappear."*

*The Navy sent search teams to the area. However, they made no contact with any ships nor discovered any debris that would have indicated a ship had sunk.*

*Your orders are to transform your motorhome into aircraft configuration and begin a search and possible rescue starting at the ship's last known coordinates. We suspect foul play. It is feasible the ship was high jacked, probably by the Chinese. If you find the Zumwalt, you are to discover what happened to the crew and their officers. If you cannot rescue them, you are ordered to sink the ship and everyone aboard. We cannot let the technology of that ship fall into the hands of any foreign powers.*

*Please confirm your orders and execute immediately.*


### <u>Time To Get Up—Joshua</u>

I awoke to the echo of Caleb's voice in my mind. *Sorry to wake you, bro. We got orders from The Apostle.*

I remained in bed as Caleb downloaded all of The Apostle's messages into my brain. I didn't know he could do that. It seemed every day I was learning about some new ability of his.

When the download was complete, I briefly considered getting up. Before I could move, Caleb thought to me, *No point in getting up. Chanlina and I will take care of transforming to aircraft mode. It will take a couple of hours to reach the last coordinates of the Zumwalt. Go back to sleep.*

Before I could protest, I fell back to sleep. I attributed it to another of Caleb's talents.

When I awoke again, a couple of hours had passed. I woke up the rest of the crew and briefed them on our new orders. Most of them were still half asleep until Simone looked at the closest sim-window. "We're flying? Over the ocean? Oh my!"

We were at 20,000 feet, cruising at 400 knots and completely cloaked. A few minutes later, we were directly over the Zumwalt's last suspected location.

Chanlina interrupted our sight-seeing. "What type of search pattern do you want to use, Captain?" I wasn't sure if she was speaking to me or to Pearl. Before I could reply, she added, "Since the Zumwalt is supposed to be super stealthy, I recommend we drop down to 5,000 feet, slow to 200 knots and begin a spiraling out pattern, keeping a one-mile distance between passes. I believe a spiral search would be better than a grid search for this mission. I also recommend we launch our surveillance drone to 15,000 feet. It can give us a warning of any approaching bogies, both ship and aircraft, up to a radius of a hundred miles."

Pearl looked at me and shrugged. I assumed she wanted me to make the decision. So I answered, "Whatever Chanlina suggested is fine with me."

"Sorry Joshua," replied Chanlina. "Pearl is the assigned captain of this vehicle."

Pearl interrupted, "Joshua is the assigned leader of this search. He will be making all search related decisions. Please follow his orders."

"Understood, Captain. What are your orders, Commander Joshua?"

I thought I detected a smile along with her response. "As I said, Pilot in Command, your suggestions are approved. Please have your copilot assist you in the search." Now everyone was smiling.

*Wait a minute*, interrupted Caleb, *Why am I only a copilot? I should be …*

Chanlina had slammed the door on Caleb and now the smiles turned to laughter as we began our descent, slowing as we went. At the same time, I noticed on the control panel the surveillance drone had been launched.

I said to the team, "The search has begun as ordered. Let's have breakfast."

Search and rescue missions are usually boring, *very boring.* Once the search pattern had been entered by Chanlina and Caleb into our advanced AI computer system it was even more boring than usual. We could eat our breakfast, play video games, read an eBook or snooze without interruption until we received an alert.

An hour after the search began, we got our first alert. Our surveillance drone had picked up a cargo ship sailing westward. When we zoomed in on the ship, the computer identified it as the *Xiang Hua Men*, owned by the Nanjing Ocean Shipping Company headquartered in the Jiangsu Province, China."

"Wait a minute," protested Bill. "That's not a Chinese flag they're flying off the stern."

"You're right," replied Mark. "It's a Panamanian flagged ship owned and operated by a Chinese company."

"Why would they do that?" asked Simone.

"I worked at Terminal 6 in Portland for a few years," answered Mark. "It was common for ships to be owned by a corporation in one country and registered in another. I wasn't quite sure how it worked, but I think it was a way to save money on taxes and port fees. Some countries don't allow ships from specific countries to dock at their ports. Having them registered in a friendly country could give them access."

"Interesting note," added Chanlina, "this boat was captured by Somali pirates in 2012."

"Pirates in 2012?" asked a surprised Bill. "I thought pirates were part of ancient history. What happened to the ship?"

"Wikipedia says they eventually captured the pirates. None of the crew was injured or killed."

Pham raised an interesting question. "Do you think that ship could have been the one who brought the helicopters to attack us at Denali?"

Caleb asked his own question, *Why don't I pay a visit to our Chinese brothers and see if I can find out if they were involved in the attack?*

"I think that is a great idea," answered Agent Hong. "Perhaps you can tone down the 'Chinese brothers' comments. These men are not my brothers. I was born in China, but raised in America and lived there since I was five. I consider myself an American."

There was an uncomfortable pause, then Caleb replied, *I didn't mean to offend you Joey. You are part of Team Joshua and that makes you a true brother to us all. My attempt at sarcastic humor was over the line. It won't happen again.*

Bill added, "Don't take his comments personal, Joey. You know how us black folk don't have a lick of sense. Just have a donut and relax."

Bill's attempt at humor was spot on and everyone got a chuckle out of it, including Joey.

"Okay," he acknowledged. "I was overly sensitive. Where's my donut?"

### <u>Paying My Chinese Brothers A Visit—Caleb</u>

The *Xiang Hua Men* is a large cargo ship, however that doesn't mean they have a large crew. On a cargo ship the size of *Xiang Hua Men,* they would have between 20 to 30 crewmen. That would include the captain, and usually around four additional officers. I was surprised to find out the crew of the *Xiang Hua Men* had nearly 75 men and women. A bigger surprise was only about 25 of them were Chinese. The biggest surprise was the majority of remaining 50 were wearing U.S. Navy uniforms. What was going on?!!!

Before I transported back to our vehicle, I went into time distortion mode and checked the identity of every person in Navy uniforms. Then I checked the roster of the Zumwalt crew. It was a perfect match, from the captain to the seaman third class.

All that took me a day and a half of distorted time, but only about fifteen minutes in real time. When I returned to our aircraft and told them what I had found out, there was stunned silence for a few minutes.

Simone was the first to comment. "This doesn't even seem plausible. Are you sure—"

Before she finished her question, Chanlina interrupted, "I just did a quick confirmation check. Everything Caleb said is true. Now that we know what's happened, I suggest we try to find out why and what's going to happen next."

We tried brainstorming but came up with nada. We continued to follow the ship. When we discovered it, it was leaving Norris Sound, apparently heading toward the Bering Sea. If we backtracked, it looked as if the ship had been anchored off-shore from Unalakleet, a small town with a population of about 700, but it had both an airport and a riverport. The airport was just a stone's throw from the shoreline. I did a quick trip to check out if there had been any helicopters brought ashore from the ship. Their records showed eight attack helicopters, one larger chopper and one heavy lifter had been moved ashore on barges. A week later, all of the helicopters had left for Denali National Park. The *Xiang Hua Men* remained anchored.

Joshua and Pham decided to speak to the riverport master. The aircraft descended to sea level, remaining cloaked as it morphed into the surface boat configuration and headed to the riverport.

The riverport master was a Native American. He was a big man, heavily muscled with long black braids that hung over his shoulders. He wore Levi jeans and a dark green wool shirt covered by a heavily padded brown vest. On his feet were what I would call mukluks. As we came into his office he looked over Joshua's shoulder at our boat.

"Is that your boat at the end of the wharf?" he asked in a deep, gruff voice. Joshua nodded. Before he could say anything, the port master said. "Very strange."

Joshua said, "It's a new Navy design."

The port master shook his head. "Not what I meant. Two days in a row I see very strange looking ships."

Joshua pulled out his phone and showed the man a picture of the Zumwalt. "Is this the other ship?"

"Depends," he answered.

"Depends on what?"

"Depends on who you are."

Joshua pulled out his creds and handed them to the port master. He studied them for several minutes before handing them back and said, "So you are the Special Agent in Charge for Homeland Security. I'm the Special Agent in Charge of Unalakleet Riverport." His stoic face slowly smiled. "What can I do for you, SAC?"

He identified the other ship as the Zumwalt and added, "Very strange. All the crew from the funny-looking ship got off and waited on the pier. A few minutes later, tenders from the cargo ship brought a replacement crew who went aboard. The first crew got into the tenders and headed out to the cargo ship. Very strange," he repeated.

"Why was it strange?" asked Joshua.

"None of the crews ever came to my office, not even one person from either crew. They disrespected me, I'm the Special Agent in Charge."

Joshua and I headed back to our boat, climbed aboard and moved down the river into the Norris Sound. We cloaked and transformed into the aircraft configuration. We sent a surveillance drone to track the cargo ship and we went after the Zumwalt.

### Peak-A-Boo, I See You—Pearl

We sent out every surveillance drone we had to search for the Zumwalt. Most of them were sent to the west based on the assumption it was heading toward a Chinese port. One drone was sent toward Vladivostok. I know it's a Russian port, however it was the closest port near China. Maybe the Chinese would pay the Russians a healthy fee to dock in their port just to confuse our search.

We even sent a couple of drones to the east as well. It was a remote chance they would head east, but we needed to cover all possibilities. The Zumwalt could cruise at 30 knots (35 mph), which would give them a range of a little more than 800 miles per day. The Zumwalt left Unalakleet two days before. If they cruised without stopping, they could be within a circle of 3,000 miles diameter. They could be anywhere.

We weren't the only ones searching for the Zumwalt. The Navy went on high alert status as soon as the ship was declared missing. When we shared our Unalakleet intel with the Navy, they committed a small task force of ships and planes in their attempt to find the missing destroyer, however, our search capabilities were much more sophisticated. We had the best chance of finding the Zumwalt. When you added in the capabilities of our two spirits, I felt confident we would find the missing ship.

When Caleb and Chanlina dedicated their efforts to the search, I truly became the captain of the new War Wagon. I was so used to communicating with them, I really missed hearing their voices as they interfaced with the computer. However, even without them, our AI computer system continued to work flawlessly.

Joshua suggested we fly east toward Anchorage. When I asked him why, his reply was, "It's just a hunch."

The computer set us on a direct course to Anchorage. Traveling at 400 knots, we would arrive in about an hour. Ten minutes later, Chanlina said the *Xiang Hua Men* had anchored at a small port city on the coast of St. Lawrence Island in the mouth of the Bering Strait.

Twenty minutes after that, Caleb contacted us. *Tally ho! I found the Zumwalt.*

It turns out we were the closest of the search teams and locked in on the Zumwalt's location. It would take us fifteen minutes to have visual contact, assuming they didn't change course.

Five minutes after Caleb's first report, he contacted us again. *You need to hurry. I was so focused on finding the Zumwalt, I wasn't paying attention to any other ships in the area. It looks like the Zumwalt is preparing to attack the* Oasis of the Seas. *They're traveling the outside passage, no port cities in… Oh my God! The Zumwalt just launched one of those hypersonic missiles. It blew a huge hole in the port side of the cruise ship!* The Oasis *is dead in the water… it looks like the crew of the Zumwalt are going to board* the Oasis… *Pirates! I think they must be pirates. Hurry up, bro. People are dying!*

### <u>Send In The Marines—Joshua</u>

Chanlina was back aboard and took control of the computers. "What are your orders, Commander Joshua?"

"Stay cloaked and strafe the destroyer from stem to stern. Make us move while you strafe. They will probably return fire if they can lock on to where our attack is coming from."

"Roger that, Commander. Beginning moving strafe," she replied.

"Caleb, do you have a count of how many pirates went aboard?" I asked out loud.

*I counted a boarding party of at least a hundred. The strafing has stopped any further boarding. They entered through a huge hole in the side of the ship. It looks like it was where the sea level hatch used to be. The damage looks like it's above the waterline and extends up three decks.*

"I want to get aboard and see what the pirates are about," I turned to the crew and continued. "Simone, Mark and Pham, gear up." I looked over at the two FBI agents and said, "You don't have to join us. Why don't you stay and provide protection for the War Wagon?"

Joey looked at Bill. He nodded back and continued to get into his body armor. Joey turned back to me and said, "We're going with you. The more the merrier."

I turned at the place where Chanlina's voice was coming from and ordered, "Chanlina, take us on top and drop us off as close to the bridge as possible."

Before she could respond, we heard the sound of bullets pinging off our armor plate followed by one very powerful *boing* from a deck gun.

"Caleb, what type of deck guns do they have?"

*They have a twin gun weapon system shooting 30 millimeter rounds. I think that was what rang our bell a few seconds ago.*

"Take that gun out. Use the rockets if need be, but take it out now."

As Chanlina began a rapid climb above the top of the cruise ship, I heard two rockets being launched from our tubes, followed immediately by a resounding explosion. We moved past the bow of the boat and were deposited on the top of the bridge. Chanlina immediately did a swooping dive and made sure anyone on the deck of the Zumwalt was dead or dying.

I contacted Chanlina, *Can you tell me if you see any pirates on the bridge?*

She responded immediately. *I checked after I dropped you off. I saw the captain and several of his officers. The main door to the bridge is closed and barricaded. All the officers are armed. No pirates in sight, but it's just a matter of time.*

*Good work, Chanlina. Can you tell Pearl to radio the captain and let him know we are coming? I don't want him to think we're pirates storming the bridge.*

A few minutes later, a hatch in the bridge's overhead opened and a junior officer poked his head out. "Don't try anything, I'm armed." He paused then, in a shaky voice, said, "Please identify yourselves."

"I'm Special Argent Joshua Brown with six members of my crew," I said.

"Please come down the ladder one at a time. Any funny business and I will shoot you dead." His voice sounded strained as he backed down the ladder with his pistol drawn.

I was the first one down the ladder. Both of my Desert Eagles Auto Mags were in their holsters. I was followed by the other six of my team with their pistols in holsters and assault rifles slung over their shoulders.

Mark was the last one down, holding Sarge in his arms. As he stepped onto the deck, he turned his head, and in a low voice said, "If you're really going to shoot someone you might want to click the safety off."

The junior officer looked at his Glock and then at the captain. Captain Johansson said to him, "Stand down, Lawrence. Please holster your weapon."

After brief introductions, I spoke with the captain. "What can you tell me about the attackers?"

"A man who said he was the captain of the Zumwalt told us to heave-to for boarding. I asked him if his ship was having problems and volunteered to assist him. He responded by threatening us, saying if we didn't shut down our propulsion system and open the sea level cargo hatch, he would blow a hole in the side of my ship. I asked him to stand by while I got authorization to let him board. It was a stalling technique, I used the few minutes to alert my security people. While they were arming themselves, I told the Zumwalt captain I would open the hatch, but first we had to move cargo so he could board us. His reply was, 'Too late, jerk off. You're a dead man.' Then he fired the missile at us."

He stopped to gather his thoughts before continuing. "It was terrible. The explosion killed most of our security people. Those who survived were either unconscious or severely injured. A large group of men and a few women boarded through the huge hole in our starboard side. The first thing they did was kill the remaining security people. All fifty of our security people are dead now."

As he told me of the attack, tears began to flow down his cheeks, and we could hear the pain in his voice. He paused as he reached up with both hands to cover his face, sobbed and gestured to his first officer to continue.

"We broadcasted a warning throughout the ship for all passengers and crew to go to their quarters and lock themselves in. We told them we were under attack by pirates, then contacted our operations office and informed them, too. They said they would send help, but it might take a while before they arrive. They told us to tell the passengers not to resist and they would be reimbursed for any losses they might incur. We broadcasted that message just before you joined us. By the way, how did you get here so quickly? Wait, how did you end up on the bridge's overhead?"

"It's a long story," I answered. "I'll tell you after we repel the pirates. Pirates are thieves, they want to steal things like money, expensive jewelry and whatever else is valuable and small enough to carry back to their ship. They also want to make sure you don't sail away leaving them stranded."

Agent Hong added, "This is going to be what the police call a smash and grab. They want to get your wealth and leave before the cops arrive. Based on that, I would assume they will focus on your vault where your safety deposit boxes are. It's usually where your passengers would store the most wealth. Their next targets would be your most expensive passenger suites moving from suite to suite as fast as they can. They probably assume they have less than an hour before the cavalry comes calling. We've been hunting these guys for several days, they didn't expect us to find them so quickly."

"They will probably be knocking on the bridge door any minute now," Bill added. "Do you have a captain's quarters attached to the bridge?"

"Yes, right there through that door," the first officer answered, gesturing toward the starboard side of the bridge.

"Do all of you have weapons?" asked Joey.

"No," replied the first officer. "About half of us have guns."

I took over. "I want all of you to get into the captain's quarters and lock the door behind you. Do not open that door unless we give you a special knock, one knock, followed by two knocks and then three knocks. If anyone knocks on the door and doesn't use the code knock, fire several shots through the door and remain inside."

The junior officer tentatively raised his hand. I acknowledged him and he said, "It's a metal door. I don't think our bullets will go through it."

"Good point. If they don't use the code when they knock, remain silent. If they break the door down fire into the opening immediately. Time to get into the captain's quarters and lock the door. We'll be hunting down the pirates."

# CHAPTER 12
# WAR WAGON VS PIRATES

### <u>Where Is The Treasure Buried?–Caleb</u>

I was our source of intel on where the pirates gathered. There were six pirates with assault rifles on their way to the bridge. It was going to take them awhile: I shut down the elevators, so they had to climb eighteen floors to reach the bridge deck. The climb was going to slow them down some by the time they get to deck 18. There was a central hallway that ended at the only access door to the bridge which looked like a bank vault. It would take some time to get it open.

The safety deposit boxes were located on the main deck amid ship. I transported inside the vault to check stuff in the boxes. There were close to 1,500 boxes. I distorted time to get a quick estimate of the value of the things in the boxes. There must have been at least $10,000,000 in cash, jewelry and even some gold, both coins and nuggets. There were even diamonds, rubies, emeralds and sapphires. I had no idea what they would be worth, but I was sure it would come to several more million. There would have to be twenty pirates, maybe more, working on emptying all the safety deposit boxes.

Last but not least would be the large luxury suites, which I guessed the remaining 50 pirates would hit in groups of twos and threes. According to the accommodations listed in the ship's guide, there were nearly 175 luxury suites. That would mean each team would hit almost nine suites. If I were a pirate, I would start with the biggest luxury suite and work my way down until it was time to bug out.

The only other possible target would be the casino. They must have a lot of cash on hand. I did a quick pass through their bank and counted at least a $1,000,000 all in one place.

We took stock of the four locations we needed to cover— the bridge, the safety deposit boxes, the luxury suites and the casino— and dispersed accordingly.

## Eeny Meeny Miney Moe, Where Do the Pirates Go?—Joshua

A hundred pirates against eight Team Joshua members. Sounded like good odds to me. I prioritized our targets. Mark and Sarge would take out the pirates attacking the bridge. Pham, Joey and Bill would focus on the deposit boxes, and Simone and I would hit the casino. As soon as our first target was successfully eliminated, we would take out the pirates hitting the luxury suites. Caleb would provide us with intel and special assistance when needed. Chanlina would keep an eye on the Zumwalt and make sure they didn't try anymore attacks against the cruise ship. Easy as pie. At least I hoped so.

## Guarding the Bridge—Mark and Sarge

The security camera outside the door to the bridge showed the hallway was still empty. The junior officer opened the door and quickly closed it behind me and Sarge. We hurried down the hallway to the first intersection and turned left. We turned again onto the starboard side and waited. I accessed the view from the security camera on my combat iPad and watched until the six pirates cautiously made their way up the hallway, checking their six every few steps. When they got to the intersection of the two hallways, they stopped and did a quick peak to one side, then the other.

Sarge and I remained quietly hidden as I watched their movements on the iPad until one of the pirates shot out the security camera. The last thing I saw was one of them reaching into his satchel and pulling out something that looked like a block of C-4 explosives. They were going to blow the door. It was now or never.

Sarge and I silently moved to the corner of the intersection, waited a moment, I clicked off the safety on my assault rifle, and thumbed the selector switch to fully automatic. I leaned down and whispered into Sarge's ear, "Attack and destroy, now."

He bolted around the corner and streaked toward the pirate who was watching their six. Sarge was on him before he could pull up his weapon and get a shot off. He hit the pirate so hard it knocked him off his feet and onto his back, knocking his rifle from out of his hands.

Before the remaining pirates could turn to see what was happening, I stepped around the corner and strafed the remaining five. They never got a shot off; I killed the one with the explosives first, the others were quick to follow.

In my command voice, I yelled, "Sarge, front!"

He stopped chewing on the pirate's throat and quickly ran to me, sitting to my right. I reached into my ammo satchel and took out a towel to wipe the pirate's blood from his muzzle. I reached into the bag again and grabbed Sarge's favorite treat which he gently took from my hand. As he chewed, I patted him on the head and praised his attack. "Good dog, Sarge, good kill."

I stood and ejected the empty magazine from my assault rifle, reached into my ammo bag again and pulled out a full magazine. I loaded it into my weapon and clicked on the safety.

I turned to Sarge who was closely watching my every move and said, "Let's find some more pirates."

Sarge barked his approval and we headed to the casino to see if Joshua and Simone needed any help.

## Aces And Eights At The Casino—Simone

All of us headed out through the bridge's steel door into the hallway with Mark and Sarge. At the intersection we parted ways, as they turned left, and we went right to the freight elevator which Caleb had briefly turned on. We got off on the main floor and all five of us cautiously moved toward the registration counter with the vault containing the safety deposit boxes just around the corner.

It was eerily quiet and dark as we walked down the main walkway. There were all kinds of shops and restaurants, yet not a soul to be seen. Most of the venues were locked up tight with lights turned off. It felt like we were on a ghost ship. As we got close to the registration counter, we began hearing voices. We moved off the main walkway and waited in the shadows.

It was a large group of pirates all wearing Navy uniforms with various rank insignias. They were all carrying flashlights and we scuttled behind chairs and couches in the lounge area of the darkened lobby to hide from the light. They were laughing and congratulating themselves for all the money they had stolen from the casino. One of them yelled in a boisterous voice, "Can you believe how easy it was to break into the casino bank? They had only two guards."

"What were they packing?" asked one of the other pirates.

"They both had .38 caliber revolvers. Only 12 bullets between them. Who did they think they could stop with those peashooters?" laughed a third pirate.

"Did you see how Chuck almost cut one of the guards in half with his assault rifle before the peashooter cleared his holster? What a rush!!!" shouted a fourth.

They stopped at the registration counter and the apparent bank vault leader asked the casino leader, "Well congratulations. How much do you reckon you got from the casino?"

"At least a couple of million," he replied. "We didn't stop to count it. It could be twice that, maybe even more. I'd never seen so many packets of $100 bills in my life."

"Well, you head on up to the luxury suites and see if you all can get a lot more. The others have a head start on you, so you better hurry. Don't forget to have a little fun with the ladies while you're at it." He checked his watch. "We have to be back aboard our destroyer in about thirty minutes. Get moving."

"Good luck on opening all those safety deposit boxes. See you back at the ship," said the casino leader. He turned and headed for the elaborate staircase with about twenty pirates in tow.

Joshua and I decided to make a quick call to the casino to see if there were any survivors. Joshua wondered why the casino guards hadn't left the bank. All the ship's crew were supposed to have abandoned their stations and headed to the crew quarters.

We would be joining Mark and Sarge at the luxury suites while Pham, Joey and Bill focused on the action at the vault.


## I'm The Intel Man—Caleb

When Mark and Sarge were done taking care of the steel door to the bridge, I began searching the four decks of luxury suites. The most expensive suites were on deck 18, the same deck the bridge was on. Unfortunately, the bridge was at the forward end of the ship and the suites were at the aft end.

I did a time distortion search of the thirty suites on deck 18. Six of them were already hit by the pirates. They killed seven passengers and raped three women.

When Mark and Sarge arrived, they eliminated one of the pirate teams and were already pursuing another. Joshua and Simone had just arrived on deck 18. Unfortunately, five more pirate teams were about to join with more coming shortly behind.

I did everything I could to slow the progress of the pirates and keep them from killing more passengers. I made sure their doors were locked and bolted closed. I opened the safes and displayed all the money and jewelry on the beds and had the passengers lock themselves in the bathrooms. It seemed to be working.

I told our team members what locations were already hit and which suites were next on the pirates' lists. It ended in a gunfight in the hallways.


## It's Dying Time—Joshua

Simone and I were just turning a corner when we spotted two teams of pirates banging on the doors of two suites across the hall from each other. I drew both of my Desert Eagles .50 caliber semi-automatic weapons and shot two of them in the head while Simone put two kill shots from her Beretta in the third man's head and heart.

The pirate team across the hall scrambled to retreat, shooting wildly as they turned into an adjacent hallway. Unfortunately for them, Mark heard the shots and was coming up the hallway with Sarge leading the way.

The first pirate to turn the corner was hit by Sarge before he even saw the dog. Sarge hit him at full speed, staying low and chomping down on his genitals with his massive jaw. As they tumbled to the ground, they knocked down a second pirate who stumbled over them. Mark shot him before he could defend himself. It was a good grouping of bullets centered on his heart.

Sarge was shaking his prey like he was a chew toy, while the man screamed in agony. Mark shot him in the head to put him out of his misery.

I took out the last pirate with two simultaneous shots, one in each eye.

A third team of pirates showed up and immediately began firing at us. It took a little longer, but eventually we got them all too.

A member of a fourth team poked his head around the corner to see what was going on. Big mistake. Mark shot and killed him before he could even register what was going on.

The man's partner turned and ran, but Sarge was faster. When Mark ordered, "Sarge, attack and destroy, NOW!" The dog was off in a streak of gray and black fur. The pirate turned as he ran and tried shooting Sarge. He was too slow. Sarge grabbed his shooting hand in his mouth and bit down so hard, it severed the man's hand clean from his arm.

The man screamed in agony and attempted to crawl away. Sarge spit out the hand, sending the pistol clattering to the floor, then sprung onto the man and bit down hard on his neck. He stopped screaming.

We had taken out four pirate teams in less than a minute. Ten minutes later, with Caleb spotting for us, we'd taken out nine more teams with no casualties to our side. Caleb said the other teams seemed to have disappeared.

### How Safe Are Safety Deposit Boxes?—Pham

While Joshua and three teammates were eliminating the pirates who were hitting the luxury suites, Joey, Bill and I were preparing to stop the pirates from looting the safety deposit boxes.

From the shadows of the dark lounge next to the lobby area, we had a perfect view of the vault door. It looked like they were going to use C-4 to blow the door and get access to the vault. Joey noticed one of the men was handling what looked like a battery-operated power drill. Bill countered that it was a lock puller.

When I mentioned I'd never had a safety deposit box Joey told me, "Every box has two locks, one for the passenger and one for the banker. When a passenger needs to get into his box, the banker unlocks his first, then the passenger opens his lock, and they remove the box. Each key is different for security reasons. A lock puller is a device that bypasses the key locks by pulling them out of the door."

Bill looked at the door and whispered, "It would be nice if we had a bazooka. It wouldn't damage the vault door very much, but it would certainly take out some of the pirates and mess up those who survive."

"How about grenades?" I suggested in a low voice.

"Do you have any grenades?" whispered Joey.

I reached for my satchel and pulled out a flash bang grenade.

"Wow," Bill exclaimed softly, then mouthed, "How many?"

I held up six fingers.

We moved behind a nearby counter a little closer to the vault, but still in the shadows. Each one of us took a flash bang out of our satchels and held it in our throwing hand. We laid our second one on the countertop, unslung our assault rifles and laid them on the counter along with an additional magazine. We were ten feet apart as I raised my hand, showing a closed fist on my non-throwing hand.

I raised one finger, and we pulled the pins, on two fingers we cocked our throwing hand, on three we threw the grenades into the midst of the pirates. We immediately squatted down behind the counter, closed our eyes, and covered our ears, as the three grenades exploded.

We waited a few seconds then stood up, grabbed the assault rifles and opened fire on the pirates as they stumbled to their feet, deaf and dumb. It was all over in a few seconds. Nobody moved except us. They were all dead.

### The Zumwalt Strikes Back—Chanlina

Ever since we took out their deck guns, the Zumwalt had gone silent. Everything seemed to have shut down. We'd been monitoring all their electronic emissions continuously since Caleb had called out "Talley Ho." Those emissions continued until we blew away their deck guns. A minute later, those emissions stopped.

None of the remaining crew showed themselves and none of the crew who went aboard the cruise ship attempted to return. With the emissions shut down, I'm not sure the pirates who boarded the cruise ship knew the Zumwalt was under attack.

I followed the battles of Team Joshua until the fighting was over. Caleb kept me informed. At best, he could tell there were only a small remnant of pirates who survived. I was sure Joshua would want to interrogate the survivors. There were so many questions as yet unanswered.

### Tell Me What You Know or Die—Joshua

There were thirteen pirates who survived. They all surrendered when they found out they couldn't make it back to their destroyer. Mark and Sarge were standing guard at the gaping hole on the starboard side. Mark had removed the gangway which connected the cruise ship with the Zumwalt. One look at the battle damage the destroyer sustained was enough to convince them there was no escape. We confiscated their weapons and locked them up in the ship's three brigs with the captain's approval. Once we'd notified him that the fighting was over, he took back command of his ship. He selected some of the crew and appointed them as temporary security guards, putting his junior officer in charge.

We were able to reclaim most of the money and jewelry the pirates attempted to steal. Bill jokingly asked if we were entitled to a finder's fee. Joey volunteered himself and Bill for the task of removing the bodies from the crime scenes explaining, "When Bill and I were detectives with Portland PD, we had way too many bodies to take care of. Most of them were pretty gruesome. They ranged from car accidents to murders. You never get used to it, but you do learn to deal with it."

To me, the saddest thing was to hear how many passengers and crew members were killed by the pirates. Twenty seven bodies were discovered. The captain had received instructions from the cruise line's headquarters. This cruise was over. All passengers and crew would be transferred to another ship and taken to the nearest seaport where they would be flown to any location they wanted. The cruise line would cover all expenses, including a full refund. It was the least they could do.

The dead were to be stored in the ship's refrigerators until they could be offloaded onto a transport vessel. One of the ship's passengers suggested it would be a waste of money to store the pirates and take them ashore saying, "Why not just chop them up and feed the pieces to the fish?"

Unfortunately, maritime law did not permit this type of treatment, but I have to admit it sounded like a good idea to me. Besides, we still needed to identify who the pirates were and where they came from.

I started the interrogation process early in the afternoon of the next day, one at a time.

One of the leaders, who had been involved in ransacking the luxury suites, was up first. He had taken a bullet to the shoulder yesterday. It wasn't life threatening, but I'm sure it hurt like hell. Caleb was assisting me as my lie detector. Spirits have a knack to know if a person is telling the truth. He suggested we hold back on the pain meds. I agreed.

"What's your name?" was my first question.

He was strapped onto a gurney, gritting his teeth in pain. He managed to say, "Get me some pain meds and I'll tell you."

I smiled at him and replied, "Tell me your name first, then I'll give you the meds."

Still gritting his teeth, he managed to say, "Davis… My name is Jefferson Davis. Now get me the damned meds."

Caleb thought to me, *He's lying. His real name is Harley. Harley Davidson. His father was a biker and named him after his bike.*

"Tell me, Jefferson," I asked. "Were you named after the Civil War Confederate president?"

"I told you my name. No more questions, get me the meds."

"Not yet," I said with my meanest sneer. "I believe your daddy named you. But it wasn't Jefferson, was it, Harley?" I paused for dramatic effect. "You lied to me, Mr. Davidson. I can tell when you're lying, so you don't get any pain meds. I'll just move on and let you live with the pain for a while longer. See you in an hour or so."

"Wait!" he shouted as I stood and headed to the cell door. "Who told you my name?"

I stopped, turned my head to study him, then said, "Why, you did, Harley. You told me you are Harley Davidson. Your daddy gave you that name because he loved his Harley motorcycle more than he loved you. Don't you remember? I'll get you your pain meds now."

I returned with a hypodermic filled with a clear liquid. "This lidocaine will take away your pain, for a while at least," I said as I poked him in the arm and pushed down on the plunger. Almost immediately, his demeanor changed. He looked at me and laughed, "You are one dumb shit, Mr. Interrogator. Don't bother me with any more questions, I'm not telling you nothing."

"Anything," I corrected. He looked confused. "You should have said, 'I'm not telling you anything.' It seems you're the dumb shit."

Before he could come up with a rebuttal, I added, "By the way, one little detail. Beside the lidocaine, that needle also contained sodium pentothal, better known as truth serum. Just a little bit will make you tell me everything I want to know. Too much and you die. You should be feeling sleepy. Just close your eyes, this will all be over soon."

As his eyes began to flutter, Caleb asked me, *Did you really put sodium pentothal in the needle?*

*Hell no! I just believe in the power of suggestion,* I replied. *I'm going to ask him questions. Tell me if he's lying.*

For the next ten minutes I berated and interrogated. Caleb said he never lied once.

I called a brief meeting with the expanded team and quickly briefed them on what I found out from one of the pirate leaders. "All the pirates, the men and women who came aboard the cruise ship, were mercenaries. They were hired to steal as much as they could, then return to the Zumwalt. A skeleton crew of Chinese sailors was operating the destroyer and didn't take part in the raid. The leader of the crew was a senior colonel in the Chinese Navy. He briefed the mercenaries on where to plunder aboard the cruise ship and specifically ordered them to murder anyone who resisted the raid.

"I asked the merc leader for details of how he ended up on the Zumwalt. He said a man who claimed to be a high-level member of our government used the dark web to contact almost 500 mercenaries. After a series of interviews they selected a hundred for the mission. They were paid ten grand apiece upfront, plus a promise of a percentage of the take from the cruise ship. The man who had done the interviewing never gave his name and always wore a mask when speaking face to face.

"Once the one hundred were selected they were briefed by an anonymous man claiming to be an admiral, and boarded onto a Chinese ship, the next step was to sail to a remote seaport. That was probably Unalakleet, at the far east end of Norton Sound. Someone in our government gave the captain of the cargo ship the coordinates for the Zumwalt. It sailed toward the Zumwalt's coordinates and pretended to be in danger of sinking. They sent out a short range SOS. The Zumwalt responded and was captured. The US Navy skeleton crew from the ship was executed and thrown overboard. The mercs and the Chinese crew boarded the Zumwalt to immediately set sail for the cruise liner. They had no idea what happened to the cargo ship once they left Norton Sound.

"We know the *Xiang Hua Men* sailed back north toward Norton Sound and is currently docked at a cove on St. Lawrence Island, right at the beginning of the Bering Strait."

"Why would the Chinese do this?" asked Pham. "It has to be some type of setup to—"

Before Pham could continue, Chanlina was in our minds. *Everyone needs to get back aboard the War Wagon right now. A pulse of energy from Zumwalt crashed our cloaking device. Caleb said they're scrambling two attack helicopters from their aft hangars. I'm going to drop down to sea level next to the port side cargo hatch. You can jump aboard from there.*

### I Thought We Were Invincible—Pearl

When our cloaking device went down, I was shocked. I thought we were invincible. Chanlina attempted to reboot the cloaking software, but to no avail. She kept getting the same error message, *The cloaking device is no longer available, please try again later.*

While Chanlina struggled with the cloaking problem, I watched the Zumwalt and saw two attack helicopters being towed out of the aft hangar by a robot tug. I couldn't tell if the choppers were drones or manned. As soon as they were clear of the hangar, they began spooling up their rotors.

I didn't wait for them to be launched, I took over fire control and ordered the two attack birds to be vaporized. It didn't work. I repeated the order and got the *please try again later* response. I took manual control of the War Wagon and squeezed off two unguided rockets at the attack choppers. One chopper was destroyed as I grabbed the manual flight controls. The second one had just lifted off as we climbed vertically, cleared the top of the cruise ship, crossed to the other side, and dove down to a hover near the port side cargo bay.

I opened the War Wagon's hatch and the automated gangway extended as all seven of Team Joshua sprinted across into the War Wagon. Sarge acted as rear guard and was the last one aboard. I closed the hatch and did a two-G vertical climb just as the Zumwalt's attack helicopter cleared the top of the *Oasis* and opened up with the Chinese version of its Gatling gun. Mark took manual control of our own Gatling guns, all four of them, and made Swiss cheese of the attacker. It burst into flames just before it crashed into the ocean.

I didn't wait around for the next surprise and instead headed to the closest of a chain of small islands that formed the outer boundary of the inside passage. Ten minutes later, we were sitting on the ground in a small clearing surrounded by huge evergreen trees, wondering what the hell happened. While we took a few minutes to decompress, we received a brief radio message from the *Oasis* captain.

"Ahoy Team Joshua, all of us aboard *Oasis of the Seas* owe you our lives. We cannot begin to tell you how much we appreciate you showing up when you did. I want to mention two things before I sign off. First, a rather odd message for Mr. Mark Riley from my junior officer. Something about how he will never again forget to take the safety off. I'm not sure what that means; perhaps Mark can figure it out. Secondly, as soon as you disembarked from our ship, the Zumwalt left us. It was heading northeast at 30 knots. I hope that helps you sink the bastard. Good hunting, Team Joshua. *Oasis* out."

# CHAPTER 13
# WHAT WILL THEY THINK OF NEXT?

### How Bad Is It?—Caleb

Chanlina, Pearl and I began trying to figure out how the Chinese were able to shut down our cloaking device, followed by our weapon systems controls. We ran a complete series of diagnostic tests on all three of the AIs. That took some time and I decided to see how everyone was handling the after-combat shakes. Don't get me wrong, many people handle combat without any emotional trauma, especially those who have survived several firefights. However, sometimes even the most seasoned combat veteran will have issues.

Pearl wasn't doing too well. Her performance during combat was spot on. She did just the right thing at just the right time. After we landed, she stepped outside for a little fresh air and began projectile vomiting. Before she lost consciousness, Simone joined her and held her close. Both women shed a few tears and Simone offered a few words of reassurance. Ten minutes later Pearl was back at work, one hundred percent focused on the issue at hand.

When the diagnostics were completed we had some not-so-bad news. Chanlina informed the team in her young girl voice, "The Chinese didn't steal our cloaking technology, they just jammed it. The same goes for our weapons systems. They projected some extremely powerful, very high frequency noise that took our systems temporarily offline. Everything works fine now."

Pham asked, "Why didn't they take out all our systems? Why just those two?"

I answered, *Each of the War Wagon's systems operates on a unique frequency. They probably found one by trial and error. That's why it took them so long.*

"How can we fix it so they can't jam them the next time we encounter them?" asked Joshua. "Even if we change the frequency, they could still find it and shut us down."

Chanlina replied, *Yes, they probably could if all we did is stay with one fixed frequency for each system. However, we're not going to do that. Our AIs are developing a variable frequency oscillator interface, or V-FOI for short. Once they have programmed the interface to accept the V-FOI, it will be statistically impossible to jam.*

"What does that mean in regular English?" asked a confused Simone.

I answered, *It means it would take a thousand years of trial and error to come up with the correct variations in frequency.*

"Sounds like pretty good odds to me," replied Joshua. "How long will it take to have the V-FOI operational?"

*A week or two,* answered Chanlina.

"Make it one," said Joshua, a look of determination on his face. "I want to intercept the Zumwalt before it meets up with the *Xiang Hua Men.*"

For the next few days, we didn't have much to do. I decided to keep an eye on the Zumwalt. I visited the ship almost daily to check on its location. I also wanted to see the people who had figured out how to jam our cloaking device. I listened closely to their conversations, committed them to memory in my spirit brain and translated them to Pearl. I didn't need to translate for Chanlina; like me, she understood every language known to man (and woman).

The gist of what they were saying was how superior their computer skills were compared to the lowly Americans. I was surprised they hadn't injured themselves with all the back slapping they did. They were looking forward to returning to China and receiving their well-earned commendations from the Tribunal, in spite of their failure to loot the *Oasis's* treasure.

I seriously doubted these clowns would ever return to China. I asked Joshua if I could scuttle the destroyer. He asked me to wait until he knew more about what the Chinese really wanted. Then and only then, could I sink the Zumwalt. I could hardly wait.

Then the other shoe dropped. Not only had they been able to shut down our cloaking device, but they were also very close to having their own. While they were determining how our system worked, they were able to reverse engineer their own device.

I was shocked at first, but by digging deep into their design, I was able to find their Achilles' heel. They were using the same steady-state frequency we'd been using. We could crash their device whenever we wanted.

Every time I made a new discovery aboard the Zumwalt, I shared it with the members of Team Joshua. The last surprise was that the Zumwalt was not going to rendezvous with *Xiang Hua Men.* Once they had proved their cloaking device worked, they changed course and headed directly toward Xiamen, the PRC seaport located a stone's throw from Taiwan.


### Tag, You're It—Joshua

As soon as I found out the Zumwalt was heading for China and not going to meet up with *Xiang Hua Men,* I gathered everyone together. That included both Chanlina and Caleb.

It took the better part of an hour to locate all of the team. While Chanlina and the AIs were working on the finishing touches of the V-FOI, I'd released the team for a few days of R & R. The small island we had landed on wasn't Wonderland, but it would do very nicely. Pearl and Simone took nature hikes around the island. They discovered some type of fruit growing wild next to one of their hiking paths. We ran it through our food processor and decided it wouldn't kill us. It had a mildly sweet taste and added to the limited variety of food stocked on board. Pham and Mark went fishing. Our protein supply was running low so it was nice to resupply our cooler with freshly caught saltwater salmon.

Bill, Joey and I remained close to the War Wagon and began working out. Since we didn't have any weights on board, we did almost all of our exercises with body weight. On the second day, Joey found an assortment of fairly large rocks (Bill called them mini boulders) and we began taking turns lifting them. We also did some jogging around the clearing. We set up an estimated one-mile circuit and began timing ourselves for one, two and three mile runs. It felt good to get out in the fresh air.

I'd given Chanlina one week to get the upgrades to our cloaking device finished. She did it in four days. It was time to get back to work.

"Caleb discovered the Chinese techs aboard the Zumwalt have built their own cloaking device and are now heading toward China," I began. "We won't be able to track them, but don't forget, we have a secret weapon. Its name is Caleb. He is going to be able to track the location of the Zumwalt as it heads to a seaport in China, which I suspect will be Xiamen. It has a large naval shipyard where they might try to reverse engineer the Zumwalt and build their own version of the ship, complete with their recently pirated cloaking device."

Pham asked, "Do you think they might use the copies of the Zumwalt to attack Taiwan? It's only about a hundred miles across the Taiwan Strait to the main island. A friend of mine who is from Taiwan told me the PRC built a huge structure made up of Chinese characters on the cliffs above Xiamen facing the Kinmen Islands, a part of Taiwan that's only a mile or so from mainland China. He said it translates as: We will soon be one nation."

If the Chinese want to use the Zumwalt ships to attack Taiwan, why would they use the Zumwalt they hijacked, then sail all the way across the Pacific Ocean to attack a cruise liner? Once they had the Zumwalt, why not sail directly to Xiamen?" Joey asked.

That was a good question. Chanlina had the answer, *Because they wanted the War Wagon's cloaking device. Once they have the cloaking device all their warships and aircraft can be cloaked. They can hide all their ships and planes and no one will be able to say for sure China was to blame for the attack. In fact, they might say they were trying to protect Taiwan and send their troops there to protect their Chinese brothers from further attack.*

We all sat quietly, considering Chanlina's comments. I agreed with most of what she said, however, I had a few comments of my own. "I'm sure the PRC wants to eventually absorb Taiwan just like they took over Hong Kong, Macau and a number of islands in the South China Sea. I think what they really want is us. They want all the advanced technology available in the new War Wagon. The cloaking device was just a part of what they wanted, I believe their ultimate target was the cold fusion reactor. It was the first thing they went after. They thought Pearl would sell it to them, and tried to kill her when they found out she was feeding them bogus design data."

Pearl sat down abruptly when I brought back memories of what had happened to her and Pham. I was sorry to have to bring that up, however painful it might have been, but I needed to show how their attempts to take control of the War Wagon escalated. "Their next step was on *Wonder of the Seas* when three of their men attempted to steal our vehicle. The step after that was to steal our vehicle at Denali National Park when they brought a small army of helicopters to take it from us. It was there they found out about our cloaking technology and our ability to morph from motorhome to war wagon to aircraft. Their latest attempt gained them the cloaking technology and more detail on what our combat capabilities are."

There was more silence as they thought about what I'd said. Simone was the first to respond, "So you're saying everything they did was to figure out a way to capture the War Wagon. What about *Xiang Hua Men*?

"A ruse to delay us so the Zumwalt could get to *Oasis of the Seas.* The crew of the cargo ship are cannon fodder, just like the mercenaries aboard *Oasis.*"

"So what happens next?" asked Pearl. She seemed to have recovered from her brief moment of distress.

"We wait with our new and improved cloaking device inactive. As soon as they realize we're not following them, they'll turn off their cloak. They want us to follow them so we will follow at a distance with our own cloak offline."

"What will they do next?" asked Mark.

I answered with a smile, "I have no idea, but I bet it'll be exciting."

## Let The Games Begin—Joshua

The Zumwalt had a four day head start on us. They were traveling at 30 knots for four days before we lifted off from our island retreat. During those four days they could have traveled 3,300 miles. Once we were airborne, we traveled at 400 knots so it took us a little over eight hours to catch up with them. Caleb updated their location every hour. He confirmed they were heading toward Xiamen.

We approached them cautiously. They were 1,500 miles from Xiamen with their cloak deactivated. They stopped 500 miles from the Chinese shipyard. They were waiting for us to catch up. They wanted us to find them.

I wanted to see what they would do when we approached them with our super cloak (Chanlina's name for our upgraded device) deactivated. When we were a little over 100 miles from them, they fired up their engines and began moving again. They'd seen us and wanted us to follow.

We kept our distance and remained uncloaked. I was expecting an update from Caleb and he contacted me right on time. *As soon as they spotted you, the skeleton crew got busy. When they detected us and you were uncloaked they were really pumped up. The acting captain called someone for orders. They're sending reinforcements. They think we've fallen into their trap.*

*One other item of note, the* Xiang Hua Men *was reported to have collided with an iceberg in the Bering Sea. They were taking on water and the Chinese captain reported they were sinking. Only a few of his men survived and the ship went down by the stern.*

It turned out the reinforcements Caleb mentioned were unprecedentedly substantial. They'd scrambled both aircraft and ships. I was curious how they thought they were going to capture us.

I knew they wanted all the advanced technology the new War Wagon could offer. If they shot us down, they'd lose that opportunity and once we were cloaked again, it was very unlikely they could shoot us down. It reminded me of an old adage: **You can't kill what you can't see.** Despite my confidence, I had a feeling there could be some wildcard the opposition could play to overcome our advantages. For the life of me, I couldn't imagine what it could be.

We continued to close the distance. The Chinese armada was at least fifteen minutes away, the aircraft would be first to arrive. Just before we were in range to attack, the Zumwalt activated their cloaking device. Chanlina sent a high energy pulse towards them, destroying their cloak. At the same time Caleb activated our new and improved version of the cloak.

Pham and Mark launched the two attack drones. We had upgraded the drones with the new cloak so the Chinese would never see them coming. My goal was to send the Zumwalt to the bottom of the sea, or as Caleb colorfully suggested, *to Davey Jones's Locker.*

The two drones fired all their weapons until they ran out of ammunition. They fired their guided missiles at the waterline. Those rockets were packed with very high energy explosives. The first round took out the ship's propulsion system. The second round blew gaping holes in both sides of the ship and it began taking on water. We backed off to let the skeleton crew abandon ship as the first of the Chinese aircraft arrived.

The ships were still out of sight as two flights of four fighter jets began looking for us. We took our time as our computerized weapons' systems targeted the first four planes. We were hovering directly above the sinking ship, about a hundred miles from the Chinese mainland. We waited patiently for the jets to come into range. That's when it happened.

The sky went black, just for a moment. There was a feeling of vertigo, like we were falling into a gravity well. An instant later, we were in daylight again. Except the sun wasn't in the right place, in fact we couldn't see any sun at all.

"Oh shit!" shouted Chanlina's avatar. "We're in a Wonderland bubble."

## Inside the Chinese Bubble—Chanlina

Except it wasn't the Wonderland we were used to. It wasn't a sunny day with puffy white clouds and beautiful flower gardens. We materialized inside a huge room with high walls and a few barred windows. Only two bare lightbulbs cast dim light on the concrete floor. The seven of us were dressed in prison uniforms with manacles on our feet and arms. Heavily-armed Chinese prison guards kept close watch on us as we were ushered toward what looked like the throne of an ancient king. Its wrought iron details and pure gold highlights were blinding and overwhelming.

Caleb looked at me, eyes wide. "Why are you looking at me like that?" I asked, and realized my voice was the voice of an old woman.

I turned to look at the spirit's avatar on the throne and screamed, "What have you done to me, you miserable excuse for a demon? What have you done?"

"SILENCE, YOU OLD CROW!" the spirit screamed back at me. "Do you not realize I can destroy you all with the snap of my fingers? You will bow to me now or I will destroy the man-whore you call Caleb. I warned him never to challenge me, and yet here he is."

Joshua interrupted as I stood speechless with fury and rage. "What do you want from us? I assume it's the technology of our War Wagon. So, why isn't the War Wagon here for you to take? And what happened to our attack dog?"

Caleb's avatar spoke up, "You're not back in China now. I think your powers are limited here. If you're still so strong, why don't you prove it, you ancient pile of decaying shit!"

The demon avatar smiled wickedly and replied in a calm voice, "As you wish."

Caleb's image seemed to freeze, then vanished with a slight popping sound as his prison clothes and his manacles fell to the ground with a muted metallic *clunk.*

Joshua screamed in rage and terror. "You destroyed my twin, you arrogant son of a--"

"It's okay, Joshua," I interrupted. "He destroyed Caleb's avatar, not his spirit. I can create a new body for him any time I want."

The demon spirit's face broke into another evil grin as he said, "You're bluffing. I know who you are and what you are capable of. Go ahead and try it. Make a bigger fool of yourself in front of the so-called Team Joshua."

"Your wish is my command," I said with a smile. "Return to me lover boy."

The rest of the team wasn't sure who was doing the bluffing. Simone seemed to be approaching a panic attack and Joshua wasn't doing much better. Pham took Pearl's hand to steady her. She had kept them closed ever since she'd been trapped in the bubble. I thought I detected Joey and Bill getting ready to rush the demon avatar's body, even though they were still manacled with guards watching them. They must have thought humans couldn't be affected by spirits, even in the bubble. Once this was over, I needed to update them on the limitations of humans in Wonderland.

There were two pops in a row. The first one returned my avatar to the younger version of myself dressed in a long, flowing robe. The second pop made Caleb reappear as if he were going swimming, dressed only in a too-small pair of Speedos.

The entire team broke up laughing at the absurdity of Caleb's outfit. He didn't seem bothered by his lack of clothes. His new and improved avatar turned and rushed the throne. He grabbed the demon avatar around the neck with both hands and began to strangle him. Before Caleb could apply killing force, everything went black for a second and all of Team Joshua materialized inside the new War Wagon.

Everyone was now wearing the same clothes they had on when they left for the Chinese bubble. I set up a smaller one in the middle of the War Wagon's bridge.

Joshua shook his head and asked me, "Can't you dress him in less revealing attire?"

"Oh, sure. I've gotten so used to seeing his avatar nake—"

Joshua raised his voice and interrupted her, "Too much information."

I shrugged my shoulders and a similar robe to mine appeared on Caleb.

The War Wagon was still in airplane mode with our cloaking device fully functional. Sarge was greatly relieved to have the team materialize again. He had been cowering in a corner near the port side hatch, waiting for our return.

The entire crew was emotionally exhausted from the ordeal. After a short interval of silence to gather our thoughts, Pearl was the first to ask, "What the hell just happened to us?"

### **What the Hell?—Joshua**

Suddenly, The Apostle was standing in our midst. He didn't materialize slowly like somebody who'd beamed from the starship Enterprise (sorry, I'm also a devoted Star Trek fan, the one with Captain Kirk, Picard not so much).

He turned to us and asked, "Is everyone all right?"

The Apostle looked at each of the team members. When he came to me, he said, "I bet you have questions about what just happened."

"Hell yes, we've got questions," I replied.

"Okay, let me see if I can answer a few of them." The Apostle paused for a moment then asked, "Did you notice anything missing?"

"Only the new War Wagon and Sarge," answered Chanlina. "Animals and machines aren't permitted inside a bubble."

"Almost right. Intelligent animals and complicated machines are not compatible with bubbles. Do you remember when everything went black for a second? It happened twice, when you were first taken from the War Wagon, and again when you were returned back aboard."

"I remember," I affirmed, the rest of the crew nodding in agreement.

The Apostle gave us all a reassuring smile and began his explanation. "The Chinese bubble you were in was very primitive. It resided on the hanger deck of the Chinese's newest aircraft carrier named *Fujian*. Our experts on bubble design and transporting think what I'm about to tell you is what happened. However, I would consider their opinions a guess at best.

"Even though the War Wagon was cloaked when this took place, there was a brief instant when your cloak was inactive when the War Wagon's cloaking device changed. The Chinese were able to lock on to the War Wagon. When they were ready, they transported their entire bubble to the War Wagon and captured you. Their tech was sufficient to provide avatars for Caleb and Chanlina. We have no idea how they were able to dress and manacle you in the prison setting. We think they had help from a very strong ancient spirit to make Caleb disappear. Fortunately, Chanlina was able to recreate his scantily clothed avatar. When Caleb attempted to strangle the actor who was simulating the demon avatar, the Chinese decided to shut it down. Apparently, they have an auto-return feature on their transporter for emergency situations. I think that decision was made because the actor who played the demon avatar was *Fujian's* commissar, the government's leader of the ship."

Chanlina interrupted. "How were they able to make my avatar look like a decrepit old lady?"

"Again, we don't know for sure. My best guess is the ancient spirit had something to do with it."

I was really upset about what had happened to my team, especially to my brother. "So what are we going to do about this? We can't let them go unpunished. I think we need to strike back as soon as we can."

The Apostle looked at me for a moment before he asked, "You are one very sophisticated weapon surrounded by nearly a dozen military ships and even more fighter aircraft. How do you propose to fight back?"

I looked at The Apostle with determination in my eye. I furrowed my brow, puffed up my chest, and said, "Give us a couple of days. This team will come up with something unbelievably awesome."

The Apostle looked me in the eyes and replied, "I believe you will. Keep me informed."

With a slight *pop,* he vanished.

# CHAPTER 14
# URANIUM INTO LEAD

### Two Can Play This Game—Chanlina

I was furious at the Chinese for depicting me as some old, weak, female character who would faint away at the first sign of violence. I wanted my revenge. I let Caleb interface with the computers while I planned a strategy. The plan would have to incorporate more than my revenge. I wanted it to include a solution to stop the Chinese from any further attempts at capturing the War Wagon. I had a vague idea of how to plan my attack, but I needed more information.

I needed to contact a superior spirit guide. I decided to reach out to The Apostle and work up from there, if need be. However, I had to work fast. I didn't want *Fujian* to return to port. I wanted to attack while they were still at sea surrounded by an armada of ships to protect them.

I contacted The Apostle. *This is Chanlina requesting a spirit guide meeting with The Apostle.* Instantly, I was at the traditional Wonderland setting, blue sky, puffy white clouds, flowers, trees, birds and a myriad of other beauties. The Apostle was standing near a round, glass-top table with two comfortable looking chairs. He was holding two glasses in his hands as he said, "Chanlina, it's so good to see you in this familiar setting. Have a seat. Do you like lemonade?"

I took the glass from his hand and sat down across from him, took a sip, and asked, "Could we have hard lemonade?"

"Of course," he answered. The next sip had a bite to it and I nodded my approval. He looked relaxed for a Sunday morning, dressed in attractive casual clothes. I matched him with a similar outfit of my own. Our avatars were in their (our?) late twenties and enchantingly attractive. It was the relaxing setting we needed.

He took a sip of his drink and asked, "What can I do for you?"

"I'm considering a plan to shut down the Chinese from any further attempts to hijack our new War Wagon and I need information about the limits of a Wonderland bubble."

"Why don't you tell me what you have in mind and I'll tell you what I know?" he replied.

"Okay," I said. "Can we encapsulate *Fujian* in a Wonderland bubble and then move the bubble to a yet-to-be-determined place?"

"Wow! No one has ever asked me something like that. I need to invite an arbiter."

An instant later an ancient avatar appeared, he looked like he must have been at least 200 years old. "What should I call you?" I asked.

"Arbiter is what I am and who I am. Before you say anything else, I need to inform you of a few rules. Please pay close attention. Rule number one: Spirits cannot intentionally harm a human for any reason. Any spirit who is charged with violating that rule is entitled to a hearing. If found guilty, that spirit will cease to exist. Rule number two: Spirits can interact with humans only when that interaction is approved by an arbiter on a case by case basis. Rule number three: Spirits who are bonded to a human have permission to interact with that human at any time unless forbidden by an arbiter. Rule number four: Spirits are permitted to interact with other spirits but not allowed to do them any harm. If a spirit claims another spirit has violated that rule, a hearing will be held and if the charge is upheld, that spirit will cease to exist. That about covers it. What is your question?"

I explained to the arbiter what had happened to me and my human friends, and what I proposed to prevent them from repeating additional attacks. The arbiter sat quietly with his eyes closed until I was done. As soon as I was finished, he opened his eyes and said, in a very calm voice, "Your request is denied."

Appalled, I blurted out, "On what grounds?"

He stared at me for a moment, shook his head, and said, "Your plan violates several of the rules I just stated. Based on what you described, the rules would cause you to cease to exist ever again. I understand what your human friends and associates went through, but you are forbidden to interact with humans as you described. Were there any Chinese spirits who assisted in the kidnapping?"

I shook my avatar head. "To the best of my knowledge, no real demons or spirits were involved."

Both our arbiter and The Apostle sat up straight and looked at each other.

The Apostle looked down at his hands as the arbiter turned to me and said, "I need to correct something you said. The word 'demon' is to be used only to describe a fallen angel. Spirits are what remain when humans die. They are two distinctly different creatures."

The arbiter's avatar took a deep breath and let it out slowly before he continued. "I sympathize with you and your human teammates. You and your team are a unique entity. I will assist you in any way I can, but the rules still apply. Have The Apostle contact me when you come up with other ways of reaching your objectives. As soon as you find one which meets your goals and the rules as I stated to you, I will gladly approve your plan."

### Let's Get Together And Figure This Out—Caleb

When Chanlina approached me after her meeting, she shared what went down. I suggested we bring the entire team in on it. In order to come up with a plan and still have time to execute the mission, I suggested we go back to our Wonderland bubble and freeze time until we figured something out. That way we could take all the time we needed to come up with a mission plan that would pass muster with the arbiter while *Fujian* was frozen in position.

All of the team agreed and Pham checked on the location of the Chinese aircraft carrier. It was still almost a hundred nautical miles from Xiamen. I really loved Wonderland. I have so many good memories of my time there with Chanlina. But this was going to be a very different type of visit.

We spent the better part of a week brainstorming what we wanted to achieve, followed by how to go about accomplishing our goal.

Before we began, all of our human team members made their daily calls home. Once inside the bubble, we control time. Inside we can match time outside if we wish. However, once inside we can speed up or slow down time. When I say we are going to freeze time, I mean inside the bubble time accelerates to the point where everything outside of it looks literally frozen.

From my perspective, the best thing about being a spirit inside the bubble is we get to have avatars. Those avatars can be duplicates of when we had human bodies or something completely different. We can also pick the age we want to be. For example, Chanlina was over 200 years old when she died, however, she chose her avatar to be how she looked in her late twenties. One downside is spirit avatars cannot exist outside the bubble.

There are two other very important features of bubbles. The first is that human beings can enter the bubble and co-exist with the avatars of the spirits. Secondly, once inside the bubble, it can be transported to wherever in the world we want it to go.

Two days of planning produced a pretty good plan. We ran it by the arbiter. We were disappointed when he didn't approve it. We went back to the drawing board, made changes to the plan, and thought we had made the necessary corrections. They both bounced that one too. On the third attempt, our plan was approved.

Before we had begun our final planning, The Apostle had stepped into our bubble to offer some suggestions. Actually, he asked us some thought provoking questions. The first question being, "What is the top-level goal of any nation?"

After some mild discussion, we came up with an answer. Joshua said, "To protect and prosper its citizens."

"Excellent," was The Apostle's response. "How do most nations accomplish that goal?"

Chanlina answered immediately. "By attempting to rule the world. To be the strongest, and to use that strength to dominate all the other countries."

"And just how do they dominate those other countries?"

Simone answered, "Through wars and subversive means of stealing another nation's strength."

"And just how effective are those actions in maintaining their dominance? How long do they remain in power and what are the costs of maintaining dominance?"

"The Roman Empire lasted for over a thousand years," Agent Hong answered. "In present day, probably a few hundred years. The cost of war in terms of loss of human life has grown exponentially during those years. With the development of nuclear weapons, there is the potential for destroying civilization as we know it."

The Apostle's avatar stared at Joey Hong for a moment. Before he could speak, Agent Bill Cody said, "I taught him all that stuff." Everyone began to laugh, except Joey, who shot daggers at Bill.

"All right, Agent Cody," said the avatar. "Answer me this. Who are the two strongest nations at the present time?"

Bill smiled and said, "That's an easy one, the United States and China."

The Apostle followed with, "Do they both have nuclear weapons that could decimate the Earth?"

"Absolutely," replied Bill.

"Then don't you think you should all tread carefully as you plan for your retaliation? It would be best if they never knew you had foiled their plans so completely. One final question. Are you aware of recent upgrades to *Fujian?* They have replaced the steam powerplants with two state of the art nuclear reactors, similar to the set up on the American aircraft carrier, *USS Gerald R. Ford.* They have also upgraded their electromechanical aircraft launch systems. You might want to consider these features as you plan your attack. Good luck to you all."

With his closing comment, The Apostle vanished from our bubble.

### Let The Games Begin—Joshua

We took The Apostle's comments to heart. With Pearl on our team, we had the world's most renowned nuclear physicist. We asked her if she could shut down *Fujian's* nuclear reactors so they would never be usable again. Her initial comment was a little disconcerting. "I'm not sure. My expertise is really fusion reactors, not fission reactors which are used in submarines and aircraft carriers. What do you want me to do?"

"Well first of all, let me tell you what we don't want you to do," I answered wearily. "We don't want you to cause them to explode like an atomic bomb. We also don't want you to make them leak deadly radiation like the Chernobyl nuclear powerplant. We just want them to stop working and never be able to work again."

"Oh, is that all?" she replied sarcastically. "The only way to make that happen is to get rid of the uranium. That should be a piece of cake."

"Really?" asked Caleb's avatar.

"Of course not, dufus," answered Chanlina's avatar. "But maybe we could change the uranium into something else."

"You can do that?" Simone asked.

"Like turning lead into gold?" ask Joey, "I thought that was just a myth."

Bill added, "Hey, Alvin Maker turned iron into gold. If he could do it, why couldn't we?"

"Who the hell is Alvin Maker?" questioned Joey. "Are you making this up?"

"No man, Alvin Maker was a character in a book written by Orson Scott Card," answered Bill. "I didn't make it up, Card did."

"Enough of this crap!" shouted Chanlina. "Caleb and I should check out the *Fujian* reactor to see if this is possible. I know a few ancient spirits who claim to be able to do the lead-into-gold trick. I want to see if they really have that ability or are just blowing smoke."

### Lead Into Gold, How About Uranium Into Lead?—Chanlina

Caleb felt he should lead the meeting with the ancient spirit since he had more afterlife experience. I told him I would lead since I had been human almost two hundred years longer than him and had more contact with the ancient spirits. He pouted a bit, or at least his avatar did, before he acquiesced. To throw him a bone, I asked him to join me at the meeting.

Working through The Apostle, he put us in contact with a very old spirit who specialized in doing the very thing we were interested in. He took the time to also give us some information he thought we might not know about the spirit world.

"There are several types of spirits who make up the spirit world," began The Apostle. "First, there are spirits like Caleb who are bonded to a related human being. There are also standalone spirits like Chanlina, whose interactions are mostly limited to other spirits. However, I can interact with a lot of humans and several spirits. Most spirits are generalists; they know a small amount about a lot of different things. Fortunately, their knowledge grows over time and various interests. The other category are specialists. They know an incredible amount of detail regarding very few things."

The specialist The Apostle introduced us to was an expert in nuclear physics, both in the human world as well as the spirit world. He called himself the Wizard which Caleb and I found very amusing. The Wizard was only capable of interacting with other spirits.

We met in a standard bubble with our normal avatars, fully dressed, I might add. The ancient spirit wore a long purple robe with a hood that covered most of his gray hair, which flowed into a long gray beard that in turn covered most of his face. He also had a very large, mystical gold necklace imbedded with bright green emeralds and held a knurled wooden staff that reached above his head. Combined, it all gave him a very regal appearance. Or maybe he was truly a wizard in his human existence and emulated it as a spirit.

"How may I help you?" he asked in a deep, gravelly voice.

I posed the question, "Is it possible to change uranium into lead?"

His response was unexpected, "Why do you want to go to the trouble of changing uranium into some other non-radioactive metal? It would be easier to convert uranium 238 or plutonium 239 into an isotope which is not radioactive. Or, you could wait for it to decay."

"How long would it take for those two radioactive materials to decay?" asked Caleb.

"Plutonium has a half-life of 24,000 years, while uranium takes 4.5 billion years to decay," said the spirit jovially.

"That's not helping," replied Chanlina as she glared at him. "We need something that we can use quickly and can't be reversed. How would we go about converting uranium or plutonium into a non-radioactive material?"

He answered, "I assume it would be very similar to how they transformed uranium into plutonium, with an atom smasher. By the way, what type of application are you looking at?"

Caleb answered, "The powerplant for an aircraft carrier."

"Why didn't you tell me that in the beginning?" He asked, with annoyance in his voice. "Uranium-238 and plutonium-239 are used for weapons. Reactor powerplants for ground-based power and ships use a different isotope, uranium-235. The fuel pellets for ground based reactors are typically three percent U-235; for ships they would be HEU, for High Energy Uranium. It would contain twenty percent U-235."

"What's the half-life of U-235?" asked Chanlina.

"Only 700 million years!" he replied with a smile. "However, if you can convert it to U-237, it has a half-life of six days. Does that help?"

"Yes, but we don't have access to an atom smasher," I said, then asked, "Do you know of an alternate approach?"

"Of course," he answered, but said nothing more.

We looked at him for a few seconds before Caleb got frustrated and asked, "Could you tell us what that might be and how to use it?"

"I call it my doodle bug, but you can't use it," he replied.

"Why not?" I asked.

"Because it's mine and no one, neither human nor spirit, knows how it works. It's proprietary, a carryover from when I was a human being in King Arthur's court."

We were both speechless for a few beats before Caleb asked, "So your human name was Merlin?"

"Perhaps," he replied with a smile. "Or maybe I'm just messing with you."

We assumed the latter explanation. "Could you be persuaded to make your … your doodle bug convert the U-235 in the aircraft carrier's reactor to U-237?" I asked with as much politeness and decorum as I could muster.

"Of course, but why don't I convert it to gold?" he mused." I bet that will open a few Chinese eyes."

"Let's just stick with U-237," I replied.

"I wouldn't recommend it," said the Wizard. "I forgot to mention that once U-235 is converted to U-237 it's rather unstable and beta decays into Neptunium-237 which is very high in radiotoxicity. In other words, it becomes lethal and results in a very painful death.

I looked over at Caleb and saw him shaking his head in frustration, then I turned back to the Wizard and said, "In that case, we'll settle for gold."

"Gold would be too obvious," countered Caleb. "Remember, this shouldn't point back at us. It would be better if the Wizard changed the uranium to lead."

"That's so mundane, but if that is your final decision, I will concur," said the Wizard, with a touch of disappointment in his voice. "When do you want me to make this happen?"

"How long will it take to make the conversion?" I asked.

"Let's see," he murmured to himself. "A hundred kilos of uranium, I have to get by the shielding, so on and so forth, my best guess would be around…" he paused briefly and closed his eyes as if he was lost in thought trying to come up with a difficult solution. When he resumed, he said, "five to ten…" He paused again and stared at us with a Cheshire Cat smile.

"Come on, man," said Caleb. "Don't keep us in suspense. Is it hours, days, weeks?"

"I was thinking more like nanoseconds."

## The Next Step—Pearl

I have to admit, I was mildly miffed when Chanlina briefed us about what would be done to *Fujian's* reactor. After all, I do have a PhD in nuclear physics and my expertise is in fusion reactors, however I'm still knowledgeable enough in the fission reactors. It sounded like the Wizard spirit was some kind of nut case, and if I were there, I could have helped the discussion along and hopefully bypassed some of his messing around. I was nevertheless amused when he implied that he was Merlin and a close friend of King Arthur.

I don't doubt the Wizard spirit has the ability to almost instantly turn U-235 into lead. My concern is what will be the negative fallout of the conversion. The atomic weight of the uranium is 235 compared to the atomic weight of lead is 207. It means the Wizard's doodle bug has to strip away 28 pieces of subatomic particles from each uranium atom. That is known as fission, and fission releases energy. It could be a lot of energy, perhaps enough energy to destroy the aircraft carrier, or possibly even the entire armada.

I approached Joshua to explain my concern and he contacted The Apostle who in turn set up a second meeting with Caleb, Chanlina and the Wizard. Joshua decided to join us. Since we were all still in the bubble, or an extension of it, *Fujian* wasn't going anywhere. We could take our time to ensure we weren't going to start WWIII.

The meeting was set in an adjacent bubble for the sake of privacy. The rest of the team was busy going about gathering as much information as they could on the Chinese armada, with special emphasis on the aircraft carrier.

Pham, Mark, Simone, Joey and Bill were each assigned specific ships and studied how they were positioned in the armada. Most of the aircraft had returned to either the airbase at Xiamen or landed aboard the aircraft carrier. Two Chinese recon drones were the only things flying with the exception of our cloaked War Wagon hovering directly above *Fujian*. From our perspective, outside the bubble, time stood still.

Someone had set up a separate bubble for Sarge to play in. It was a forest setting with a wide variety of wild animal avatars. He was having the time of his life. When he caught one avatar and bit down on it, the avatar would vanish completely for a moment, then reappear somewhere close by and the game would repeat until Sarge was totally fatigued. Then all the animals disappeared until he was ready to go again. One or more of us would stop in to visit Sarge during one of his rest periods to feed and play with him. Mark would usually visit a couple times a day.

Inside the bubble it was always a bright sunny day, outside the bubble it was always 1300 hours.

We set a time for the meeting to begin, 0900 hours bubble time. Everyone was there including the Wizard. A large, round picnic table materialized with the Wizard sitting in one of the chairs, smacking his lips as he gestured to the rest of us. "Please take a seat, I'll be with you in a moment. It's not often I get to eat a delicious meal."

His avatar became a blur as he finished off his food in record time, wiped off his mouth and hands on the napkin and returned to normal bubble speed. He smiled warmly at all of us and said, "It so good to see you again so soon. And this time you've brought reinforcement spirits. I don't believe we've met."

"My name is Joshua Brown and this is Pearl Intelligent. She has a PhD in nuclear physics from Cal Tech and is the creator of the first small cold fusion reactor."

I watched the Wizard carefully as Joshua introduced me. Both Caleb and Chanlina watched him as well to see how he would react to me being a human and not a spirit. At least, not yet.

When he realized some of us were humans, he stood abruptly, knocking his chair to the ground behind him. "I'm not permitted to speak with humans. Why… What are you doing? I could be banned from bubbles, I could lose my existence. I must leave immediately," he managed to squeak out as he continued to back away from the table.

Before he could disappear, Chanlina grabbed one of his arms and Caleb took the other. "Relax Wizard," said Chanlina in a soothing voice. "This meeting has been approved by the highest level of spirits. Your existence is secure. Dr. Pearl has a few questions for you. Once you answer them this meeting is over."

I could see him start to relax as Chanlina continued to reassure him everything was going to be all right. Caleb picked up his chair and guided him to it. He gingerly sat down, avoiding looking at me or Joshua. In a low voice he said, "Ask your questions, Dr. Pearl. I will do my best to answer them."

"Can you tell us how your doodle bug works?" I asked.

He waited a moment before answering. We weren't prepared for what he was about to say. "I really don't know. Not for sure anyway." He paused again then added, "May I give you some background information?"

I was too shocked to say anything. Joshua took the lead and said, "Certainly Wizard, take your time and share your background with us."

He nodded with the smallest of smiles. "Several hundred years ago when I was a coal miner in what is now Pennsylvania, I was searching one of the numerous tunnels looking for a new vein to mine. I was pretty far removed from the rest of the miners when I came across something strange. It was embedded under a piece of rock I'd just chipped from the tunnel wall.

"It looked like a nugget of greenish rock that was slowly pulsating. It was about the size of my fist and it reminded me of a beating heart. I used the tip of my pick to pry it from the wall and cleaned off the debris.

"I could feel it pulsing in my hand, and it felt good. I'd turned to walk back to the rest of my gang to show them what I found when a tingling feeling that started at the tip of my ring finger that quickly spread up my arm and into the rest of my body. It wasn't painful, in fact it was almost a pleasant feeling.

"When it reached my head, I swear it began talking to me. I couldn't exactly hear a voice *per se,* but something seemed to suggest to me to keep this find a secret from everyone. It explained if I complied with its wishes, I would become a rich and powerful creature.

"I can tell by the expressions on your faces you think what I just told you is some kind of fabrication. I promise I'm telling you the absolute truth. Let me prove it to you."

He reached into a pocket of his robe and pulled out a small round box. Inside was a heart shaped, translucent, green stone. A soft light emanated from its center, pulsing about seventy beats per minute.

He removed the stone from the box, sat it in the middle of the table, and said to us, "Ladies and gentlemen, let me introduce you to my doodle bug. Feel free to touch it if you wish. Let it tell you what it can do."

No one made a move to touch the doodle bug. We all sat with our hands in our laps staring at the pulsating stone.

"I forgot to mention, once I walked out of the mine, I never returned. I became famous, rich and powerful, just as the nugget promised. I had no idea if it was a living organism or some type of construct built by an alien race. What I do know is it bonded with me almost immediately. As long as I was within a few feet of it, we were connected. When I was killed in a train accident, it died too."

He closed his eyes for a moment, pausing to catch his breath. "The good news was, its spirit remained bonded to me. In our world, it would be like a spirit bonded to a spirit."

He leaned back in his chair and said, "Dr Pearl, please direct your questions to the doodle bug's avatar. It will answer you truthfully. It never lies; I don't think it is capable of lying."

I stared at the pulsating green stone and asked, "Doodle bug, how can you change uranium-235 into lead without causing a nuclear explosion?"

It replied immediately, "A worthy question Dr. Pearl."

The doodle bug's voice was soft, but easy to hear. I detected no accent. I couldn't tell if it was a male or female voice. Before I could speak, it responded, "I can change my voice to whatever you prefer, Doctor." It said again in a voice that started as a deep baritone and moved up the scale to a high soprano. "Just tell me what you prefer."

"Your initial voice would be fine, I would like all of us to hear what you have to say."

"Very well, let me begin. I was created to be a problem solver. The problem you presented and the solution you required is relatively simple. I would solve the problem by approaching the nuclear core of the reactor and change the composition of uranium-235 into lead by rearranging the atomic structure of each atom. This would be similar to splitting the U-235 atoms in a fission reactor. If not controlled, it would lead to a catastrophic explosion. To keep that from occurring, I will act like control rods used to control the heat generated by the fission reaction of the uranium. I will absorb the stray subatomic particles, thereby prohibiting a nuclear explosion."

"What do you do with all the subatomic particles?" I asked.

"I transition them to another dimension where they can be safely dispersed. That dimension contains no life forms and never will. It is used as a dumping ground for entropy."

Joshua spoke up. "I'm afraid you lost me when you mentioned other dimensions and entropy."

"Are you familiar with n-dimensional physics?"

"I have no idea what you are talking about," answered Joshua.

"I do," I answered. "I always thought it was an abstract mathematical concept rather than a reality."

"Then I'm afraid I cannot explain any further. I hope I can ameliorate your concerns by saying I have done what you have asked hundreds of times before. I have never had any problem with changing one metal into another. You will either have to trust me or find another solution to your problem."

# CHAPTER 15
# PAYBACK IS A BITCH

### Decision Making Time—Simone

We met in the main bubble after the Wizard and his doodle bug had departed. It was lunch time and we sat around a large table that could have been a buffet there was so much variety of food. From soup to nuts, pastas, salads and a dozen different types of sandwiches. Whoever manages these bubbles does a great job of meeting all our needs. Oh, I forgot to mention they served us drinks too, nothing alcoholic at lunch except beer, but a wide variety of teas, coffees, soft drinks and water.

A standing rule was, whenever possible, we didn't discuss our missions while we ate. The avatars of Chanlina and Caleb always joined us for our meals. A few of us were surprised the avatars could eat, drink and enjoy all other bodily functions. Chanlina told me in private that avatar sex was better than when she was human. My face flushed with second-hand embarrassment. That was entirely too much information.

When lunch was over, we got down to business.

As a service avatar cleared away our dishes, Joshua went first. "I'd like to get a debrief on what you found out about *Fujian*."

"Let me give a quick overview to bring everyone up to speed," began Pham. "The armada consists of the *Fujian* aircraft carrier, three guided missile cruisers, an assortment of five destroyers and frigates and one nuclear submarine. They also have two recon drones circling the ships nonstop night and day. One of them flies at 2,000 feet altitude, the other at 3,000 feet. Our perspective has them frozen in time so we can't identify the flight patterns.

"They're presumably searching for the War Wagon which is situated directly above *Fujian* at 5,000 feet and remains cloaked. The AI computers are controlling the Wagon and it's not emitting any electromagnetic signals. At the time we froze reality, all the ships were at battle stations on high alert. Also, there were no other ships or aircraft within range of our surveillance equipment or spy satellites. It's just them and us. Of course that could change quickly once everyone is back in real time."

Mark looked at Caleb's avatar and said to the team, "Caleb did a quick but thorough check of the carrier before he broke out to the meeting with the Wizard. Tell them what you found out."

Caleb was still nursing a beer. He set the bottle down and replied, "The *Fujian* is the newest and most advanced of the four Chinese carriers. Only *Fujian* is nuclear powered. The upgrade to nuclear reactors has put them on a par with the American carrier, *USS Gerald R. Ford*. Like *Ford*, they also have two separate reactors aboard the ship which supply all the power needs. I believe if we somehow shut those reactors down, the carrier will be dead in the water.

"Because their catapults are electromechanical, they will be shut down as well. That means none of the aircraft aboard the ship will be able to launch, with the exception of the three helicopters they have in their aircraft inventory.

"The entire fleet of remaining aircraft are now tied down on the flight deck. The hangar deck is totally empty of any aircraft. That deck was turned into a temporary bubble generator and transporter. It has not yet been taken down."

Joshua broke in. "If the ship has no electrical power at all, how will that impact the crew? Remember, the arbiter told us they would not approve of any plan that could result in the loss of human lives."

Mark spoke up to address Joshua's concerns. "When the flow of electricity is shut down, everything stops. No lights, no ventilation fan, no juice to power equipment or to launch onboard weapons. They won't even be able to drop or weigh their anchors. However they do have battery powered emergency lights in all the hallways and crew quarters. They also have six gas turbine-powered electric generators that can produce very limited energy. Certainly, they would have enough to power up their ship-to-ship communication systems and contact all the other ships in the armada.

"If I were the captain, I would have most of the ship's 5,000 crewmen taken aboard the other ships in the armada. I would keep a skeleton crew aboard to guard the ship but send the others home. It would take less than five hours to reach the navy seaport at Xiamen. I'd also radio the base commander and request backup and ocean-going tugs to pull the carrier to shore.

"I'm not saying nobody will die, but if they follow normal procedures, I don't see why they can't get through this emergency without loss of crewmen."

"Okay," Joshua replied. "Good answer, Mark. I think the arbiter would accept your answers."

Josh paused for a moment then asked a second question. "If the Wizard's doodle bug is successful in turning *Fujian's* reactor fuel from uranium to lead, why don't we also use it on the nuclear sub?"

I stepped in to add my two cents. "I don't think that would be a good idea."

"Why not?" asked Joshua.

"*Fujian* has been operational with the reactors for only a few months. It's likely to take months, perhaps years, to determine the uranium is now lead. On the other hand, their nuclear sub has similar but smaller reactors. Joey, you were the one covering the submarine. What can you tell us about it?"

Joey tapped a few places on his iPad and a picture of a submarine appeared on the big flat panel monitor floating in the air to one side of the table. "This is the submarine traveling with the armada. It's a type 093A Shang-II class nuclear powered attack submarine and is considered one of the best attack subs in the world. It's been operational for almost two decades.

"The sub has two nuclear reactors in tandem in the middle of the boat. They both use uranium-235 for fuel. No surprise there. It is supposed to be able to do 35 knots submerged. It is equipped with advanced acoustic stealth technology which makes it almost impossible to detect with traditional sonar.

"It carries 22 torpedoes launched from six forward tubes. There are no rear tubes. They recently added a vertical launch system located behind the sail for launching supersonic anti-ship/land attack cruise missiles. They also carry subsonic anti-ship missiles, a couple of different types of underwater torpedoes, and rocket propelled bottom mines.

"The sub has a crew of one hundred and a very different command structure. There are actually two captains in command. One is the military commander; the other is the political commissar who is not military. Supposedly, they have equal authority but when they disagree the commissar can override the military leader."

"That's pretty impressive," added Joshua. "How many 093A subs do they have?"

"Counting this one, there are four in operation with two others in dry dock for upgrades," replied Joey after quickly checking his iPad.

Joshua turned to me and asked, "Okay, Simone, why do you think we shouldn't turn the sub's uranium into lead?"

I looked over at Josh and answered, "Since *Fujian* has only been operational with its two reactors for a few months, they might accept the idea that it was due to some kind of unknown malfunction in the reactor. However, when two nuclear powered ships in the same armada seem to have similar malfunctions, they might smell a rat, especially when the sub has been operational for more than twenty years without any problems."

Joshua looked around at the rest of the team and said, "That's Simone's opinion. What about the rest of you?"

Agent Hong was the first to reply. "If we shut down the nuke reactors on the sub, it's more likely many of the crew members will die. First of all, it's very unlikely both reactors would shut down at the same time and secondly, the sub has no backup power sources. If it's submerged, it's never going to resurface, which will result in the deaths of the entire crew.

"We're in an area where the ocean is very deep. Based on the data I have, without the reactors to provide power, the sub won't be able to maneuver. It won't be able to blow the ballast tanks, which will cause the ship to sink. In this part of the ocean the sub will sink below its crush depth. The sub will implode and all hands will die. I'm told the arbiter will not permit any action by a spirit that is likely to cause the death of a human being."

"How about if the sub's on the surface when the reactors shut down?" asked Joshua, playing Devil's advocate.

"As soon as *Fujian* declares an emergency, the sub will submerge and began searching for bandits," Hong answered.

Chanlina's avatar suggested, "Let's take out the sub first, then go after the carrier."

I was the last to speak up. "We still have the problem with two nuclear power ships shutting down at the same time."

Joshua looked around at each of us and asked, "Any final questions, comments, concerns?" When nobody spoke up, he added, "Thank you all for your input. It was obvious you spent a lot of time researching this issue. As team leader, I'm the one to make the decision." He paused for a moment then closed with, "We will limit our attack to the carrier. If the arbiter approves our plan, we will move forward as soon as possible. Caleb and Chanlina, I want you on the bridge of *Fujian* to provide feedback on how the two captains of the ship respond to having their nukes shut down."

The plan was approved. The Wizard was contacted and he agreed to have his doodle bug turn the uranium into lead. We would go back to real time at 0900 hours ship's time the next morning. At 0905 hours, Caleb's and Chanlina's spirits transported to the bridge of the carrier. At 0910 hours, all hell broke loose.

### The Bridge Over Troubled Waters—Caleb

Chanlina and I transported to the bridge of *Fujian* promptly at 0905 hours. Our spirits took a quick look at the bridge crew and easily spotted the navy captain and the political commissar. They were both dressed in navy blue uniforms with enough gold braid to pay the national debt. Each sat in large, comfortable captain's chairs about ten feet apart. Each had their own yeoman bringing them morning tea. They seemed to be ignoring each other as they sipped their tea and scanned the other armada ships through large tinted windows.

The crew went about their duties like precision clockwork. At 0910 hours, things changed abruptly. They had been cruising at a comfortable 20 knots in the middle of the armada when the large numerical chronometer hit the magic number.

There were two seconds worth of flashing red lights and alarm klaxons, then everything went dark. The morning sun was at their back and provided meager illumination, leaving the bridge in murky shadows. At the same instant, every piece of electronic equipment shut down simultaneously. For a brief instant, there was total silence. It was interrupted by absolute chaos. The bridge crew was running back and forth, yelling and screaming, trying to determine what had shut their equipment down. It brought to mind a scene of a Chinese fire drill I had seen in a movie many years ago.

The ship's navy captain was out of his chair in a flash, attempting to give orders for his people to settle down. However, the political commissar spilled his hot tea into his lap and jumped up screaming in pain. His yeoman ran to his aide, but slipped in a puddle of tea, lost his balance, and crashed into a nearby crew member.

A few seconds later, the battery powered emergency lights came on, things began to calm down. The commissar's yeoman managed to get to his feet and helped get him to his quarters at the back of the bridge. He left his boss lying in bed, moaning in pain while he attempted to contact a medic to attend to the tea burns. Unfortunately, he couldn't get through. All the lines were dead.

He quickly ran to the naval captain and said in Mandarin, "Captain Liu, the ship's communications system is not working. I need a doctor for the commissar. What should I do?"

The captain stopped his discussion with his subordinate officers and turned to the yeoman. "Is something wrong with the commissar?"

he asked. I was surprised he would stop giving orders to his officers to check on the commissar.

Chanlina was reading my thoughts. She thought to me, *The captain needs to stay in the good graces with the commissar. It must be a top priority to make sure he's not seriously injured.*

The captain told the yeoman to go to the ship's medical facility and bring back a doctor to examine the commissar. The medical facility was several decks below the bridge and about a hundred meters aft. The yeoman immediately ran through an open hatch and down a passage way to the nearest ladder.

The captain turned back to his first officer. "We need to find out what happened as quickly as possible. The power is off on the bridge and we cannot communicate with the rest of the ship. Did you attempt to get the emergency power system up and running?"

"Of course, captain. It was the first thing I tried," answered the first officer. "Nothing happened when I pushed the start switch."

"Get one of the petty officers to accompany you to manually get those gas turbines back up and operational. Perhaps, if we can get them generating electricity, we can get our com system functioning again."

The first officer left in a hurry and the captain turned to other priorities. Fifteen minutes later, the bridge lights came on and all of the ship's bridge electronics began to reboot. When the ship's com system was functioning again, he sent an all-hands message to the ship ordering the status of all the ship's systems. Before he could finish his message, several incoming calls were being made by most of the ships in the armada.

He punched up the button on the com system to make contact with the captain of one of the cruisers. "Captain Liu are you aware you are slowing down? I believe your propulsion system is no longer functioning. If that is true, we calculate you will be dead in the water after several hours. If you cannot get your power system operational within that time, you may begin to drift with the current. Please let us know if we can be of service."

"Thank you, Captain Wang. Thank you for informing me we have lost propulsion. It appears I will need the assistance of many of the ships in the armada. I will get back with you soon. Please be on standby ready to assist."

Captain Liu stood motionless for several minutes after the cruiser's captain disconnected. I could tell by looking at his wide eyes and clenched jaw that he was stunned and had no idea what to do next. He knew the emergency power generators would not be able to supply the power needed to move the ship. If I were in his shoes, I'd be planning the best way to abandon ship.

Instead, the captain seemed to snap out of his reverie, grabbed the handset and contacted the commander responsible for the nuclear propulsion system. "Commander Zhang, what is the status of our propulsion system? I was informed by one of the cruiser captains our propulsion system is no longer operational. Was he correct?"

The commander replied, "I'm afraid he was correct Captain. Both our propulsion units are no longer functioning."

"What part of the systems are causing this problem?" the captain asked, fully aware there were numerous subsystems required to work correctly in order to get his ship moving again.

"We determined the problem is with the nuclear reactors. Looking at our data monitoring system, the fission reactors are no longer functioning. In less than a second, the reactors went from the desired setting just like it had been doing when we set sail for Xiamen ten hours ago, then they dropped to zero. The data indicated the fuel was no longer radioactive. We pulled the fuel rods completely out of the nuclear material, but to no avail. Neither reactor is producing any heat. I'm sorry to report, but I have no idea how to reverse this situation."

As soon as he disconnected from the power system commander, he received another critical message. "All ventilation systems are inactive, almost all of the crew are finding it increasingly warm and very difficult to breathe. It's worse on the lower decks. What are your orders sir?"

He punched the button for the ship-wide PA system. "All hands, this is your captain speaking. All crew members, I repeat, all crew members are to abandon your stations and form up on the flight deck. You are to move in an orderly manner with the crew from the lower decks to leave first. Follow the orders of your officers. That is all."

While I was tracking the ship's naval captain, Chanlina had been following the political commissar as he was removed to his quarters. Apparently, the tea was very hot, enough to be scalding. She had used her spirit powers to raise the temperature of the tea to boiling just before she made sure the yeoman dumped the entire cup of tea into his boss's lap.

### Damage To The Political Commissar—Chanlina

I followed as the yeoman helped the commissar into his quarters on the starboard side, behind the bridge. I watched intently as he removed the man's pants and underwear and had him lie on his bed. I noticed it wasn't the standard issue bunk bed the rest of sailors slept on; it was queen-sized and deep with a Chinese label.

When the yeoman ran into the small bathroom adjacent to his quarters to fetch a washcloth, I inspected the damaged area. His entire groin was bright red. I thought I detected a few heat blisters on his most delicate parts.

The yeoman returned with the washcloth dripping cool water. He took great care to lay the cloth on the affected area without scrubbing.

"I need pills, pain pills!" yelled the commissar. "Go get a doctor and bring him to me. Tell him to bring me his strongest pain pills. I am in great agony and may be ruined for life!"

The yeoman ran from the room as I stayed, watched the commissar moaning and groaning on his grandiose bed. After a few minutes, the suffering noises subsided and he sat up, took a bottle of water from his nightstand, and took a long swig. He laid back down and poured the rest of the water onto the washcloth covering his manhood. He seemed to be doing much better. I couldn't have that.

I looked at the soaking wet cloth and decided it was much too cool. As I continued to inspect the cloth, I heard gentle snoring sounds. I did a quick mind probe as he continued to slumber and discovered the commissar had been the one performing as the ancient spirit from the ships hangar deck. I was sorry Caleb didn't have the time to strangle the bastard. I absolutely could not tolerate letting him go without appropriate punishment.

As I gazed at the cool damp cloth, I noticed it began to rise. He was having some perverted dream. That was insufferable, so I pinned the cloth to his groin and flash fried his uplifting equipment. I got exactly what I hoped.

He sat up in agony, unable to remove the cloth. The odor of burning flesh filled the room as he fainted from the intensity of the pain.

When the yeoman arrived with the doctor in tow, they were shocked at what they saw. The cloth had slipped down onto the thick pile rug that covered the deck, exposing a well-charred portion of his body. The erect member would be erect no more. It now had a black, sooty appearance with patches of yellow and red.

As I exited the commissar's quarters, I heard the doctor yelling at the yeoman, "What happened here? You said he had some minor burns from hot tea spilled in his lap. What did you do to him, yeoman? What did you do?!!!"

### All Hands, Abandon Ship—Joshua

We watched from the War Wagon as the aircraft carrier continued to slow and the cruisers maneuvered alongside to take on the carrier's crew. We monitored the chatter between the ships and learned heavy lift helicopters were in route to assist in the evacuation. Simone suggested the choppers were probably for the officers. Chanlina's spirit was pretty sure the captain would remain on the ship until everyone else had been removed. There was a hint of humor to her thoughts. *I'm positive the political commissar will be on the first chopper. After all, he's the political leader; he'll have to debrief the Chinese leaders on why their multibillion-dollar aircraft carrier is a floating pile of junk.* She paused for a moment and when she communicated to us there was definitely a touch of laughter. *I understand the commissar needs some medical attention before he addresses the leaders. He sustained some unfortunate burns during the chaos.*

Caleb's spirit interrupted any further comments Chanlina might have been planning to share. *Chanlina! What did you do to him?*

*Not much,* she replied with a shrug. *I didn't kill him, if that's what you're worried about. At least he was alive when I left him.* She paused for a moment before sheepishly adding, *There's always a few injuries during a conflict.*

Before either of our two spirits could share any additional comments regarding the condition of the ship's commissar, Mark brought something to our attention. "The submarine was in position at the rear of the armada up until a few minutes ago. I saw her beginning to submerge. So far, the high tech scanner on the War Wagon permits us to track her, but if she decides to go deep, we may lose her."

"Can you tell us where the sub is now?" I asked.

"She's making a large circle around the armada. According to intel I gathered, that's pretty standard when something goes amiss with any ship in an armada. She's searching to see if there are any additional threats to the ships."

"Would they consider us a threat?" asked Bill.

"Absolutely," answered Mark. "But while we remain cloaked, they won't be able to detect us."

Pearl asked, "Where is the sub now?"

Mark checked the readout on the threat status monitor. "They're almost directly under us."

I did a quick check of our ride's status. Everything was in the green. I said, "I don't see any further need to remain with the armada.

We've accomplished our goal. Let's head back to more friendly waters. Pearl, do you agree?"

She nodded and said to the computer controller, "Chanlina, take us to our home base."

Chanlina responded, *Would that be at the Boeing ARL?*

"Of course not. It would be at the base named in honor of me, Pearl Harbor."

There was a mixture of laughs and groans from the team, including myself. Pham said, "Since when did you develop a sense of humor, my love?"

"I've always had one," she replied. "I felt this was the right time to bring it out."

Chanlina interrupted, *Aye aye, captain. Heading for home at your namesake base, Pearl Harbor.*

# CHAPTER 16
# FROM THE FRYING PAN INTO THE FIRE

### Heading To Pearl—Agent Joey Hong

The aircraft configuration of the War Wagon made an easy turn to the right then left the armada behind. I watched through the faux windows as we began to accelerate and climb to our cruise speed and altitude. For the first time in several weeks, I began to relax. We'd successfully completed all our mission objectives. It was time for some R & R. I reclined my seat, closed my eyes and thought about meeting up with Lili in Hawaii.

I had just dozed off when I saw the flashing red light through my eyelids and heard the warning message, "Cloaking device off line. Cloaking device…"

I opened my eyes and sat up. Joshua was shouting, "What's happening, Chanlina? We need that cloak!"

Mark shouted to the team, "Two Chinese drones are closing in!"

Pearl screamed, "Chanlina, launch our drones. Attack code A1."

There was no response from Chanlina. The enemy drones began strafing our starboard side with 30 mm machine gun fire. Our drones never launched.

Joshua, yelling loudly at Caleb to be heard over the sound of the machine gun rounds playing a tattoo on both sides of the War Wagon, demanded, "Where is Chanlina? Why isn't she responding?"

*She's here, Josh, but we're locked out. She can't hear us and we can't hear her. I think someone has disconnected her from our computers too.*

Joshua turned to Pearl. She looked stunned and Joshua had to grab her by the arm and shouted in her ear, "Get us on manual mode. We have to fight back or we're all going to die."

Pearl seemed to understand and turned to face a control panel. She quickly switched us to manual control. Then she toggled the switch to reengage the cloaking device. It didn't work. She tried again and got the same results. She moved to the flight control and weapons switches. She pushed several buttons and was met with green lights. She yelled loud enough for all of the team could hear, "We're on manual control … Pham, Mark, launch our drones and get theirs off of us."

Pearl shut off the alarm. I heard the sound of our drones being launched. They quickly took care of the Chinese drones. They weren't very well armored and our own 30 mm Gatling guns made Swiss cheese of the attackers.

It was eerily quiet. "Is everyone okay?" asked Joshua in a normal voice. "Anybody injured?"

"We're all good, boss," Mark answered; Sarge gave a reassuring bark.

"I want you and Pham to stay at the drone controls until we're out of range. Pearl, do you know how to get the cloaking device back online?"

She answered, "No. Sorry, I have no idea how it works. I just wish Chan—"

Before she could finish her sentence, the alarm went off again. WARNING, INTRUDER ALERT…WARNING INTRUDER ALERT…

All of us jumped up from our seats and began searching for intruders. Mark said a few words to Sarge who promptly came on guard, ready for action. The rest of us checked our weapons and did our best to keep them out of sight.

The warning continued as three well-armed men materialized in the rear of the compartment. They were dressed in black body armor, including what appeared to be bullet proof masks that covered their entire faces. They were armed with what looked like short-barreled machine guns used for close quarters warfare.

The soldier in the middle spoke first. "Turn off your alarm so we can converse without shouting." His English was perfect with just a hint of an accent. "Lay your weapons on the deck and step back. Do it now or you will all die."

One by one, we placed our weapons on the deck and took a step back. Joshua was the last to follow the intruder's order. He laid one of his Desert Eagles on the deck and reluctantly stepped back.

Pearl pushed a button and shut off the alarm in mid-sentence.

I spoke in Mandarin to the three men in black. "Who are you and what do you want from us? We are not responsible for your misfortune. We were only observers. Please depart from our aircraft."

The leader replied back to me, also in Mandarin. "Your Chinese has a strong American accent. We know you, all of you are responsible for what happened to our aircraft carrier."

Bill had been listening to our conversation. He understood a little Mandarin, but spoke it poorly. To take the attention of the intruders away from me, he said in broken Chinese, "Wrong you are. Lie stop. Go away!"

Two of the attackers began chuckling, but the leader yelled at Bill in English. "You stop! Your attempt at speaking Chinese offends me."

It was Simone's turn to distract them. "How do we know you're real? You could be projections—"

The lead attacker turned to Simone and asked, "How can I prove to you we are not projections?"

Before anyone had a chance to respond, his gaze shifted quickly back to Bill and he fingered the trigger of his gun. He shot two rounds straight into his chest, sending him off the deck and slamming into the bulkhead.

Pearl let out a piercing scream, momentarily drawing the attention of all three the Chinese soldiers.

In that instant, two things happened simultaneously.

Mark made a quick hand sign to Sarge who had been waiting anxiously for orders. The attack dog launched himself like a linebacker sacking a quarterback. He hit one of the attackers full-force, knocking him into the rear bulkhead and sending his weapon skittering across the deck. The impact of the blow knocked his helmet and facemask off, leaving his head unprotected. He screamed until Sarge clamped down on his throat, abruptly shutting him up, as Sarge began shaking the man's body back and forth like a giant chew toy.

While Sarge was taking care of business, Joshua reached behind his back and pulled his second Dessert Eagle from his waistband and shot the leader in the forehead, right between the eyes. His facemask offered no protection from the .50 caliber bullet that penetrated his mask and blew out the back of his head.

Before the leader had crumbled to the deck, Joshua fired two additional rounds at the last of the attackers, the first demolishing his weapon, the second blowing out his knee. The man fell to the deck screaming in pain. The force of the bullet not only ruined his knee, but it completely ripped the lower part of his leg from his thigh. Blood was pumping out of his stub. If he didn't get a tourniquet on what remained of his leg, he was going to bleed out quickly.

Simone and I hurried to see if Bill had survived the shooting. He was moaning and mumbling to himself, "This really hurts," he managed between clenched teeth. "It hurts like a mofo."

We looked for blood, but stopped searching when I touched his chest and discovered he had his body armor on under his shirt. "Get up slacker, you aren't wounded."

"What ju mean I ain't wounded. My pride be wounded, dat man-in-black he done dissed my Chinese speakin'."

I helped him to his feet and sat him down in a chair. "I'm really glad you had your body armor on, partner. I don't know what I'd do without you."

"Yeah, who gonna buy you donuts," he said with a smile.

When Simone realized Bill wasn't wounded, she quickly got a med kit and tended to the disabled soldier. She squatted down in a pool of the man's blood, Joshua leaning over her shoulder as she applied the tourniquet to his injured leg. "Do you think he'll survive?" he asked.

"Hard to say," she answered as she gave the man a shot of morphine. "He's lost a lot of blood."

Joshua sounded worried as he said, "I really need to question him. I need to find out how they shut down our cloaking device, which ship they came from, how they managed to get aboard, and a million other things that are eating at me."

Just as Simone was finishing up, the alarm sounded again: WARNING, INTRUDER ALERT…

Pearl got up and walked to the manual control panel to cancel the alert. As she pushed the button, she said to no one in particular, "We're done with the intruders, so just shut the hell up."

A fourth intruder materialized behind her. He grabbed her around the waist as she began screaming, attempting to break free. Pham tried to stop him, but the new intruder shot him with his pistol, pushed a button on his belt and they both disappeared.

The whole abduction took ten seconds, maybe fifteen. Pham was writhing on the deck where Pearl had been standing. Simone hurried from the one-legged soldier to Pham and began checking out his wounds. The rest of us were so stunned, we just stayed frozen. This can't be happening. What do we do now?

### Next Steps—Caleb

Joshua approached the one-legged soldier and started his questioning. The morphine shot reduced most of the pain in his leg, allowing him to remain conscious. We quickly found out he spoke no English.

Joshua decided to have Agent Hong be our link to the soldier. I was designated to be the lie detector. We operated as a version of good cop, bad cop.

"What is your name, soldier?" Joey asked in a friendly voice.

"I have no name for you," he replied, with a feeble attempt at a sneer.

I sent a brief shot of pain through his damaged leg and noticed him trying to hide a wince. Just one of my many spirit talents.

'Did that hurt a little?" asked Hong. "Every time you don't answer one of my questions or lie to me you will feel pain. If you refuse to answer, we will remove the tourniquet and throw you out the hatch. You will certainly die, either from loss of blood, or from the impact when you strike the ocean. Do you understand?"

He nodded as I gave him another shot of pain.

"So sorry, I forgot to tell you, you must answer vocally. Let me—"

"I understand!" he said tensely. "My name is Mao. The name was selected by my father who was one of our beloved Chairman's supporters."

"Where did you come from when you came to our aircraft?"

"From my submarine," he answered immediately. Caleb confirmed he was being truthful.

Hong asked the next question. "Where did the other soldier take our captain?"

"Do you mean Pearl, the nuclear physicist?" he asked.

"Yes."

"She was taken aboard my submarine."

"How were you able to come aboard my aircraft undetected? When did you sneak aboard?"

He looked confused by my question. "We didn't sneak aboard, we transported from our submarine inside your aircraft as soon as we were able to neutralize your hiding device."

"That can't be true," interjected Mark. "We're at least fifty nautical miles from the armada by now. I'm still able to track the submarine as the boat makes surveillance passes around the ships while *Fujian's* crew are being taken aboard the others."

"What's our current speed and altitude?" asked Joshua.

"We haven't moved since our cloak went down. We're hovering at 5,000 feet."

Simone had been assisting Pham after he had been shot in the shoulder. She gave him a small dose of morphine for the pain, he looked half-stoned. He managed to whisper to Simone, who in turn passed his message on to the team. "Pham says there's no way they could transport one person ten miles, let alone four people fifty miles. He says the soldier has to be lying."

Caleb messaged all of us, *He's not lying. At least he believes what he told us is true.*

Hong repeated the information still speaking in Mandarin and waited for the soldier's response. We were all surprised when he began laughing. Hong asked him, What causes you to laugh?"

"I laugh because you don't know. I thought sure you Americans with your superior technology would have discovered us by now."

"What are you talking about?" asked Hong, an edge of concern in his voice.

The soldier looked at each of us with an expression of superiority. "The armada has two submarines. One is the 093A attack sub you know so well. Apparently, you have no knowledge of my submarine, a model you Americans call a boomer. My submarine is type 094. It carries four ICBM missiles armed with nuclear warheads. From our present location, our missiles can easily reach your West Coast.

"At the present time, my submarine is submerged directly under your aircraft, barely a mile from its poor, exposed underbelly. That's well within range of our transporting device. You were easy to find once your cloaking machine was neutralized. Once we made the proper connection, it was easy for us to transport inside of your aircraft and kidnap Dr. Pearl. She will ultimately reveal the secrets of cold fusion reactors. She will remain in China for the rest of her life."

He checked his chronograph on his right wrist. "I will be returning to my ship immediately. Unfortunately for you, your ship will be destroyed soon after I leave. All of you and your prototype War Wagon will be destroyed by a tactical nuke."

In an instant he was gone, leaving his amputated leg behind.


### We Got To Get Out Of This Place—Joshua

"I've got a visual on the boomer," reported Mark. "He's telling the truth, it's beginning to surface directly below us."

I contacted Caleb, *Can you create a bubble around the War Wagon and transport us out of here?*

He answered, *I can try, but I sure wish Chanlina could assist.*

Mark broke in, "She's on the surface, they're taking the protective shell off the VLT."

"What's the VLT?" asked Simone.

"Vertical Launch Tube," answered Mark. "They can fire a variety of missiles vertically instead of through torpedo tubes."

"Can't we manually get away from them?" Hong asked.

Joshua shook his head. "Only Pearl and Chanlina know how to fly this thing. We're sitting ducks. Caleb, how's the bubble coming?"

I responded, *No joy, Josh. All my attempts are being blocked by an unknown source.*

The next few moments were a blur. Mark shouted, "They're launching!" At the same time, Chanlina's spirit returned and took control of the computers. There wasn't enough time to escape the missile, but she rolled the aircraft on its side as the missile screamed by us before it could arm the nuclear bomb.

That was the good news. The bad news was the missile sheared off the top rotor and we began losing altitude rapidly. Chanlina rolled us back upright and began to autorotate to slow our descent. Simultaneously, she ordered the computers to morph the aircraft into its mini-submarine mode. That would normally take at least 60 seconds, we had only 10 before we hit the water hard and quickly disappeared under the surface.

We continued to sink, our human crew had to keep clearing their ears as Chanlina increased the pressure inside the boat. If she hadn't raised it, the outside water pressure would have crushed us like a beer can in a foot stomping contest.

She was able to stop the descent at 200 feet and we remained motionless for several minutes as she ran a series of diagnostics. One of the AI computers had gone belly up. Praise the Lord we still had two completely functional ones. We'd lost one of the four propulsive pods. She thought it had sheared off on impact with the water.

Another one was barely functional. Some of the external plates that provided a low drag configuration had been damaged, but none were missing.

The miraculous news was the boundary layer control system was completely intact. Without it, our surface drag wouldn't permit us to exceed 10 knots. With it, we should be able to make at least 30 knots, hopefully more. Our recon sensors were also fully functional. We located the boomer sub and it appeared to be leaving the area, heading back to join the armada.

Approximately half of our weapons were functional, most of them were small torpedoes and mines. All of us wanted to sink the boomer sub, but only after we had rescued Pearl. In order to accomplish that, we had to see if we could cautiously sneak up on the sub. There was a very real concern the boomer sub might launch its ICBMs at the West Coast of America.

So, we identified our next steps in the order of importance:

1.  See if we can catch up to the sub
2.  Rescue Pearl
3.  Stop the sub from launching an attack on America

It was time to prevent World War III.


### <u>Where Do We Go From Here?—Chanlina</u>

I thought I was dead. No, wait. I'm already dead. It would be more accurate to say, I thought my spirit was waning and would eventually wink out of existence. It was like I was encapsulated in a box with clear plastic walls. I could see Caleb through the walls but we couldn't communicate with each other. I thought the walls were slowly closing in on me.

My thoughts became incoherent until I had a vision of the War Wagon in aircraft mode being attacked by a missile from a submarine. It terrified me to think Caleb and my human friends were under attack. I had to do something quickly or they would perish. I couldn't bear the thought of letting them die.

Suddenly, I began to feel as if I was having an adrenaline rush, which was ridiculous; spirits don't have bodies, much less adrenal glands. Nevertheless, my pseudo-adrenaline rush energized me. I broke through the walls of the box and into my aircraft, took control of the computers and managed to avoid the missile from destroying us. Unfortunately, we were severely damaged. I only had a few seconds to begin morphing into the submarine configuration. We were less than halfway through the transformation before we crashed into the sea.

I desperately wanted to be with Caleb, to be in our Wonderland bubble and have our avatar bodies. I wanted to be able to embrace him, to kiss him, to be able to cry on his shoulder and hear him tell me everything was going to be all right. I pushed all those thoughts into the background. Hopefully, they would be realized later if I could keep us all from dying.

Miraculously, we did it. Not only did we survive, but we also managed to complete the transformation into the submarine configuration, albeit with considerable damage. I had the two surviving computers run a complete diagnostic evaluation of our sub. The results indicated we were intact and would be able to continue with our mission. We wouldn't be pretty, but occasionally even the ugly girl gets to dance.

I couldn't wait any longer. I contacted Caleb, froze time on the sub and spent a week in Wonderland with my husband decompressing. Praise the Lord for his mercy!

### What Do We Know &d What Do We Not?—Joshua

I was surprised to see Caleb and Chanlina so relaxed after our ordeal with the Chinese boomer sub. The rest of the team was still strung out, and with good reason. Pearl had been kidnapped, Bill and Pham had been shot and, last but certainly not least, we discovered a Chinese boomer sub may be getting ready to start a nuclear war.

While the human members of the team recovered, along with one dog, I sent the cheery spirits to recon the boomer. I wanted to find out how Pearl was being treated by the Chinese. In less than an hour they returned to share what they'd found out.

Caleb began the briefing with some good news. *First of all, Pearl is being treated well. She's sharing quarters with two female officers. One of them speaks passable English and they're making sure to treat Pearl like a VIP. One interesting fact, the English speaking officer attempted to console Pearl on the loss of her boyfriend and all the other members of her team. Apparently, they believe the aircraft crashed into the ocean with no survivors.*

Pham interrupted, "Pearl thinks we're all dead. She saw me get shot. She might think the man who captured her killed me."

Pham was almost on the verge of tears. I could only image the trauma he was experiencing, both physical and emotional. Chanlina came to his rescue. *Don't worry, Pham. We were able to reassure her you survived the shooting. We told her all of us are alive and planning to rescue her as soon as possible.*

Pham nodded and turned his head away from us, as tears of relief flooded from his eyes.

*We also checked out several of the sub's crew, including the captain and the political commissar,* Caleb continued. *No one mentioned anything about attacking America. They were all very excited about having captured Pearl and couldn't wait to get her to China. They seem convinced she would share her knowledge of cold fusion reactors. Everyone seemed to be patting themselves on the back for a very successful mission.*

Caleb paused for a moment. I could tell there was some bad news coming. *While we were aboard, the commissar did an all-hands report to the crew. He announced one of their leaders from the Tribuna sent them a letter of commendation for the entire ship. The four men who were involved in the capture of Pearl would get hero badges for their efforts. He went on to say they were ordered to return to Xiamen at the best possible speed. Chanlina found out that was 40 knots. If we want to catch up with their sub and rescue Pearl, we're going to have to find a way to slow them down.*

### How Fast Can We Go?—Simone

Our propulsion system had been off line while we preformed the diagnostic tests. Once Chanlina had checked the results, she spoke to us through the AI computers. "Let me give you a short overview of what's going to happen. First, everyone needs to strap in, that includes Pham, Bill and Sarge. Next, I will bring the propulsion system to standby. Fortunately, the boundary layer control unit still functions. I can manually adjust it as needed to optimize our speed. This will be a check run; however, we will be trailing the boomer sub to maintain contact as best we can. Unless there are any questions, let's get started."

There weren't any. "Let her rip, Chanlina," I shouted.

"Aye aye, Captain," she replied. "Ripping now."

We could feel the drive system vibrate slightly as we inched forward. As we accelerated, our mini sub twitched a little, but Chanlina was making manual corrections to keep us on our desired heading. After a few minutes, she gave us a brief status report. "Ten knots, on course, still accelerating." A few minutes later, "15 knots, getting a little ragged." We could feel a vibration throughout the ship getting louder every second. When she hit 20 knots, there was a loud banging noise as the ship skewed abruptly to port. Chanlina quickly throttled back and let the sub glide to a stop.

Mark unbelted and moved to a monitor, scanning the underside of the ship. "Looks like we lost another propulsion pod. We've only got two left, both at our aft end."

Caleb did a quick visual at the underbelly and reported, *Yeah, it doesn't look good. At best we can make 10 to 15 knots. We need to find another way to stop the boomer and get Pearl back.*

### What Are Our Options?—Joshua

We brainstormed a boat-load of options, pun intended. I told them to shout out every idea they could think of for rescuing Pearl, even the dumb ones. I said we'd weed out the worst and focus on four or five of the best ones. We spent two days in bubble time settling on what we thought was the best idea. It came from Chanlina and Caleb.

They suggested a small transport bubble. Chanlina would revisit the sub in the middle of the night and check out where Pearl was quartered. If she was not being restrained or didn't have a guard on her all night long, Chanlina would create a bubble around Pearl and transport her directly to Pearl Harbor. Total real time for the mission would be about five minutes, provided the two female officers were either sleeping or on duty. Pearl probably wouldn't wake up until she was safe and sound at Pearl Harbor.

After Pearl was relocated, Chanlina would return to the War Wagon, create a bubble around Team Joshua and transport them to Pearl Harbor as well.

"What about the War Wagon?" I asked. "Do we just abandon it? Or maybe scuttle it? That's like a billion dollar investment rusting away on the bottom of the ocean. If the Chinese find out about it, you can bet your pension they'll have a scavenger team dredging the ocean floor until they find it."

I asked Caleb, "Can you create a bubble around the entire vehicle and transport it back to the Navy base?"

*Maybe,* he replied. *I need to get a hold of The Apostle. He'll know or can refer me to a spirit who could answer your question.*

"Okay, but first things first. Go get Pearl safely back to Pearl Harbor."


### Smash And Grab—Chanlina

Caleb and I made some minor adjustments to our original plan. For the first part of the mission we would both check out where Pearl was being held. I would enter the quarters to see if the two female officers were present. He would check to make sure someone didn't walk in unexpectedly.

It was 0200 hours when I quickly checked the quarters where Pearl was being kept. The entry door was locked from the outside. I assumed it was to ensure Pearl didn't go wandering about the sub. I unlocked the door, but left it closed as I drifted into the room. The room was small. As with all submarines, only the captain and the first officer were assigned comfortable quarters. On the Chinese sub, I was sure their political commissar had the biggest room.

There were three bunk beds against the bulkhead farthest from the entry door. I estimated the distance from the door to the bulkhead was about six or seven feet. Each of the beds where hinged against the bulkhead and could be folded up to give the room more floor space. To the left of the door was the head, a small bathroom with only a sink and a toilet. On the right was a desk with a computer, small light, and a very small chair.

The room was dark, the only light was in the head glowing dimly. The top bunk was empty, folded up and secured against the bulkhead. The middle bunk had a Chinese woman dressed in a T-shirt and panties. She was snoring softly.

On the bottom bunk was Pearl dressed in the same clothes she'd been wearing when she was taken. Her eyes were closed and she was whimpering. Maybe she was having a bad dream.

I thought this was going to be easy. Then Caleb thought to me, *Incoming. Be careful!*

The door slid open and a tall Chinese woman in her mid-twenties slipped into the room wrapped only in a towel. Her hair was wet, I assumed she had just finished her shower. I remembered submarines had shared showers with very stringent time restrictions. She let the towel fall to the deck while she reached up to lower the top bunk. She murmured something softly and a man came through the door and slid it shut behind him. His towel joined hers on the deck. They embraced, kissed a few times then climbed into the top bunk, being careful not to wake anyone.

Caleb's spirit joined me. *How's it going so far?*

*It was going great before the other girl and her lover boy decided to play hide the pickle,* I thought back to him. *This better not take too long.*

After ten minutes had gone by, Caleb commented silently to me, *I'm getting excited. How about you?*

*Not now, Caleb!*

A few minutes later we heard heavy breathing followed by grunts and groans and a few gasps, then silence, followed by a few giggles.

The man lightly slapped the girl's backside then carefully climbed down to the deck. He picked up his towel, wrapped it around his waist and slipped out of the room, closing the door behind him.

We waited a few minutes until we heard snoring from all three bunks. Caleb created a very small bubble that enveloped Pearl. He willed it to slide out of the bottom bunk and I quickly moved inside. My avatar popped into existence dressed in a Chinese officer's uniform just in case someone burst into the room … again.

Caleb quickly transported the bubble with Pearl and Chanlina's avatar inside and arrived at the Tripler Army Medical Center near Naval Station-Pearl Harbor. I went with them, of course. I helped move Pearl from the bubble to a bed in an empty room. She had continued to sleep through the entire escape. She was going to be in for a big surprise when she woke up.

# CHAPTER 17
# RECOVERY OF THE MINI SUB

### What To Do With The War Wagon?—Caleb

I requested a visit with The Apostle and he graciously accepted my request. Chanlina strongly suggested, almost pleaded, she also attend. She pointed out to me that now that Pearl was convalescing at the hospital along with Pham, she had the most experience handling the War Wagon. She was right and The Apostle didn't object so we ended up together with The Apostle at a standard Wonderland bubble.

The Apostle dressed our avatars in very conservative clothing, while his was dressed in a business suit with a white shirt and a red power tie. I'd never seen him dressed like that. I figured he must be going to a high-level business meeting after our visit, or had just come from one.

"Have a seat at the table," he said pleasantly, then added, "Refreshments?"

We declined.

"Then let's get to it," he said. "It's my understanding you wish to transport the remains of the War Wagon from its submerged location in the Pacific Ocean to somewhere in the continental United States. Is that correct?"

"Yes sir," I replied. "Chanlina and I, along with Joshua, suggest the War Wagon be transported to the Boeing ARL facilities."

"Why that location?" he asked.

Chanlina answered. "First, because it's a secured facility. Secondly, because all the techs who built it are the most qualified to disassemble the components and determine what can be salvaged. Thirdly, when Pearl is released from the hospital, she is the most qualified person to evaluate the condition of the cold fusion reactor. Fourthly—"

"That's enough, Chanlina," The Apostle said with a chuckle. "You had me at secondly. You're approved to move the War Wagon to Boeing ARL. Good hunting." Then he added, "Please notify everyone on the team, your government is flying out the families of Mark, Bill and Joey. They will be flying first class from Portland to Honolulu on a chartered airplane. They will be meeting up with the rest of the team later today. We've made reservations for everyone at the Hilton Hawaiian Village on Waikiki Beach for as long as they want to stay."

The Apostle departed Wonderland with a pop and the bubble dissolved quickly. Chanlina and I were at the Pearl Harbor hospital along with the rest of the team. Pham and Bill were checked out by the hospital doctors and released. Pham lied next to Pearl in her hospital bed, both smiling at each other.

When we shared the news with everyone about the families coming to visit and staying at a luxurious hotel right on the beach for as long as they wanted, there was surprise, followed by laughter and clapping. Sarge started barking and running in circles. He stopped in front of Mark and looked up expectantly. Mark leaned over, patted Sarge on the head, then told him, "Yes Sarge, Maria and Serina will be coming to visit us." The dog barked loudly and plopped on the ground in front of Mark waiting for him to rub his belly. Mark added, "Yes Sarge, I'm happy too."

We debriefed the team emphasizing The Apostle's approval. Joshua gave us our orders to recover the War Wagon and take it to Boeing ARL. He said he would contact Boeing and let them know they would be receiving the remains.

Before we left, Pearl thanked us both for extracting her from the Chinese sub. She blushed when we told her about her pseudo-roommate having sex in the bunk above her. "I can't believe I slept through that," she responded.

We said our good-byes, told them we would get together with them all in Everett, then transported to the last known location of our sub. We found it on a barge being pulled by a Chinese salvage tug heading for Xiamen.

### <u>On A Slow Boat To China—Chanlina</u>

I was really pissed off. *What I wanted to know is how they found it. All the players on the Chinese sub were sure it went to the bottom. The armada was heading for home with both subs, cruising away from where our own was submerged, a hundred feet below the surface. How in the hell did they find it so quickly, get a salvage tug to the site, haul it aboard and then head for home? That's impossible!*

Caleb attempted to calm me down. He suggested, *Maybe they have spirits we don't know about. Maybe only a few of the crew on the sub even know about spirits. You know how secretive the spirits can be. Or maybe somebody in our own government told them where to look.*

He was right, but I was still upset. *So what do we do now? We can't let the tug get to Xiamen.*

*How about we sink the barge? We lose the War Wagon, but at least the Chinese don't get it. If we're smart, the tug crew will think the wagon was too heavy for the barge.*

Caleb's suggestion perked me up. *If we're really smart, we sink the barge and once it's a couple of hundred feet below the surface, we bubble the wagon and transport it to Boeing. Caleb, my love, if I had a mouth I'd kiss you.*

He replied, *If I had a peck—*

*Don't say it! Don't even think about it until we get the payload to Boeing ARL. After that, I'm all yours, naughty boy.*


### <u>Time To Get Busy Again—Caleb</u>

I did a quick check of the tug and the barge it was towing. The ocean-going tug was huge and built for salvaging a variety of heavy items. It had a crew of eight and a gangway that extended from the aft end of the tug onto the barge. The barge had two large cranes, one positioned on the port side and the other on starboard. They were located halfway between the forward and aft end of the platform. Each crane had two operators. There were also a series of inflatable pontoons on each side of the barge to keep the deck from sinking below sea level. This was really heavy duty equipment, capable of handling the War Wagon with ease.

I thought I saw a possible weak link, actually there were three of them. They were the thick cables which attached the tug to the barge. One end of the cables was secured to the three bollards equally spaced across the boat's stern. The other ends of the cables were attached to similar bollards equally spaced across the forward end of the barge.

I was pretty sure I could "create" an accident by weakening the cables until they snapped. I didn't have to break all three; the crew might get suspicious if they all broke at once. Two would be better, especially if one of the side cables broke first, causing the middle one to snap from the increased load, which would result in the barge slewing out of control. With a little assistance from Chanlina, I was sure we could get our War Wagon to break free from its tie-downs and slide into the sea, never to be seen again by the Chinese.

The plan looked good on paper (or wherever we stored our ideas). Now it was time to see it in action. To aid us in our task, the sea began to get rough. Six foot swells added more stress to the cables. Chanlina and I combined our spirit powers to weaken the port side cable. We wanted it to look like there might be a material flaw in it. We worked on the "flaw" for several minutes and it was finally spotted by one of the crew. The tug boat captain reduced his speed, but he had to maintain enough speed to handle the tug in the now choppy sea.

We gave it one final push and the cable snapped, swinging wildly back toward the tug. It caught one of the deck hands across the chest, knocking him overboard into the sea.

Almost immediately, the second cable snapped on its own and whipped into the pilot house at the forward end of the tug, crushing whoever was inside. The boat was losing control. Less than a minute later, it was floundering in the high sea.

With only one cable remaining, the barge began to slew to starboard, being battered by the rough waves. The tie-downs designed to secure the War Wagon to the barge began to fail. One of the crane handlers who was trying to get aboard the tug was hit in the head by a tie-down bolt and fell into the ocean, swallowed up by the thrashing waves immediately.

The waves had grown to monstrous proportions now and the barge was swept up the backside of one wave, rolled over the top and came screaming down the front, building speed all the way. It reminded me of a roller coaster at an amusement park, except with a very different ending. The barge T-boned the tug. The boat broke into two pieces and sank quickly. The entire crew went with it. We watched as the barge was caught up in a whirlpool, slinging off bits and pieces of our minisub as it spun around. Eventually, the barge tipped and what remained of the War Wagon was slung off into the sea and disappeared below the waves.

We followed it down and gathered what we could, created a bubble around it and transported it directly to Boeing ARL.

We were able to meet our mission objectives. We denied the Chinese access to our prototype War Wagon. That was the good news. The bad news was we could be found guilty of killing human beings. We didn't intend for it to happen, but it did. In the legal sense, we didn't murder anybody. However, it could probably be considered manslaughter. We weren't sure if the penalty for manslaughter was as severe as murder.

There would be a hearing; we'd have to appear before the Tribunal of Spirits. If found guilty, we would be put out of existence… forever.

### Here Come Da Judge—The Apostle

The arbiter and I sat down in a secure bubble to go over the details of the case. Since he was counselor for Caleb and Chanlina, he would be the one to defend them if their case went before a Tribunal.

As was the custom, the arbiter spoke first. "Let me review the spirit laws dealing with the death of human beings, as pertains to spirit involvement. There are three classifications of human deaths. There are natural deaths, manslaughter and murder. We don't need to spend much time defining natural deaths, but for completeness I will give a few examples: old age, illness and accidents not involving spirits.

"Manslaughter involves the unintended death of a human being when a spirit is involved. If a spirit observed a human being killing another human being, it would not be charged with manslaughter. Even if the spirit could have taken actions to prevent the murder, it would not be charged. If a spirit is responsible for providing a weapon to a human being and that human being accidently or intentionally kills another human being it will be charged as an accessory to either manslaughter or murder.

"The last case concerns the two spirits operating under your authority. The information you provided me about the incident in question would indicate there was no intent to kill the crews of the tug and the barge. The fact that they intentionally caused one of the connecting cables between the tug and the barge to fail is, in my opinion, not grounds to charge them with any degree of manslaughter. If we are forced to go before a Tribunal, what I have stated will be my defense."

He paused for a moment to see if I had any questions. When I didn't respond he continued. "I feel I should warn you, the spirits representing the Chinese will push for murder charges against Caleb and Chanlina, with annihilation as their punishment. They will claim our two spirits committed cold blooded murder of eight Chinese crewmen on the tug and four crane operators on the barge. They say the murders occurred to permit them to steal the remains of an aircraft which had crashed at sea. Since the crash occurred in international waters, any abandoned vehicle can be claimed as salvage."

"That's outrageous!" I said. "If all of their sailors were killed, regardless of how it happened, they have no witnesses."

The arbiter shook his head. "They say they have a spirit witness of the murders and theft."

"How do you plan to argue against their witness?" I asked.

"Our plan is to put the avatars of Caleb and Chanlina in the witness stand separately. As you are aware, witnesses are not able to lie when in the witness stand. Unless the Chinese witness has found out a way to beat the compulsion against lying, we should be all right."

"I don't have a good feeling about this," I said warily.

"Neither do I, Apostle," the arbiter admitted. "Neither do I."

### Preliminary Hearing--Chanlina

*They said what?!!!* That was my comment when The Apostle gave us the news about a Chinese spirit witness. Caleb was too stunned to reply at first. I sensed he shifted to self-defense mode. *I think we should do a little snooping to see what they are planning.*

The Apostle would have none of it. *If you get caught trying to tamper with evidence you might as well kiss your existence good-bye. I agree we need to find out as much as we can about how they're going about this charade, but neither of you can be involved in spying. This may come as a surprise to you two, but I have a team of excellent spirit sleuths who will do just fine getting the information we require. For now, why don't you two head to Wonderland for a while. I'll contact you before the hearing and communicate what my other team finds out.*

The Apostle hurt my feelings. I mean, I was happy about his suggestion to spend time in Wonderland with my Caleb. However, I was hurt to find out he had other spirits like us, maybe even better than us. I sighed a bit then thought, oh well, life goes on … you know what I mean.

The hearing was scheduled to take place in two days. We wondered why it would take so long, but it turned out humans would be included in the hearing. I thought it would be limited to only spirits. I wasn't sure if that was a good or bad thing. I found out the humans who were allowed to attend were to be observers only. They weren't permitted to testify or talk, just watch the proceedings.

Only two humans from each side were permitted to enter the bubble and they sat behind a low wall that separated them from the spirits. Before entering, all humans were required to undergo a series of scans to prevent any type of recording equipment or weapons to be brought into the courtroom.

Joshua and Simone took their seats on the left side. On the right side representing China was a high ranking officer in the China's Navy. He was wearing an admiral's uniform. The other man was dressed all in black with dark glasses and a white cane. I assumed he was blind.

Caleb and my avatars sat at a table on the other side of the low wall. We were joined by the arbiter's avatar who would represent us. There was only one spirit avatar sitting behind the table representing China's interests. He was a large Asian man with a permanent scowl etched on his craggy face. He wore a blood red robe with a hood that covered most of his pure white hair and beard. He walked slowly with a cane to steady himself as he approached the prosecution's bench and carefully sat down.

We all stood as the avatar for the spirit judge who would hear our pleas sat down behind his bench. "Please be seated," he said. "Since this hearing involves two different countries, I have been selected to oversee this hearing. I have no affiliation with either the United States nor China, therefore I am neutral. You may address me as Judge Juan.

"I have had the chance to review the charges filed by both countries and I must clarify a few things. This is a spirit court, and as such we make no rulings regarding human beings other than their interaction with spirits. We make no rulings that deal with property rights of any kind. The only issue we will address is whether the spirits Caleb and Chanlina killed human beings in order to regain human property. Will you both take seats in the witness boxes, please?"

As our avatars walked to the two boxes, Judge Juan said, "For our human visitors, once a spirit is seated within the witness box they are unable to tell a lie. I understand that is not the case with humans."

The judge turned to me first and asked, "Chanlina, did you, or did you not, take part in murdering one or more of the human crew on the tug boat and barge?"

I replied, "No your honor, I did not murder any of the crew!"

The avatar of the Chinese spirit stood up so abruptly he knock over his chair. He slammed both fists on the table and shouted at the judge, "She's lying. Somehow, she has fooled the witness box. I demand she be retested with a new box!"

Judge Juan let him rant and rave for a few more moments. When he stopped for a moment to catch his breath, the judge interrupted with an exceptionally calm voice, "That will be quite enough of that, sir. Sit down and compose yourself or I'll have you removed."

Slowly, the man righted his chair, sat back down and said apologetically, "My apologies, Your Honor. I got carried away by the blatant lie of the Cambodian assassin."

I was furious and about to rip the man's avatar a new one when the judge raised a hand to silence me. An avatar, I assumed he was a bailiff or an aide, approached Judge Juan and whispered a message.

The judge gave an expressionless nod. "It has come to my attention there has been an error in procedure. Two days before a hearing is held, both the prosecuting spirit as well as the defense spirit are required to provide the court with their credentials. My list of spirits does not include any credentials for the prosecuting spirit. "

"My apologies, Your Honor," replied the avatar in the red robe. "The original prosecutor was suddenly taken ill. In my country I am know as The Ancient Spirit of China my given name is Chin-A. My credentials are now available for your review."

Silence hung over the bubble for what felt like an eternity as the judge read over the spirit's documents. When he finished, the judge stood and performed the deep bow required for a most ancient spirit, then added, "Your credentials are approved sir."

Caleb's avatar began laughing. He laughed so hard tears were running down his cheeks. Finally, the judge took his gavel and rapped it on his table a few times. "Silence! I will have silence in my courtroom!" He turned his stern gaze at Caleb and asked, "What do you find so humorous?"

Caleb wiped his face with his sleeve to dry his tears and said, "I'm sorry your honor, but this is not the avatar of an ancient spirit. It's not even an avatar. This is a sophisticated projection created by the Chinese and programmed to manipulate the court. We ran into a similar projection a few days ago and were able to shut it down. They are using the same approach in an attempt to sway your decision regarding us. I'm sure he would love to show you videos they fabricated that show Chanlina and I murdering the crew of the tug boat, but none of it is real. With the court's permission, may I show you what a fake he is?"

The judge nodded and Caleb walked over to the image of an ancient spirit who stood up and turned toward the judge. "Your honor this is preposterous," he said in a pleading tone. "This will prove nothing."

"Nevertheless, I will permit it," replied the judge.

Caleb stood in front of the image and was mildly surprised to see a smile forming on the projected face.

Caleb glanced at the judge who gestured for him to continue. Caleb turned back and said, "Please observe." He attempted to push his hand trough the projection's image. It was met by what appeared to be a solid body of an avatar.

Caleb took a step back, shocked at the failed test. The prosecutor stepped forward and said, "Let me show you *my* demonstration." He struck Caleb in the face with his fist, knocking him to the floor.

I was shocked. It really was an avatar, maybe even the avatar of the spirit of Chin-A, the first true emperor of China. We were doomed.

### Prepare For The Tribunal—Joshua

After the hearing, Caleb and Chanlina were overcome by a combination of fear and anger. Chanlina was deathly afraid they were going to cease to exist. At the same time, she wanted to destroy the fake Chin-A's spirit along with its avatar. She couldn't let herself believe it was the real Chin-A. The arbiter tried to point out that spirits can't kill spirits. Her response was if she were going to die again, so would the fake Chin-A.

Caleb was convinced whatever struck him was not truly an avatar. He felt it was some type of construct impersonating an avatar, therefore he wouldn't be punished if he destroyed it.

It took them a while to calm down. Judge Juan scheduled the tribunal two weeks from the hearing date. I promised them the team and I would do everything in our power to make this right. We had two weeks to find out how the Chinese had fabricated such a believable story. The worst part was Caleb and Chanlina were going to be sequestered the entire two weeks. They weren't allowed to assist us in proving their innocence.

That wasn't as bad as it appeared. Caleb had given me a blow-by-blow of what took place during the recovery of the War Wagon's remains. It wasn't just dialogue, it was visual too, in real time. Because of the way we were bonded, we could share everything in greater detail than just dialogue. It was like I was with him during the recovery of the War Wagon. I could see what he saw, feel what he felt. I knew for a fact he and Chanlina did not murder the crews. I needed to find out how to get Caleb's images of the War Wagon recovery to the Tribunal. I needed to get The Apostle's opinion.

Some of you may be wondering if Caleb shared everything with me, including his time with Chanlina in Wonderland. The answer is absolutely not!

### Planning Meeting—The Apostle

When Joshua approached me about having a visual account of the destruction of the tug, the barge and the death of the crews, I decided it would be best to share this information with our arbiter. By my way of thinking, it was one more piece of evidence to substantiate they didn't murder anyone.

I set up a private bubble for the three of us to plan how to rebut the so-called evidence that would be presented by the Chinese.

The arbiter's avatar spoke first. "Let me familiarize you with the procedures of this spirit tribunal. The tribunal will consist of three spirits, all who have extensive backgrounds in criminal spirit proceedings. This tribunal will set a new precedence. For the first time, a spirit tribunal will have representatives from America, China and a neutral country. In our case, the neutral country representative will be Judge Juan from Spain.

"There are many legal spirits who believe this should not be permitted. Human beings have allegiance to all the various countries in the world. Spirits aren't supposed to have similar allegiance. I share that position. However, higher ranking spirits than I have decided to permit this unique trial."

I wondered what possible reason could there be for making this unique exception, however, the arbiter did not offer any speculation. Instead, he moved on to outline our defense. "To the best of my extensive experience, the accuracy of the witness stand has never been challenged. When in the box, a spirit cannot lie. It's not a lie detector, it's a lie preventer. The challenge by the Chinese council is ludicrous. I doubt the American and Spanish judges will permit a replacement witness stand.

"In addition to the testimony of our two witnesses, we have visual evidence from five different spy satellites corroborating the evidence, two were from the United States, one from Australia, one from Japan and the last one from Taiwan. The Chinese also had two satellites in the area. They claim one of them had been jammed by the Americans, but the second one shows a very different set of data. This one has pictures of Caleb and Chanlina with assault rifles shooting the ship's crew members."

"Wait a minute!" interrupted Joshua incredulously. "Caleb and Chanlina are spirits. They have no bodies. Without bodies, they can't hold assault rifles. They weren't in any bubble until after the tug and barge were destroyed by the storm. That means there were no avatars who could be seen or recorded."

The arbiter's avatar nodded and replied, "You'd think that was the case, but the Chinese claim they have a new device that can detect spirits visually. We'll get the chance to review their evidence before the trial begins. Similarly, we will have to give them our evidence. One final note, we have requested Chin-A submit to a spirit evaluation test. We want to verify the being who was present at the hearing was a real avatar of real a spirit."

### Show Time—Chanlina

Caleb and I waited outside the tribunal courtroom bubble. I've never felt so nervous in my life. Caleb seemed confused; he couldn't accept all these horrible things were happening to us. We'd played by the rules and yet the rules seemed to have changed drastically.

We would be the last ones to enter the bubble. Joshua and Simone were seated in the observation section on the left side of the bubble behind a low wall. On the right side were two Chinese humans. One was the admiral of the Peoples Liberation Army Navy (what a weird designation). The other was the man dressed all in black with dark glasses and white cane. He appeared to be speaking to the admiral. However, if he was, the admiral wasn't listening.

Avatars of The Apostle and our arbiter were seated at the defendant's table in front of the low wall, close to the bench where the three judges would sit. On the right side was the prosecutor's table where the supposed avatar of Chin-A's spirit sat.

When the avatars of the three judges walked in, everyone stood and waited for them to sit down. They were dressed in black robes with Judge Juan in the middle. He said in a firm, no nonsense voice, "Please be seated. Please bring in the defendants."

We moved through the wall of the bubble and our avatars popped into being, encasing our spirits in a human form. We walked down the center aisle, through the low gate and sat down at the defendants table.

The three judges stared at us briefly before Judge Juan said, "This tribunal is now in session. Chin-A please make your opening remarks to this tribunal."

The Chin-A avatar stood, approached the three judges and said, "Your honors…"

That was as far as he got before a strange buzzing sounded. It seemed to begin as a very low frequency with matching low intensity. Chin-A seemed frozen, then turned slowly and stared at the blind man sitting next to the Chinese admiral. The blind man's mouth moved rapidly as the buzzing grew louder and the frequency escalated.

I glanced at Joshua. He seemed to be holding a very small transmitter in his left hand as he used his right to turn up the volume. He was watching Chin-A who now seemed to be trembling. As the volume increased, so too did Chin-A's vibrations.

The blind man stood up holding the white cane in his right hand. He was now speaking incredibly fast in Chinese as he turned his head toward the Chin-A. All at once, three things happened: The white cane blew apart in a shower of electrical sparks. The blind man collapsed into a heap on the courtroom floor and the Chin-A creature, who was apparently neither spirit nor avatar, seemed to come apart at the seams. A rainbow of colored fluids seeped from the body of what must have been a droid.

Caleb began shouting, "I knew he wasn't the avatar of Chin-A. I just knew it!"

Suddenly, a brief darkness descended over the courtroom. When it lifted, there was the ghost like image of the spirit of the real Chin-A. The chaos from a moment before became totally silent, as if a volume control knob was turned to zero. In that silence, the spirit began to speak, "It is with great remorse I address the court. The current Chinese government has shamed me by adding my name to their deceptions. The current three rulers of my creation will be punished accordingly." The ghost image turned toward Caleb and me and said, "I apologize for the actions of my people, both in human and spirit form. They have shamed not only me, but my nation as well. I hope you can forgive us. You have my word this will never happen again."

The ghost began to fade until it could be seen no longer. Everything slowly returned to normal.

The trial was over. The ruling of the Tribunal was that China was guilty of fraud and half a dozen other crimes. All charges against the spirits of Caleb and Chanlina were dropped.

The Chinese admiral was arrested and faced charges from the World Court. In addition, a variety of economic sanctions were made against China.

Joshua had his hands slapped by the tribunal for bringing a weaponized sonic generator into the spirit court. He was ordered to never do it again. Joshua apologized to the court and promised to never do it again. Which proved the old adage: It's better to ask for forgiveness instead of permission.

The expanded Team Joshua met in Hawaii for a party. It was to be a mission-ending celebration, but with an added surprise. It was a double wedding, between Pham and Pearl, and Mark and Maria. A Navy chaplain volunteered to hold the service with the rest of the team members pitching in to serve as best men and bridesmaids. Even Sarge and Serina helped out as ring bearer and flower girl. When the wedding services were over and official papers signed, the party really began.

# CHAPTER 18
# END OF THE ROAD

### The Final Gathering Of The Team—Joshua

We gathered back at the Hilton Hawaiian Village to celebrate the acquittal of Caleb and Chanlina. I'd made arrangements at the hotel to use one of their several banquet facilities for our party. The banquet room was located on the third floor which had an expansive, open air lanai.

We'd all met up in the late afternoon for cocktails on the lanai. It had a terrific view of the beach, the ocean and the surrounding park directly below us. The hotel staff was busy setting up for a luau and the Hawaiian band was rehearsing the music for the entertainment portion of the show. I was looking forward to seeing the beautiful Hawaiian sunset everyone raved about.

Caleb and Chanlina had created a complex bubble that permitted their avatars to join the party while still having the access to the lanai and everything that went with it. I'd spoken with them immediately after their acquittal, before the court bubble disappeared.

Chanlina was the first to share her experience. "This was the most bizarre thing that ever happened to me either as a human or a spirit. I was terrified Caleb and I were going to lose our existence. I was so surprised when Joshua used his sonic disrupter and destroyed the android who was pretending to be the avatar of a spirit. I have no idea how the Chinese were able to get him past the security spirits."

Caleb added, "I thought we were all going on a relaxing pleasure cruise. It was supposed to be a vacation. I don't think it was much of a vacation, more like a nightmare in hell. If you remember, I said the vacation was probably a disguise for a mission."

The Apostle's avatar also showed up and informed everyone the mission was officially over. The vacation, the real vacation, was still in progress for as long as we wanted.

The dinner was really great. We toasted each other and The Apostle led the way. "To the best damned team in the world. You've successfully completed every mission you were assigned to do, each one more difficult than the last. While some of us have been tortured, beaten, stabbed, shot and even killed, or at least mostly killed, we still exist as a team. Thank God for all the team members, humans and spirits alike."

He paused for a moment, then his avatar stood up, raised his glass and shouted, "TO THE TEAM!!!"

Everyone stood with him and shouted the toast, drained their glasses and threw them into the large fireplace on the north side of the room to seal the toast … forever.

It was a perfect Friday night and the Hilton Hawaiian village puts on a fireworks show over the beach every Friday as the beginning of their luau. We all gathered on the lanai to watch the ten minute fireworks display. When it was over we sat down for our own table and the delicious meal waiting for us.

After our seven-course meal of Hawaiian delicacies and many adult beverages later, we migrated to the lanai and watched the beach show. And what a show it was!

First came the Hawaiian music performed by the band. Next a large, older gentleman dressed in white slacks and a multicolored Hawaiian shirt sang. He had a hypnotic voice, deep and mellow, it was simply beautiful. On his third song, three beautiful women in grass skirts and unusual tops made from coconuts joined the performance.

The tempo changed to a fast pace and a man dressed in a skimpy loincloth danced to a pounding rhythm. He was well-muscled and handled a three-foot wooden stick like a baton while he gyrated in time to the drumbeats.

Simone was standing next to me and whispered into my ear, "He's really good, isn't he?"

Before I could answer, Chanlina's avatar added, "And really good looking, too."

I looked at the two women who couldn't take their eyes off the young Hawaiian boy strut his stuff. I felt I had to interject, so I said, "I guess he's okay if you like that sort of thing."

Chanlina looked at Simone then smiled and said playfully, "Oh, we like that sort of stuff, don't we Simone?"

Simone answered is a soft, dreamy voice, "Oh yes, we definitely like that sort of stuff." Then they both giggled to each other.

All the women squealed with delight when the lights were turned off and the young entertainer lit the ends of his baton, twirling it dangerously fast. The beat of the drums got louder and faster. He added a second flaming baton to his routine and the drums went faster still. All at once, he tossed the two spinning sticks high into the air just as the drums stopped. He caught them both and continued to spin them as the drums began again, but then they stopped abruptly, and the fires went out.

When the lights were turned on again, the young man had disappeared to be replaced by a scantily clothed young Polynesian girl who demonstrated the Tahitian version of the hula. Never in my life had I ever seen anyone move their hips so fast. It was truly amazing. I turned to say something to Simone, but she had drifted away with Chanlina. They'd apparently lost interest in the rest of the show.

The last act involved taking women from the audience to learn the hula. Some were okay and really got into it, while others seemed to be embarrassed.

Not to be outdone, The Apostle appeared with six grass skirts for all the women in our party. They were quickly tied around the hips of our women who were ushered out onto the lanai.

When the music began again, our ladies moved to the lanai and spotlights illuminated them as they did their best to imitate the Tahitian girl. They were cheered on by us and the guests at the luau. When the music ended and the dancing stopped, we decided Mark's daughter, Serina, was the best of the six. She blushed as all of us congratulated her. That included Sarge who barked enthusiastically.

When the luau was over, we sat around the tables and talked about the future. Bill and Joey had to get back to Portland. They had been on temporary leave from the FBI. They and their women would be leaving the following week.

Pham was going to Seattle with his new wife Pearl and would stay there. She had to get back to Boeing ARL to determine the extent of damage to the cold fusion reactor. Pham was brought onboard by Boeing to get his take on the technology demonstrator.

Mark, Maria, Serina and Sarge had to leave the next day. Serina had to get back to school in Portland and Maria wanted to get back to her job as fitness trainer at the gym.

Everyone had left the banquet room except Simone and I. Caleb and Chanlina took their bubble and transported to some location unknown to us. They both said their good-byes and after they left a sadness swept over me. Was this the end? Was this the last of Team Joshua?

Simone sensed my despair. "Don't get all sad on me. It doesn't have to be the end. We all need some time to decompress. I think I'd like to do some snooping to see how the Chinese were able to do what they did to us. I'd also really like to know who the American traitors were. How about you?"

I took a deep breath and let it out slowly as one thought came to mind. "I want my old War Wagon back. For all the bells and whistles of new War Wagon, I never felt comfortable in it."

Simone smiled and kissed me on the cheek then said, "I'm with you. Let's get the real War Wagon back." She paused and smiled slyly, "How about we get married first?

I returned her grin and said, "Yeah, that sounds like a plan. Hey, why did it take so long for you to propose?"

# EPILOGUE

## The Apostle

With the destruction of the fake spirit of Emperor Chin-A at the Tribunal of Spirits, this mission of Team Joshua came to an end. It was by far the most complicated mission any of them had ever dealt with. When it began, we weren't entirely sure there was a mission. The only thing we knew for certain was someone had approached Dr. Pearl Intelligent and offered her a huge sum of money to give up the design data for a small, cold fusion reactor.

At that time we didn't know who was providing the money. More importantly, the existence of such a nuclear reactor was classified well beyond top secret. Only a handful of scientists new about it and what they knew was compartmentalized. Each scientist knew only a portion of the research. Dr. Pearl alone knew the details of the entire program. So how did anyone even know there was a cold fusion program?

When she was approached to part with the design data, she contacted an associate at Homeland Security. They asked her to play along, but to feed them disinformation, a little at a time, to see if they could determine who was behind this attempt of espionage. That strategy almost cost the good doctor her life, as well as the life of her new boyfriend, Pham Bin Minh, which resulted in Team Joshua coming on board.

From then on things began to escalate quickly. There had been an ongoing program at Boeing to build a technology demonstrator. It was called The New War Wagon which was really a misnomer when you consider all the various configurations involved. It was a technology demonstrator, never considered a production vehicle. Team Joshua was tasked with providing security for The New War Wagon under the guise of having a cruise vacation to Alaska.

There were really three objectives for the cruise, the first being a three week vacation for the extended team as a reward for their successful previous missions. The second was to test the capabilities of the new technologies recently developed. Alaska provided the perfect location for those tests with hundreds of square miles of unpopulated land in the United States. The third objective was to identify who was trying to steal the cold fusion reactor design.

It didn't take long to determine China was behind the attempted theft when three Chinese nationals tried to break into the vehicle where it was stored in the cargo bay of the cruise ship. What we didn't know was if the Chinese government was to blame for the botched attack or was it some private interests within the country? It turned out, it was both.

The next attack got deadly. When several of our group had decided to go dog sledding on Mendenhall Glacier, they were attacked by a helicopter full of mercenaries. A total of seven men died that day, two were Chinese nationals, three were American mercs and two were Alaskan dog sled drivers. It was believed Dr. Pearl was the target to be kidnapped.

The presence of the American mercs led us to believe this wasn't only a Chinese operation. Americans were definitely involved. Again we felt it had to be both individuals from our government as well as from the private sector who were willing to sell information to the Chinese for a very hefty price. By definition, they were all traitors.

At that point, things got a lot more difficult. At Denali National Park, the Chinese launched a full-blown attack with the intent of capturing the War Wagon and Dr. Pearl with a fleet of helicopters launched from a Chinese cargo ship. Somehow, they knew exactly where Dr. Pearl was at all times. Their plan was to kill the members of Team Joshua, capture the good doctor as well as the War Wagon, fly them to the cargo ship and sail back to China before anyone knew what happened.

That didn't go well for the Chinese. All their helicopters were destroyed by the War Wagon. Apparently, they were unaware of the various configurations the War Wagon could transform into or its cloaking device and projection system. The former allowed us to hide from them and the latter gave them a false target to attack. It was estimated nearly a hundred of their pilots and soldiers were killed in addition to the destruction of eight attack helicopters, one heavy lift chopper and a command center helicopter.

Next came the Zumwalt destroyer fiasco where the skeleton crew of the multibillion dollar Navy ship was captured and killed. A small crew of Chinese sailors together with a large group of mercenary pirates took over the Zumwalt and used the ship to attack and plunder a cruise ship on its way home from Alaska. However, Team Joshua in the War Wagon came to the aid of the cruise ship, killed or captured all of the hundred pirates and ultimately sunk the four billion dollar Zumwalt.

While the War Wagon was busy sending the Zumwalt to the bottom of the sea, an armada of Chinese war ships was steaming to her aid or so we thought. The newly upgraded Fujian aircraft carrier was the lead ship in the armada worth at least 13 billion dollars. It was the first nuclear powered Chinese surface warship.

The Chinese had developed some new technology and were initially able to fool Team Joshua into believing the spirit of Emperor Chin-A was going to kidnap Dr. Pearl. They had developed some short-range transport device and combined it with sophisticated special effects to temporarily confuse our people. It turned out it was all a theatrical production taking place on the hangar deck of the Fujian. The humans of Team Joshua were able to escape back to the War Wagon unscathed.

In retaliation, with the help of special spirits Caleb and Chanlina, they were able to deactivate the Fujian's two new nuclear powerplants causing the entire crew of 5,000 sailors to abandon ship.

However, it should be noted that a second submarine of the armada was able to transport a team of sailors to the War Wagon, kidnap Dr. Pearl, and return to their sub. They then launched a missile which caused irreparable damage to the War Wagon resulting in its crashing into the sea. The crew was able to bubble it up and transport to safety.

That brings us to the last of the incidents involving Team Joshua and the Chinese. The spirits of Caleb and Chanlina had a plan to recover the remains of the War Wagon which was submerged beneath the sea. However, they were too late. A Chinese ocean going tug had beaten them to it and was hauling the salvaged remains back to China. Fortunately, our two team spirits were able to turn the tables on the Chinese when a storm destroyed the tug and barge. They were able to encapsulate what was left of the War Wagon and transported it back to the Boeing ARL to determine what was left of the vehicle's systems.

So let's look at the big picture. The Chinese desperately wanted the small cold fusion reactor and were willing to do anything to get it. What was the price both governments paid? I estimated the cost of the loss of the Fujian, the Zumwalt and the War Wagon at around $20 billion. In addition was the death of approximately 300 to 400 people from both navies, the civilians on the cruise ships, the mercs and the dog sled drivers on Mendenhall Glacier. And what did they get for their troubles? As far as I can see, the answer to that question is, not a damned thing!

Why on Earth didn't China just buy the technology from America? Being a Top Secret project, that was not a viable option. So they tried to steal it, like they do with all the other technologies.

But why were they so desperate to acquire the technology?

I think I might have part of the answer. There have been some unsubstantiated rumors floating around DC recently that China had some serious problems with their nuclear fueled power plants. I heard two separate reports indicating they had two reactor melt downs which resulted in the deaths of over 2.5 million people and rising due to radiation poisoning. In another report it seems they're also experiencing problems at one of their uranium enrichment plants. A more recent report says the Chinese reactor problems make what happened at Chernobyl look like a walk in the park.

It's hard to know exactly what's going on in China. The relatively new Tribunal leadership, also referred to as the Holy Trinity by its detractors, are very closed mouthed about any negative things going on within the country. Another underground political group in China is likening the Tribunal leadership to North Korea's Kim Jon-un. However, the spirit of real Emperor Chin-A appears to have corrected those deficiencies.

I want to close out this report on what I consider could be interpreted as a positive note.

First of all, Caleb and Chanlina as a going away present, identified everyone who was responsible for the loss of lives and fortunes both in China and in the United States. That included both government officials and civilian business men and women. It specifically identified those who were considered rich and famous greedy bastards. Somehow, they passed that information on to humans who swore they'd never even heard of spirits. In China, that has led to numerous public executions and no one was considered righteous, no not one. In the US it's been a little different. Some people on the list just seemed to disappear into thin air, while others have been ruled suicides. Two gunshot wounds to the back of the head don't seem a likely method of suicide, but who am I to judge?

Concerning Team Joshua, I'm not sure what will be happening with them. They obviously need time to decompress and recover emotionally from this mission, but now that everyone's getting married, their perceptions on crime fighting may be changing. I'll just have to wait and see.

I found out from a high-level spirit one very interesting fact: In China there are very few spirits. When native born Chinese men or women pass away, their spirits hardly ever develop. I asked the high-level spirit why that was. His answer was succinct: Because the Great Kahn doesn't permit it, not since the Chinese built the Great Wall to keep him out.

My reaction was: Wow! The Great Kahn sure knows how to hold a grudge!

*THE END*

# ABOUT THE AUTHOR

I've been a fan of science fiction ever since I was in grade school (a very long time ago). In those day's there were three outstanding science fiction authors: Isaac Asimov, Arthur C. Clark, and Robert A. Heinlein.

My favorite author was Heinlein. He began writing his science fiction stories for young people. His first books were categorized as Boys Books. Today, they're called Young Adults.

His stories were so believable to me, I couldn't wait to get to his latest book. As I matured, so did his books. I have read every book Heinlein published and still have most of them in my personal library. I think my all-time favorite Heinlein story is *Stranger in a Strange Land.*

My current favorite author is Orson Scott Card. Again, like Heinlein's stories, I find myself living the story as it unfolds. *Ender's Game* and *Prentice Alvin* are two of my favorite Card novels.

**If you enjoyed reading *The New War Wagon***
**you'll love the first 4 books in the War on Crime series.**

Book 1 in the War on Crime series. This book introduced the terrible accident in Afghanistan of one of the twin brothers and then moves forward to the crack team doing God's work against some very bad players in the world.

Book 2: *Joshua* recounts the three trial missions he is required to conduct without the aid of Caleb. As he moves from one mission to the next, they become more complicated and deadly.

Book 3:  The spirit of Caleb teams with his brother in *Caleb and Joshua* in a much more complicated mission; shutting down five major drug cartels. This year's Mardi Gras in New Orleans becomes deadly, very deadly.

Book 4:  They have successfully completed four complex missions. It was time to stand down and enjoy some well earned R&R. However, that was not to be. This mission was by far the most complex they had ever been assigned to.